PRAISE FOR ꓔ S
by ꓤ

"... fun, frightening, and ribald. *It won't be for everybody, but that can be said of all great writing.*"

"... delightfully weird... this story will blow you away!"

"Original, impressive, compulsively entertaining..."

"... scary and frequently hilarious..."

"... blows the genre out of the water..."

"Stephen King meets Terry Pratchett... funny and terrifying..."

"...action-rich... visceral imagery and heart-stopping horror..."

———◆◆———

"...irreverent and darkly funny. Injecting brutal scenes with almost lyrical prose lends the novel a definite otherworldly feel."

———◆◆———

"Lures the reader in fast... this is a page-turner!"

———◆◆———

PROCLAMATIONS

Except for an early morning spider that crawled into my scotch; no animals were harmed during the writing of this novel.

Women are God's best effort thus far. Men are, well... they're men. The author is sorry.

This is a work of fiction. Any human finding a resemblance to themselves... needs help.

To the readers who love this book: May all your children be beautiful, your pockets lined with gold, and your sex life rival Satan's.

EVERYONE: Give to the local Humane Society. Yes, this author does.

THE
WAYDOWNS

A NOVEL

BY

ROBERT RIFE

FOR MY DAUGHTER

Deep Portal Publishing
Polydactyl Productions
Seattle, Washington (USA)

THE WAYDOWNS

ISBN: 979-8-9862806-2-2 (Paperback)
       979-8-9862806-3-9 (Hardcover)
       979-8-9862806-4-6 (eBook)

Editing: Victoria Edwards
Cover design: Arcane Books
Interior Design by Booknook.biz.

THE
WAYDOWNS

PROLOGUE

She's not coming. It's too late now. Blood gushes from his empty arm socket, spattering onto the deck. He hears the pounding and tearing at the hatch cover. It wants the rest of him.

CHAPTER 1

IN THE BEGINNING

Thousands of years ago a spacecraft shrieked into earth's atmosphere. Crashing, it burrowed deep into the ground causing considerable discontent to the cargo. The pilots weren't too happy about it either. They would soon become a lot unhappier when the cargo ate them. The crew had no warning of the ravenous attack, so no one made it to *the switch.*

Another thousand or so years later, an exceedingly unlucky tribe of Gitchiegoomba Injuns, discovered part of the intact ship protruding from some faintly glowing rocks. Informed by their medicine man that it was a God, they immediately fell to worshiping it, making sacrifices... and consuming copious amounts of peyote. As was their custom.

Alas, damn, and golly gee! All the offerings were in vain, all for nothing. Perhaps the sickly children and old women had not been gutted properly, or there wasn't enough peyote gobbled. Or maybe the tribe hadn't jigged and chanted correctly. Perchance the medicine man was a drooling idiot, but for whatever reason, things quite literally... went to shit.

Most of the tribe became terminally diarrhetic... and the survivors nakedly waddled away on bowed legs. Descendants of these intestinally cleansed Injuns later became known as Indians, and later, American Indians, and still later, Native Americans. Evolution at work... how progressive.

Many years after the fertilizing Gitchiegoombians departed, smart and tricky white men came to these parts. And as evil and clever white men always do, they planted a flag and claimed the land. As was their custom. After accomplishing this bit of thievery, they left to appropriate other properties. As was their custom.

More long years pass, and civilization developed, creeping like a benign cancer across the territory.

Eventually, a company of surveyors operating out of Roswell, New Mexico discovered the partially buried starship.

After recovering from their own bowel tribulations, the surveyors reported their find to the proper governmental authorities. They were promptly escorted away for rewards... and permanently disappeared. As was the custom. Knowledge of extraterrestrial life must be kept from the general populace. It wouldn't be good for them... and it sure as hell wouldn't do their religion any favors.

Within days, a plain single-story white building was erected over the spot. It bore an equally non-descript business name: CONSOLIDATED CONCEPTS. And a thinly disguised military staff began exploring the starship. They discovered skeletal remains... and life. Frozen life.

Immediately, experimentation began with the alien technology and new life forms. These experiments did not go well. But they continued. They always do.

During the ship explorations, a switch was found. Found by a small group with the intelligence to guess its purpose. Properly horrified, and without a clue of how, or if, it could be nullified, they un-found it. It was to be studied in secrecy by a select few, and recommendations would be made.

So, secret studies of an incredibly dangerous control, would be made by a select few… followed with recommendations. What a military solution. What a plan. Nothing could possibly go wrong. But it did.

Storm clouds of war came in the late 1930s. Those clouds became war, as they always do. And all but one of that *select few* studying the switch wound up among the honored dead. Except for persistent scuttlebutt, the device was forgotten. But not by the one person who knew it really existed. And where.

During those early days of WW2, some frantic weaponry testing of the alien technology produced an absolute cataclysm. This holocaust resulted in the melding together of an unknown number of the ship's lower decks. It had an unspeakable effect on all lab animals within. *Human staff included.* And there was no stopping the consequences.

The ensuing mutiny, chaos, and savagery inside those areas of merged and twisted floors resulted in a permanent sealing off. All decks below 19 were not just locked down and forbidden; by wartime military decree they were non-existent. Those floors had simply vanished. It was treason to speak of them.

But whispered tales of the lost decks persisted through the years. Those abandoned regions eventually got a muttered and feared name: THE WAYDOWNS.

The Waydowns, that vast, unknown region deep in the bowels of this ancient, buried starship. A twisted place teeming with... those left behind. That's what the gossips say. They also say it had been made impenetrable.

But ways in were found. Found by some who did not tell. And those ways were used... used to dump failed experiments. Living, dead, or undecided.

This discarding procedure continues.

CHAPTER 2

PRESENT DAY: BENEATH THAT WHITE BUILDING

Far below the military white concrete structure, down past the 19 starship decks that are occupied by human researchers, are those areas that in military speak... do not exist. Officially, that persistent idea of abandoned lower decks is plain bullshit. There's no more truth in those rumors than there is in the existence of a mysterious all-powerful switch. It's total Area 51 and little green men hogwash.

But those decks are there, boiling with life. Altered and wronged creatures slither, scurry, and walk those twisted floors. They scavenge through labyrinthine, dimly lit corridors, abandoned vaporous laboratories, and flickering control rooms. They stalk, they kill, they eat, and they breed.

And some of them... some of them plot:

"God damn it, Seevee, you've got to get over this.

What you heard was only sex. I just fucked the guy, it didn't mean anything," says Tanya, leaning further over the console from her chair. Her unbuttoned lab coat conveniently slipping further open, exposing more of her. Showing more of the naked Tanya beneath. "What you heard was plain old fucking, nothing more. I... *WE* need help from those in the locked areas beneath us. If we're going to take Deck 19 and keep it, we need them. I did what was necessary."

"Seevee *LUFF* Ton! Much luff... much, much *care*... much *do* for Ton," whines the Almost, his human face twisting as he tries not to cry, unconsciously hugging himself with both multi- jointed arms.

"I know you do... *Honey*, and I... I love you back, but—"

"NO! Ton lie to Seevee, Ton no care for Seevee. Seevee killed friends, killed Almosts for Ton! Seevee carry hid Gunch for—"

"Shut up, Seevee, that's enough," Tanya says blithely.

Pushing the chair back, her coat falls open even further. Her good eye glinting as the other wetly searches for light it will never again see.

"Yes, you did kill the other Almosts for me, but they were no longer your friends. They were making plans against you. I told you so; I warned you in time."

"Seevee no never hear any them say—"

"I told you to shut up. Now come here and lay your head in my lap... baby. I'll explain things so that you can understand."

And this last remaining Almost obeys. He always did. It's called love. It can be difficult.

Further away in this convoluted maze of decks, a terrified, failed experiment runs desperately. It has been thrown into this hell because of improper development. Created far above in Deck 19's lab, it had failed the requirements. The creature had tried hard, but it was not the Übermensch that Dr. Lillith Gaust sought, not a superior human. It wasn't even close enough to be a replacement for the missing Almosts. It was garbage, just another Lab Spill. Just another failure. There were many.

This Lab Spill is being stalked, relentlessly stalked. No matter how hard the Spill tries, it cannot increase the distance between itself and the beast. The gap remains constant. Looking over its shoulder, it can dimly see the hunter's outline through the drifting haze that's everywhere in this tortured part of the ship. The shadowy figure appears low to the deck, then taller, then low again, running with a humping, side to side motion, from one wall to the other and back again. Its motion has a clopping, clicking sound. But the overall movement is always forward, always keeping the same distance back, always. The Spill is being toyed with.

Ducking into a storage room filled with shadowy rows of towering shelves, the Spill dodges among them. Scurrying down the walkways searching for an exit, it finds a creek named shit. And that's a tributary flowing through all worlds. Desperately climbing up a rack bolted to the wall, it hides among the dusty, looted crates and debris. Being still, trying to quiet its gasping breath, knowing that hiding is its only chance. It waits.

On the wall directly above, a saucer sized splotch of glistening yellow mold slowly bubbles as it breaths. Occasionally a bubble will softly pop, spraying out a few microscopic particles. That splotch is birthing. It is birthing doom.

Hearing a faint snuffling sound, punctuated with high pitched grunting, the Spill realizes the clopping, clicking, scratching sounds have slowed. But they're getting louder. And closer. Much closer. Then silence.

Peering from a crack between the crates, the Spill jambs a fist into its mouth, hoping it won't be seen, hoping it won't be heard, hoping the top shelf will be beyond the thing's reach. Hoping.

Amid a swirl of ever-present fog, the entry fills with ...

a monster. The creature is low to the ground, giving the Spill thoughts that the beast isn't tall enough, can't reach the top shelf, won't be able to climb. But then... it slowly stands, unfolding to its full height. It is at least nine feet tall. Nine feet of nightmare; it won't need to climb. Bristles form a nimbus around the huge head; a halo from hell. It looks directly at the Spill's shelf. A staccato huffing comes from the mouth. It's laughing.

<hr>

"Now, Seevee," Tanya continues, as she slowly strokes the Almost's head. "I made contact with what's behind that locked hatch we've heard sounds from. Those areas have been locked down since the mutiny, since what happened that created the Waydowns. That's many years back, a long time before you, me, and the Almosts escaped from 19. There are still people in there. Well, sort of people, what's descended from the original human staff anyway."

"What... what look like?" snuffles Seevee, trying to keep the tears and jealousy out of his voice.

"Oh, you don't have to worry, the one I met isn't near as good as you, Seevee," she answers with the unerring mind-read of a woman. *No, he's a lot better, you ugly, pathetic imitation man...he will make a good replace-ment once I get you killed off.* "I only met the one, a man called Lakker, but if he's any indication of the rest, then their area must be the ship's power source. I've seen radiation sickness before, and whatever he has sure looks like it."

"Much, much no need him, no much want—"

"Yes, Seevee, we do *much* need him. We need to find out how many others there are; what weapons they have. And we need their help to take 19. I need *humans* like me, instead of a few Lab Spills, Coilers... and you. Having those people with us could make the difference." *And Lakker told me about other things... further down... things that WILL make a difference.*

"Much no trust," quietly replies the Almost, his cheek resting on the bare thighs. Tanya including him in her statement about Spills and Coilers hurt, hurt deeply. He so desperately wants to be human for her, for Tanya. Tanya is his all, his life. This will end.

***

A monster walks toward the Spill's hiding place. Its curved haunches flex, and quills rub together, rasping coarsely. Feet make a harsh knocking sound; they're hooves. Hard, brutal and split, matching the small ones on each thick finger.

Nearing the rack of shelves, its long pink ears sway, framing feral hog eyes and upturned snout. Curving tusks shine white and wet. The bristled shoulders are level with the Spill, and hot carrion breath washes over the boxes it cowers behind. Hands reach out, shoving the boxes aside. The chuffing laugh bounces about the area.

Erupting with terrorized strength, the Spill leaps into the space above the massive, laughing head. It almost makes it.

The bristled creature isn't hungry. Not yet. It wants to play, and the shelf provides a good surface to *spread* things out. Those finger-hooves are for digging, but can be very selective and careful when probing. The fun begins. The Lab Spill screams.

Directly above the toxic Waydowns is Deck 19. Above that floor, all the other levels rise to the desert and that white building. Within 19, seated at his desk, Dr. Moto alternately rubs his bandaged head and blackened eyes, worriedly staring at the blank monitor screen. Dr. Gaust has chosen not to show herself during this little chat. This cannot be good.

It's been many days since Moto has actually seen Gaust. He'd like to lengthen the number, stretch them into never. During their last meeting, her melon sized shoulder growth had lolled about beneath a draped towel. She'd fed it bits of meat; always jerking her hand back quickly. Evidently the melon had teeth. Dr. Moto thought of it as Gaust's own personal Igor. And he shudders to think how much *little Iggy* may have grown.

Talks with Dr. Lillith Sally Gaust, the iron-willed harridan that controls all but the Waydowns, were never pleasant. Some were less harsh than others, but this one will be piercing.

"It's quite apparent that Gosteen and the woman recruit have deserted," reports Moto. "I am replacing him as security head with Private Huong. I received a report that our truck was found abandoned in Oklahoma City. I—"

"Fuck Gosteen, his bitch, and the truck, you oriental idiot. What about the Extender?" demands Lillith. Her voice is... different. Hers, but not hers. Like silk being pulled across sharp things.

"We think it's still in the area of that topside house, but—"

"THINK? Is that what you do, *Doctor* Moto? You think? It must be all you do, you fucking bucket of rice. Listen to me carefully: Where-Is-The-Extender?"

"Huong has— *we've* determined the Extender is actually in that topside house. But the bounces are erratic. The location is not constant."

"Yes, Moto, thank you for the meaning of erratic; it describes your performance. What else have you and this Huong *determined*?"

"We thin— we believe the topsiders now realize that the Extender is not a Medieval piece of armor, but that it's Extraterrestrial. They may have it covered so it can't focus and are probably keeping it locked up."

"Think. Determine. Believe. My, my, my... what a repertoire of skills you're developing. How do *you* know that they know?"

"I th— uh, I gues— um— Proby told them," he answers, not daring to say the words guess or think, and trying hard to make a definite statement. This chat has become quicksand. Deep quicksand.

"Did Proby do this tell-all before, or after he clubbed the Egg Foo out of your ass? Never mind, I don't want to hear about another of your failures. Or about that mutant Elvis shithead; that fucking Proby. What I want, is for you to get that Extender. You bring me a plan that doesn't involve another topside expedition. And I don't want it now; I want it yesterday. Mind me, man, mind me!" She abruptly ends the connection.

"Yes, O Honored Hyena, to hear you is to obey... for now. But my time draws near," says Dr. Moto, addressing the *definitely off* screen and the empty room. Defiance is best tempered with discretion. "And Egg Foo

Young is food of the filthy Chinese, you round-eye bitch."

Moto is quite the racist, and he is very democratic about. He includes everyone. This esteemed scientist thinks racism is in all peoples. He's right; it is. It's as natural as thought; it's the instinct of self-preservation. Neanderthals weren't racist. Perhaps they were an early form of... Woke.

Behind Dr. Moto is a vast room. An area that had once been the playground of that "mutant Elvis shithead; that Proby," as his creator had just lovingly referred to him. A place filled with games and memorabilia from the 1950s. All from topside thefts by that same mutant shithead, using the Extender. That breastplate attachment from an extraterrestrial spacesuit. That piece Lillith is so determined to get back. That device that opens a portal into and out of the ship; HER ship. That thing that's a time bomb of ruin for Dr. Gaust.

The mutant's chamber, lighted with flickering this, bleeping that, and other fun, no longer imprisons the Elvis/Proby creation. Or any of his kidnapped friends. But it's not empty of life. Something that's been hidden inside a long, Bowl-A- Rama game... is growing. It's beginning to spread. It's of a yellow color.

Dr. Moto keys an intercom. "Huong! Report to me at once; we have an assignment."

———••——

Back in the Waydowns, Tanya and Seevee have been hearing death screeches echoing down the corridor. This is no big deal; life is short down here, but dying can often take a while. But this noise is getting ridiculous. Tanya's patience is not... well, not patient.

"Whatever's dying is damn sure taking its time about it," says the patient Tanya. "Sounds like a Spill, but not one of ours, or it'd be yelling my name. What the fuck's got hold of it?"

"Maybe Coiler, maybe?" suggests Seevee, still kneeling before her.

"No, I don't think so. Coilers usually kill quick; they don't play with their food. And besides, our truce with them has been holding."

"Much, much no trust Coilers, much hungry all time."

"You no 'much, much' trust anybody," she laughs. Shoving the Almost away, she stands, "Get up, and let's go see what the fuck it is."

Heading toward the diminishing screams, they walk quietly. Occasionally turning down a twisted, slanting hall, dodging the debris of long abandonment, but always following those sounds of anguish.

"What we do when fi—"

"Shut up, Seevee," she hisses, "we're getting close, and I forgot the fucking gun." Pulling a scalpel from her lab coat, she looks at him, arching her eyebrows. The Almost blinks stupidly for a second, then pulls his own blade.

From a doorway directly ahead, screams fade into whimpering gurgles as the Spill finally dies. Inside, the beast lifts its head from the remains, cocking a pink ear toward the opening. A piece of gut clings to one tusk, waving slightly.

On the wall above, the blot of mold has added a few specks of itself to that surface. It's growing children.

In the corridor, Tanya and Seevee creep warily forward. Clutching the scalpel in one hand, she unconsciously rubs at a ragged facial scar with the other. Seevee protectively positions himself in front of her.

Within the room ahead, a huge head turns away from a blood drenched shelf. Nostrils repeatedly expand and contract as the monster steps toward the hall.

Seevee stops, straining to hear, motioning Tanya to halt. Only silence... or maybe... maybe not... maybe...

A boar's face thrusts itself from the doorway. Huffing sounds come from the red mouth, blowing a dangling gut shred to the floor.

Seevee whirls about, yelling, "Much run!" He needn't have bothered; Tanya is running. Much, much run.

Still standing, the creature steps into the hall, watching while Seevee and Tanya frantically look back as they turn a corner. Dropping to all fours, it starts its loping, humping pursuit. Ricocheting from wall to wall and back again, and again and again. It loves to chase. And to kill. Its master calls it Long; short for Long Pig.

With open coat flaring out, breasts flopping, Tanya races for her cabin and the Uzi. That deadly gun dropped by 19's last expedition into these diseased, cursed decks. She hears the beast's hooves pummeling down the corridor, getting louder, getting near.

Close behind her, Seevee slows to widen the space between himself and Ton. Figuring if the monster reaches them, it will get him first, and she will make it to safety. He doesn't look back. He doesn't need to; he can feel death closing in.

Careening around another turn, Tanya sees her cabin's hatch. Her lungs straining, she forces a last burst of speed, hitting the partially open door, bursting into the room.

Seeing her reach safety, Seevee speeds up. With

jointed arms pumping, knife still clutched in a bony fist, he knows she'll leap back out with the gun.

As the beast closes in, Seevee stumbles, falls, scrambling for the door. He sees it slam shut. He hears it lock.

And the Long Pig comes.

CHAPTER 3

TOPSIDE

Up on ground level, hundreds of miles from the buried ship, Rastus (no middle name) Leroy paces. This pacing man's deepest regret in life is that he hadn't killed the son of a bitch who had named him. The prick's fellow inmates had gotten that joy. Understandably, Rastus Leroy goes by RL. He has the ethics of a whore's garter belt.

As RL steps about his spare bedroom/office, he frets. He frets well. It often didn't accomplish much but fret he does. Today's fret had also been yesterday's fret, and the fret for several days previous. RL calls this thinking, and lately it's been about love. All sane people stress about that torturing, euphoric, indefinable pest.

Several days ago, he'd twisted his innards into a pretzel while working up the courage to propose marriage to his next-door neighbor. But one afternoon the woman had beaten him to it. Sort of. Jayderay had asked him to buy the haunted Roaton house; they would live there. As in together... as in she would sleep with him.

This joyful gut-punch had stunned him into a strangled "yes" and a brain-freeze. What he had not done, was get the fat diamond engagement ring he had in readiness. After that, the right moment to propose was never the *right moment*. Those slippery devils are like that.

They had slept together that night, but not in the Roaton house. No, not there; that place had... problems. Their first time had been like all first times should be... but often ain't. He was one enormous grin; she was melted bliss. The way it's meant to be.

And several of those elusive, "right" proposal moments, came and went. But being a man in love, RL was too addled to recognize them. Men in love are... well, in love. It's not a state known for intelligence.

But buying the house; that didn't require any fleeting right moment. All that required was a crook.

RL, being a congenital liar, clever, and possessing the integrity of a dead chicken, had naturally became an antiques dealer. A successful one, whose dealings shouldn't be examined too closely. Especially for legality. Perhaps best described as a benevolent viper; RL had money. So, Jayderay wanted the Roaton house... Jayderay would get the house.

As in most of his purchases, RL knew a lot more about the thing being sold than the seller did. And he hammered on the house having a reputation of being haunted. Especially since a dead body had recently been found... impaled on the dwelling's iron fence. Hanging there, it had caused quite a stir among the church group that found it. The women had used unusual language.

The Roaton place was undesirable, untenable, and a worthless dump. It was totally unfit for human habitation. The homeless in Calcutta wouldn't set foot in there. And so on, relentlessly drummed RL. Therefore, the seller (Jayderay's *former* church) should sell, should sell immediately, should sell to RL... should sell at RL's price, of course. Bend over seller, try to enjoy.

RL and Jayderay became the new owners. And they did know a great deal about the old house. Too much. From a horrifying experience, too much.

They bought knowing about its two *visible* residents. Those two, not exactly human residents. The purchase was made to keep the place from being razed, *because* of those not exactly human residents. The new owners were indebted to them; owed them big time.

That fat diamond ring is now back in RL's pocket. He's decided: to hell with the right moment. His innards continue to corkscrew. He looks in the direction of Jayderay's home, where she's currently packing.

He takes a deep breath; he's going. Nothing will stop him this time.

As RL takes this first life changing step toward being engaged... something in the closet makes a sound. It's a rather lonely, pitiful, scratching noise. *Damn it! That mouse would pick now to get caught. But if I leave it, George will get in there...*

Muttering curses, he pulls the Catch & Release trap from the closet, looks sternly at the mouse.

"Well, you weren't invited, you little beady eyed, gnawing shit." And taking the cage outside, dumps the mouse beneath a Honeysuckle vine. "Don't come back, you idiot. A cat lives in there!"

And evidently a very odd human that talks to rodents. Thinks the mouse, swiftly disappearing into the foliage. *I wonder if he talks to coat hangers...*

Back inside, RL tosses the trap into the closet, and once again steels his nerve. Fiercely gripping the ring through his jeans, he takes deep breaths, many deep breaths. All this accomplishes is dizziness. Checking the ironed creases in his jeans, tugging on the chambray shirt, finger combing his hair... he vastly improves... nothing. A man in love; a most pitiable creature.

Nearby on top of RL's desk, George the cat displays fat pink, rear toes to the ceiling. The front paws curled beneath his chin; one eye open and watching. George hadn't been bothered about the mouse; that was his human's job.

Looking at him, RL says, "George, this is bullshit," and with that profound, all-encompassing statement, he walks out. The cat's whiskers twitch, and the toes on one back foot flex; exhibiting extreme interest. And George is thinking: *RL is lucky he has a skull…it keeps his hair from falling in on his teeth.* George often has such thoughts. And he knows RL does indeed talk to coat hangers, he curses them regularly.

Marching across their adjoining drives, RL knocks at Jayderay's door, and immediately enters. Princess, greets him delightedly, bouncing about, giving a grin that dogs do so well. She adores this man who had once rescued her. He kneels, hugs her, quickly telling her she's the world best dog, and then yells out, "Jayderay!"

"I'm in the kitchen, honey," she calls back.

So far, so good.

With bowels pulsing like a boiling snake, RL storms into the kitchen, and finds her filling plastic totes for their new home.

So far, so good.

Without a hug, without a kiss, without even a simple I love you, the besotted fool drops to one knee. Extending the fat, sparkling diamond ring, he gasps, "Will,

will, will you marry me?" Not smooth, but finally... he's dunnit.

So far, so good.

Slowly turning, looking down at this sad specimen of love, brown eyes moisten, and she bites slightly on her bottom lip. With her hair up in a scarf, dirt smears on cheek and chin, that sad specimen thinks she's unutterably beautiful.

So far, so good.

"No," she answers quietly.

RL's intestines swallow his heart. Now the real fretting can begin.

———•◆•———

Quite a few miles from the spurned RL, and the cruel Jayderay:

Like something excreted by a cranky monster, the Roaton house crouches in chaotic overgrowth. It's a structure built from cursed lumber, from wood that had been murdered and bribed for. The timber had been taken from sacred grounds, and local legend tells that this dwelling hasn't forgotten its origins... that the wood used wants payment. And more than just wants, occasionally takes its due. Takes its due in people.

Through the decades, vines have engulfed the surrounding iron fence, and clutched their way up to the second floor. Abandoned gardens run riot as windows watch, like the eyes of something not quite dead. It has a lonely, desolate, poisonous appearance. Even in the searing Texas sunlight, it looks more than frightening. It looks like a place where the dead walk, and those not so fortunate sob during never ending nights. A place where much worse than murder has been done. Much worse. A place of enigmas. A place to run from. Not a place any sane person would buy.

Inside the house—inside it's worse. Ancient furniture with angry, carved faces lean crookedly on sagging floors. They've shifted through the years toward other pieces, as if wanting to feed. Desolate cobwebs holding wretched dust, coat all with a lonely skin. There are many rooms here; all are marred with memories of fear. The future holds more.

A curving staircase climbs to the second floor reluctantly, as if dreading what might be found. Framed portraits line the hallways; their watching, haunted eyes longing to close. Weak light peers through rotting drapes, while far above a stained skylight paints all with doom.

And this Roaton house has a basement, and the basement has a closet. Within that closet, a metal door occasionally reveals itself, glowing slightly. But there is no magic about this door, it just is not always seen. It came to be here long ago, came here by way of science and math; by an experiment gone horribly wrong beneath the New Mexico desert. And sometimes... sometimes this door slides open. The door leads directly into hell. The door opens into the Waydowns.

But there is love in this house. A deep, all-consuming love. A love only possible between a couple who have known the deep despair of aching loneliness, of decades passing without touch, of soul withering years without tenderness... without hope. Currently, this pair are the only *visible* residents of the Roaton house. There are others.

Yes. This house is to be RL and Jayderay's new home. The house they have chosen. The house they want. The house they have bought.

Good luck. Write soon...while you live.

CHAPTER 4

AND BACK IN THE WAYDOWNS...

As the boar creature closes in, Tanya's cabin door slams shut in Seevee's face. Hearing it lock he doesn't consider this a betrayal or treachery. Ton is just making sure she has time to grab the gun before the monster is upon them. There could be no other explanation.

Swirling to face death, the Almost clutches his knife, swiping at the air; it's all he can do. Sweat runs from his face, soaking the khaki shirt, arm joints throb and he breathes in short dry gasps.

Greedy pink eyes watch Seevee from within their wreath of bristles. It saw the hatch slam shut, leaving this man alone in the corridor. Yet the human doesn't run; only crouches waving and jabbing at the air. The hog thing is mildly curious about why it doesn't run, and totally unimpressed with the air cutting. It stops advancing, hoping Seevee will break and flee.

Seevee mops his forehead with one of his elbows; his chest vibrates with the pounding of his heart. *Seevee much not run... must make give Ton much time for gun... Seevee must fight... much fight... much fight for Ton.*

Inside the cabin, Tanya regains her breath, leaning back against the locked door. Cradling the Uzi, she idly strokes the scars on her face, rubs the blind eye, feels the healed bite marks, and the ear with its missing lobe. She looks straight ahead, remembering the near past. The time when Dr. Gaust had given her to the Almosts. For their... enjoyment. They were almost human and they had *needs*; male human needs. Seevee, their straw boss, had protected her from the worst. But he had sure taken his sweet fucking time about it.

The monster watches Seevee cower at the locked hatch; savoring his fear. Slowly rising on back legs, it walks closer. The split hooves make a muted tocking sound against the deck.

Reaching out, it repeatedly clenches its hands in the air, flexing the thick fingers. Fingers tipped with small, gore-stained hoofs. Snorting through the upturned snout, spraying pink snot, snuffling, savoring the stench of Seevee's terror. It walks closer. The massive, curved haunches ripple with muscle, and thighs rub against each other, their stiff spines muttering. It loves to play.

Seevee chokes trying to swallow; there is no saliva. Close before him stands violent death by a creature he knows he can't possibly kill. But the corridor stretches out in the opposite direction. A clear path to countless other halls and rooms. He could run; he might make it to safety. *Must no run... much soon Ton open... soon much bring gun...soon...*

Inside, Tanya sighs with disgust. *To hell with, Seevee... he's not wounded, let him fight or run. The groping, lovesick son of a bitch... but I still need him. I only fucked Lakker, I don't own him, not yet. So, I'm stuck with this damn Almost. Well, I can get rid of his gawky ass when we take 19.* She clicks the Uzi's safety off. *Do I, or not? I'm not hearing shit; what the hell is he doing? Did he run? Did the thing eat the bastard? I better wait.* She clicks the gun's safety back on.

The beast halts again, dragging out its play as it stands there, looking at Seevee. It wants him to run, wants him to scream his way along the corridor, wants him to desperately search for a hidey hole. Beneath the snout and two curving tusks, it's red cavern of a mouth falls open, the tongue lolls out. It laps at the air. The huffing laugh comes, carrying the smell of recent butchery. It crouches down a bit, legs tensing to leap.

Seeing the beast about to charge, Seevee braces himself, the knife blade dancing in the air as his hands shake. Stinging, blinding sweat runs into his eyes. *Ton come soon... much come soon...*

Quite a distance from Tanya and Seevee, a hatch unlocks. It's more or less on the same level... but in the Waydowns, such things are hard to determine. This door opens slowly, cautiously. It's the only way into this deck below the Waydowns. The only entrance into the rest of the ship that had not been engulfed by the holocaust. This portion had been spared the twisting, melting and cellular blending that created the Waydowns and its monsters. It also held the ship's unknown power source.

During the crazed time, that time when staff turned on each other, that time of mutiny, of murder and raving madness, this door had been sealed. The people behind it were safe, but all communication with the rest of the ship had been lost. Fear of those decks that had become the Waydowns, terror of its creatures, had kept the hatch sealed and locked. Now, only one man even knew how to open it.

And that hatch remained locked for decades. Until Tanya came tapping at that entry. Tanya had gotten a man inside to open up. Tanya is a woman. Women are very good at getting men to do things.

That same man now steps from the opening. Sixtyish, dressed in patches made from the remains of uniforms and staff clothing. He also wears a silly, stitched leather hat that he thinks is absolutely stud-nuts. But he doesn't appear to be well. A man whose skin looks as if gangrene had set in... and then moved out, as if it hadn't liked the furnishings.

Lakker by name, he stands just outside the room that had once been a small sanitizing chamber for the adjoining deck further in. This man wants what many of his people do not even believe in; he wants topside. He wants to see sky, sunshine, trees, oceans, and stars glittering in the heavens. Things that he only knows of from ancient video stills, and stories the original human staff had told. Originals like his parents. Things that the youngest of his community do not think actually exist, cannot comprehend. To them, there is only the ship, and whatever decks might be above. Only the ship, from which all things come, light, power, water, food. Only the ship. Always the ship. Ship without end, Amen.

This man knows better than to try finding the fabled topside without help. It was that driving need for help that led him to open up for Tanya. A woman unlike any of his tribe; a Topside Woman.

But he hasn't come out for another meeting with Tanya, not this time. Fishing an old revolver and a small metal tube from his waist-bag, Lakker prepares for a different kind of encounter. A dangerous one. He lifts the tube to his mouth.

———••———

Seevee trembles, watching the hog thing prepare to attack. He smells foul breath, hears its bristles rub together, sees the eyes glitter above snout and tusks. It's having fun.

Abruptly the beast lifts and cocks its head to one side, both pointed ears rise, twitching. Standing, it looks back down the corridor, snuffling the air.

Tanya bursts through the door, leaping behind See-vee, pointing the Uzi over his shoulder. The creature doesn't turn, or even seem to notice her. Dropping to all fours, it lopes away down the dimly lit hall, rapidly disappearing into the haze.

"What the fuck, Seevee! The bastard didn't even look at me; what the hell made it run?"

"No much know... much, much glad! ... much glad Ton come... why Ton long time not come?"

"Uh, yeah... I—had to load the gun, and it sorta... the clip kinda got jammed up. Listen Seevee, that bunch of clothes you found for me, well nothing fits but the panties, and they need washing, so you need to get busy with that. And while you're at it, do my lab coat too; it's barely white anymore. So, hop to it; I'm gonna take a nap. Oh, yeah— are you okay?"

There's nothing quite like a one-sided love affair.

Lakker finishes calling the Long Pig, puts the whistle away, keeping the gun in his hand. The creature sort of belongs to him, but it's extremely unpredictable, best to keep the pistol in sight and ready. The thing has been shot before; it knows what a gun is. This was its first outing beyond the hatch, and certainly not a planned one. Lakker had taken the beast to the doorway to judge its reaction. But seeing a manlike shape down the passage, Long had bolted. Lakker wasn't suicidal; he hadn't chased after it. Let it kill something first.

The Long Pig's normal roaming area was below Lakker's deck. That place of power, where the ship's life source thrummed constantly. An enormous and mostly unknown area thought to be the the very bottom of the ship. Only armed hunters dared to go there; some never returned. And down there, a huge not-water lake lapped gently at metal shores. No one EVER went into that.

The power place teemed with life. The deadliest was a yellow slime-like mold. It rapidly coated whatever it caught, slowly absorbing while the captured still lived.

Humans lasted indefinitely, managing a slouching, oozing walk while they were digested. And they desperately tried to talk with the hunters who came across them. The eyeless, wet glob remaining of their face, pulsed where the mouth had been. Silently screaming for help. The hunters and villagers called these desolate beings Melts, or collectively: The Yellow.

It's not exactly a mold, not precisely a fungus, nor a bacterium, or cancer. It's an alien world's form of a disease that has a terrifying name on earth. And this extraterrestrial version is... *sentient*. It is driven to multiply; driven to spread.

The boar creature lopes into view, and Lakker produces a few dried skin treats, plus a bit of ear scratching for it. He uses only one hand to scratch, as his other prudently grips the pistol. No fool is this man.

CHAPTER 5

BACK ON TOPSIDE

His proposal refused, RL is still on bent knee with the ring extended, mouth silently opening and closing. No words will come. He resembles an odd, constipated guppy. One that has just offered marriage... and been turned down. Love can hurt, even guppies.

"No, RL," Jayderay says again, gently. She need not have repeated it. He'd heard the first time. Her answer still rolls about inside him, like a hot marble. A radioactive, big and fat marble.

"It's beautiful," she says, taking the still offered ring and pulling him to his feet. "I love it—"

"YOU DO? Then why won't you—"

"Hush, RL, just hush. Come sit with me and let's talk," she says, starting toward the living room. But a flashing memory of being raped on that hard, uncaring floor turns her toward the bedroom. The rape RL has never been told about.

With Princess following, grinning her adoration,

they sit on the bed. Even being stunned into imbecility by that awful answer, RL pets and speaks to this loving animal. He knows, even more than Jaderay, that they are the dog's entire world; she shouldn't be ignored. She can't possibly know that one of her humans has just kicked the living shit out of the other one's heart.

"RL, I love you, love you with all my heart. We pretty much livin' together now, and will be full time when we get the Roaton house settled. But there's something you don't kno—" she pauses, changing direction.

"Marryin' is... it's something I've dreamed about since I was a little girl. Dreamed of me in a beautiful white dress, so happy I'm cryin' as I walk down the aisle, fixin' to be joined with my love, joined by God."

"But, but Jayderay! That's exactly what I want us to do. I want to—"

"Hush, baby. I know you do, or least you want to, because I want to. It's one of the reasons I love you; you a good man when you don't know it. Fact bein' you at your best, when you don't know it," laughing gently as she says it. RL doesn't join in; he sees no humor in this. And besides, he doesn't think he's a good man, he knows better. She looks at him steadily for a few seconds, brown eyes searching his face, her bottom lip caught between her teeth.

Taking a deep breath, she begins. "RL, I ain— I don't

have a church no more, and what's a lot worse, no God neither. When that awful thing caught me at the Roaton place and dragged me into that Waydowns, I screamed for God's help, I cried and begged for his help, and God wasn't there. He wasn't there before when I was in bad, terrible need, and I don't think he ever been there."

Her losing religion is only a bad thing to RL because it may be a long-term bad thing for Jayderay. She'd been raised to believe, by a much loved, devout Grandmother. And Southern Baptists, especially *Black* Southern Baptists, tend to be rather serious and starchy about marriage vows.

RL doesn't give a plucked partridge about vows or religion. But he does believe in God...with a passionate hatred. Yet he does pray, when driven to by the need of someone he cares for. Never for himself. He gave that up as a child... right after murdering his stepfather. That belt-happy, wife beating, fine and good Christian nightmare.

"Well, Jayderay, we could have a non-denominational ceremony, or maybe a J. P. could—"

"No, RL. No. If God bothers to show back up, then we'll marry in a church with him attendin'. In the meantime, in the meantime I'll wear this gorgeous ring and live in sin with you." She smirks at him, adding, "If your high moral standards can make do with that."

There is very little RL's high moral standards can't make do with; they are very adaptable. Like his ethics, they're as stretchy as hot licorice. He grabs her, and they fall back on the bed laughing, holding each other.

"RL! We don't have time for any mornin' time foolin' around like this. We both got tons of work to be doin' for our move," she says, making no effort to get up.

"So, who do you think is fooling, girl? Shouldn't we celebrate our engagement?"

"RL! Just what do you call what we been doin' ever night? Seems to me—"

"Well, I hadn't proposed yet, so those times don't count."

"DON'T COUNT! You 'bout to get your white butt in serious trouble, boy. I'll teach you how to treat a—"

RL interrupts her with a kiss. Their conversation becomes a bit disjointed, and quickly becomes... celebrating.

The ring sparkles. Princess thumps her tail and grins lying beside the bed. All is good. For now. But God is not through with this celebrating couple; the Deity works in strange and mysterious ways. Like an industrious dung beetle.

Quite some time later, RL floats languidly in a sea of bliss. Curtains softly filter the morning sunlight, as a ceiling fan gently stirs perfume scented air, and heaven on earth envelopes him as he drifts softly...

"RL! Don't you fall asleep like you always do. And while we layin' here, I been thinkin' and needin' us to get something clear."

"I wasn't going to sleep," he mumbles, being rudely snatched away from heaven. "So... what needs to be clear?" When a woman says she wants to 'get something clear,' the man needs to pay attention. Unless he's dead or wants to get that way.

"You kinda got a thing for that Queen Latifa woman—"

"WHAT! I do not have a—"

"Oh, shut up, you," she laughs. "Don't start lyin' before I can even finish. You do got the wants for her, 'cause anytime a movie on with her in it, your eyes get all funny. And *other* areas get frisky—"

"Jayderay! I just watch the movie, I'm not—"

"RL!"

"Well, um, well, okay... maybe I do pay a little bit more attention to, um, to her parts—I mean her act-ing."

"'Her parts' was 'zactly the right words, RL. And you better listen good to me; when we lovin' I better not never hear her name in my ear."

"I... I... well... I only watch her because she looks so

much like you, baby," says the very guilty RL, who had thought he'd been quite sly about his private lust.

"Yeah, RL, you sayin' the right thing, but lyin' as usual of course," she says with a grin. "But you mind what I said, or you liable to find *my parts* gonna be mighty hard to get."

"Yes, dear," says RL, and tries on a smile. He wisely doesn't say another word.

"That's a pretty good answer... comin' from a devil. Now, we got to get up, we got tons of work, and... Hey! Why ain— why aren't you at the shop, anyway? Not that I'm complainin', but did Frankie know you was gonna be late? That boy do get up to things when you not there."

"Frankie's as greedy as I am. He'll open up whether I call, show up, or appear in the obituaries. As to him getting up to things, hell, he does that even when I *am* there. But you're right, I need to get down there... unless you think we should—"

"No, I DON'T think we should," she laughs, scooting away from him. "Get up, put your jeans back on, and get a move on. You a engaged man now, and I expect to see a little industry from you... *outside* of the bedroom."

If it were not for women, men would accomplish very little. Poverty and starvation do not count.

Several miles away, inside the Roaton house, there are rooms that cannot be found. Except by those that walk paths unknown to *most* living creatures. In one of those hidden rooms, another very much in love couple are also on a bed. And have been for quite a while. Getting their morning exercise; they don't jog.

Love and lust, a couple of four-letter words that are often mistaken for one another. Lust is a basic animal instinct; love is a human's early glimpse of heaven. And as close as some will ever get. Both words are entwined with another four-letter word: soul. Provided the beings have one. Which, with this lusting and loving pair, is uncertain. Because they're just a little bit... different.

Shadow lies with her head on the man's bare chest. She has no coloring; she consists entirely of charcoal hues, ever changing shades of grey. Except for her eyes. The eyes have color. Brilliant violet color.

Her partner makes up for this deficit in pigment. He's lavender skinned, with eggplant colored hair, and eyes that are nearly all pupil. The couple make an exceedingly arresting sight. People not prepared for the treat, have been known to leave quickly. Very quickly, without making excuses.

"Elv-is," she says, with her always hyphenated pronunciation. "I still do not understand about this strange door in the basement closet," she says, her dark nails languidly stroking his chest. "We well know it to be a danger to this house, our home, our life... should we not block it totally? Merely barring the basement entrance hardly seems sufficient."

"No, we can't, pretty kitty," Elvis sighs, taking her hand. He's been dreading this conversation. "I gotta be able to get in there. I ... I must go through that door, into the Waydowns, back into the ship."

"NO! I will not allow it, Elv-is, I will not," she says, jerking her hand from his as she sits up. Glossy black ringlets of hair bounce and swirl about the scarred gray face, framing ebony lips, and those eyes of violet.

"I bore you going into that cursed place for Jay-deray, and I have seen the death that lurks there. I will not have you return to that horrid region."

"Shadow, honey; I have no choice. I will... I will die if I don't."

Her sable eyebrows arch, as her eyes widen, face twisting in terror. "No," she whispers. "NO! I am Roaton, I am the house, I will not... accept this. I will not permit your death." Flecks of white in the violet eyes have begun to move, like stars shooting outwards, gaining intensity. "I will not bear you going, will not bear your dying. Death will not deny me of you."

Having witnessed her anger before, Elvis wants to stop this before it goes any further. He doesn't fear her, but he fears *for* this woman. Fears what the madness within her may cause.

"Shadow! Listen to me, I don't have to go in there to stay. But I must breathe some of that air from time to time."

"I do not comprehend this, Elv-is. Why is this so? You are now living on my air and have been since first we met. You must tell me; for your love of me, tell." Her scarred, once beautiful face twists in concentration.

"Baby," he says, taking a deep breath, reaching for her hands. "I don't *know* exactly why. But I'm... I'm not... all human. I don't know what I am, not really. I was sort of invented, created in the ship's lab. And I didn't... turn out right, didn't... grow like they wanted me to. So, I must breathe at least some ship air. I'm sorry I haven't told you about not being— not being a real man. Nobody ever loved me before, and I was afraid. I AM afraid. I'm really scared that you will— stop."

As the insanity fades slightly from her eyes, a brief look of sadness flickers, but she smiles. Both cheeks dimple, creating darker pools of grey.

"Oh, Elv-is, you pretty, pretty, silly boy. I have known of this; known that you are not of total human blood from our first meeting. Not from your beautiful color, for skin stains are many. But from first I touched you, I knew. It matters not. When the house took me from a life I could no longer bear, I too, became something other than human."

Putting her maimed arms around his neck, her gray cheek against his, she continues. "But you ARE a man," her voice begins to coarsen, the insanity returning to her eyes. She looks past him, beyond him, looking into a vast pit that only she can see. "You are a man above all others, for you are MY man, and I shall love you beyond this world."

He cannot see her face as her crooked arms tighten till his neck hurts. Her eyes becoming totally white, bulging in their sockets, seeing that which is not meant to be seen. It is not her first look. As the black lips work to form words, he hears her teeth grate and grind together and her voice deepens.

"I am Roaton. I am the house. You belong to me. Always. Forever. I will not be parted from you."

Love is real. Love is magical. Love is frightening... and it can be as hard as a fucking anvil.

Something else in this room also seems magical but isn't, and it's much harder than any anvil. Off in a corner, carefully covered with a sheet, is the Extender. That disaster waiting to happen Extender. The Extender that Dr. Gaust is so desperate to recover. The Extender that will soon have visitors. Very unwelcome visitors.

CHAPTER 6

WHILE IN THE SHIP...

Huong listens boredly as that old dickhead Dr. Moto talks of his plan to reclaim the Extender.

Delicate of limb and features, with large, long lashed eyes, Huong almost fits his name, which in English is Pink Flower. The name could've caused him a lot of trouble in school. Could have, but did not. His eyes had kept him safe. After one look into those lifeless holes, all schoolyard tormentors quickly faded away. And did not return. At any school there's always another defenseless wretch. Someone else to drive closer to suicide.

Huong's big Bambi eyes are without humanity; totally without, as is their owner. If the eyes are windows into the soul, these show a brimming septic tank. He's deadly and devoid of empathy. Qualities that Moto recognized immediately while recruiting the man, as they were an excellent match to his own psyche. And the good Dr. Moto had a private reason for hiring him. One he didn't share with the lovely Pink Flower.

Had it not been for a looming trial over the murder of his missing wife and children, Huong would've told this prune of a Jap to blow a syphilitic elephant.

But Huong was very guilty, very likely to be convicted, and very likely to ride the needle. So, he'd joined the security team and became a grunt. Joined with no intention of staying, only long enough to get the huge cash sign-up bonus. And when he got his first leave, he'd disappear into the far reaches of polyglot South America.

After being driven through the New Mexico desert to a white building marked: CONSOLIDATED CONCEPTS, he'd been escorted to an elevator which lowered him 19 floors. Huong began to suspect he'd been had... as in slickly fucked. He did get his money, in cash, as promised. But he knew in his gut: No grunt ever left this buried spaceship alive.

So now he listens boredly to this Moto Jap. But quickly becomes attentive. Very attentive; they're going into the Waydowns. Huong has heard the rumor that somewhere in that maze of hell is a hidden access to an old house. A topside house. He must pack his money.

"I have an informant within the Waydowns, one that will guide us to a long-lost elevator door," says Dr. Moto.

"Goes up or down?" asks Huong.

"Neither. But that is of no concern to you at present, *Private Huong.*" Moto often put special emphasis on this recruit's lowly rank and girly name. *You little effeminate gook bitch. If you survive this expedition, I have some very interesting duties waiting for you. Somewhat sexual duties. Yes, indeed, somewhat sexual.*

"Go, prepare for entering the Waydowns. Await my orders."

With only a curt nod, Huong leaves. And prepare he will. It won't take long. Money spins the world, and he intends to get his, and take that ride.

Dr. Moto watches him go. And then, taking a deep breath, he readies himself for Dr. Lillith Sally Gaust. His visions of the delicate Huong, naked, trussed up and whimpering fade. Turning to his console, he keys the monitor screen.

"Speak!" Gaust commands. But again, there is still no visual. And her voice, like before, is different, disturbingly sibilant. It's hers, but not hers.

"Huong is prepping for our retrieval of the Extender; we will enter the Waydowns via your elevator. I intend—"

"By elevator. How innovative of you. Elevator as opposed to what? Using pickaxes? I don't give a fuck if you melt yourself and drip down there. Will there only be you and this Ho Chi Huong?"

"Yes. I felt it best to depend on stealth rather than assault. There aren't many grunts left in security with actual Waydowns experience."

"Stealth to where?"

"The, uh, the, the way into the topside house." Moto was not prepared for this question. If he admits knowledge of this entrance, then the Honored Abomination will want to know why she hasn't been told. Not good.

"So, you know where this entry is?"

"I surmise that—"

"Why, here's another of the great Dr. Moto's many accomplishments! He can *surmise*. Don't strain yourself; I do not wish to hear anymore. Get me that fucking Extender. But before you go *stealthing*, I urgently need food. I want it breathing, and bipedal."

"Dr. Gaust, so soon after your last ingest— um, so soon after the disappearance of Debra... is this wise?"

"I see you've reverted to thinking again. But you have managed to make a valid point. Has that pair of Orangutans arrived?"

"Yes."

"Bring me the female, shaved, bound, and unconscious without anesthesia. And see that you manage this without performing any of your *personal* examinations of her anus. You are to deliver this yourself. Only you. Mind me, man, mind me!"

Dr. Gaust terminates the communication without waiting for Moto's response. Failure to comply was not even a remote possibility. She is God on Deck 19, and her power and authority have grown through the decades. All decks and the white building above obey her directives. And her taming of the Waydowns is coming.

She is also the last of that long ago secret group that knew about The Switch. That bunch had blithely joked about it, even dubbing it the 'We're Fucked Switch.' And Dr. Lillith Gaust does not forget important things, most especially items like that *joke*.

Gaust shifts uneasily in a chair she no longer fits well, much as her tongue no longer fits her mouth. Her gaze flicks to a large, round container. This eight-gallon specimen display has adorned Lillith's desk for years. Smiling, she reaches out, caressing the glass sides. This jar always accomplishes the impossible... it made her smile.

Its curvature distorts viewing, making the murky contents seem to move and change. Sometimes showing what might be something identifiable... or maybe not. Perhaps it's only twisted meat within the liquid. Inside the glass, the mass occasionally seems to shift. Probably only the light through the wavy glass. Probably.

Long ago, Lieutenant Bastrop had been sent by the top brass. He had plans to shut down Deck 19. He didn't. He went missing instead. Dr. Gaust felt the removal of all his limbs, due to volume requirements, was regrettable. But the wounds had cauterized nicely. She pats the jar. *Still with me, aren't you! Ever alert, ever inquisitive. And you still watch me, don't you?* From within the glass prison, what might be an eye... slowly opens. Probably just the light again.

Still in his work area, Moto stares off into space, frowning slightly. His wizened face looking like an ancient, dried apple. A worried apple. He's a little offended by her reference to his sexual inclinations. Not embarrassed, that's not possible. But really now— on an ape? How demeaning. Still... it had been a while since the hapless and so soft Debra had disappeared.

Rubbing his bandaged head, he forces his mind away from fun to think about Lillith's changed vocal patterns. *It is not her voice, and yet... it is her voice. Why? I shall soon gaze upon the most Honored Butt-Plug... that should reveal much.*

Yes, Dr. Moto will see Lillith. He will see her for the first time in many, many days. And yes, the sight will indeed reveal much. It will be quite an enlightening experience. One he will not want to repeat. Not ever.

Behind this thinking, worried and perverted apple,

something stirs. In the cavernous game room once the prison/nursery of that shithead Elvis mutant, something yellow grows. Inside a Bowl-A- Rama is Tanya's gift, hidden there by Seevee. It extends a pod or two. It bubbles. It doesn't worry.

Directly below Moto and Deck 19, sprawls the Waydowns with its myriads of fused decks, twisted corridors, and wronged life forms. And Tanya.

As the end of her second hitch in the army neared, Tanya was approached by a group that provided trained personnel for clandestine organizations. These companies, like Consolidated Concepts, were *innovatively* funded by a military slush fund. Very slushy and very under the radar. And the pay with benefits, were beyond good.

Acceptance required a high security clearance for which she took a battery of psyche tests. She breezed through them all. Proving that, for the right money, Tanya was quite capable of seeing and taking part in highly illegal, morally reprehensible acts... and keeping her trap shut. As are most people.

But Tanya had increasingly fallen into disfavor at the new posting. She had a corrosive attitude and a smart mouth. Never with Dr. Gaust, nobody ever had a smart mouth with that woman. Never. But with everyone else, Tanya was prickly, abrasive, and basically, as she herself so delicately stated: a cast iron cunt.

Drinking heavily during work hours added to her sweet disposition. So, after repeated complaints and screw-ups, Gaust had given little sweet Tanya to the Almosts. For their play toy. This should've ended all Tanya problems by ending Tanya.

But Tanya... was Tanya. Soon after, the entire company of Almosts deserted Deck 19, fleeing into the Waydowns. Led by Tanya.

Rising from her nap, Tanya finds her freshly hand washed, nearly dry lab coat, panties, and even a bra. Seevee had been busy, but not busy enough. There's nothing else to wear. And no decent food. Except a few of the old military issue packets he had scrounged earlier. And of course, those nasty protein bars the ship continually produced. Which were marginally better than bird shit.

"Seevee! Are you out there?" she yells toward the closed cabin door. Picking up the white coat, and without waiting for an answer she continues, "Get in here."

Out in the corridor, Seevee was putting on his, also just washed, khaki security guard uniform. He wasn't about to wait for the shirt and pants to dry; he wanted to cover his body before Ton could wake and see him. Ton was disgusted by his multi-jointed arms, so naturally, he was too. Hurriedly buttoning his shirt, he opens the door.

"Yes, Ton, Seevee here."

"Couldn't you find any different food in the staff lockers? I've picked through what you found the last time. And those fucking crap cakes the ship pukes outs are killing me. They're for… things like you." Tanya isn't known for her patience when first waking. Or ever. Being stuck in the Waydowns with this last Almost for endless weeks hasn't improved it.

"No much time for look. Been washing," he says, absurdly proud and pointing to her lab coat. "Will much get food, much soon time."

"Well, you sure don't have any time now, we're supposed to meet with Moto at 19's elevator. To show him the way into that topside house."

"Moto much sneaky snake, much no trust. How Ton know when where is?"

"How I know 'when' to meet is not your concern, and a Coiler showed me 'where' that house entry is. Anyway, I need to check on something else important, and I've decided to send you."

"NO, TON! Moto much take Seevee back to lab! Much take to, to Gaust!

"Just fucking calm down, you belong to me now and he knows it. He's not gonna take you back to 19."

"NO, no, Seevee no ever come back, much no—"

"Oh, do shut up, Seevee! Try and be a man... if that's possible." *You insect looking pile of shit, if I didn't need you for a little longer you damn sure wouldn't come back... Jesus, if I have to fuck you again, I think I'll kill myself. God how I wish I could go into that topside house and just keep on running. But I must take 19; I will have that bitch Gaust. And then 19 WILL be mine. Fuck topside, I want 19... All of it. All of it. All of it.*

"Yes, Ton. Seevee go. Seevee much luff Ton." He's crushed. Her telling him to "act like a man, if that's possible" has totally shredded him. He feels he's going to his death, but go he will.

"Yeah, Seevee, I do know you *luff* me. I much, fucking much, know. Now scuttle away and go wait for Moto."

Tanya would do well to remember that even the most loyal of dogs can be kicked once too often. That old adage could be applied to an Almost. But she has other things on her mind, like touring Lakker's deck. The next level down that isn't part of the Waydowns, yet has been out of contact with the ship for decades. The deck that leads to the ship's power source... and whatever may be there.

Slipping into the freshly washed panties, she decides against the bra. *Tits are a great influencer, and Lakker sure as hell isn't immune. Him glimpsing mine peeking in and out of this unbuttoned coat will keep him distracted and agreeable. And willing to do just about anything I want.*

Above, on Deck 19, Moto has taken delivery of Dr. Lillith Sally Gaust's next meal. The caged, unconscious ape is bound at wrists and ankles, which have been twisted behind its back and fastened together.

Turning the trolley about in a slow circle, he studies the Orang with mild interest. Sticking a wooden rod through the stainless-steel mesh, he jabs the animal a few times, getting no results. It's lying on its side, so poking various areas of interest is easy. His pulse quickens as he licks his lips, swallowing loudly. *I do wonder...perhaps just a bit of hands-on examination wouldn't be noticed... No! Enough. I must not. The Honored Hemorrhoid would know; she always seems to know when I've...enjoyed myself. I must submit to the ignominious role of waiter. But my time nears.*

The good Doctor Moto is right, his time does draw near. It will be sooner and extremely different than what he has planned.

Wheeling the breathing but doomed dinner to Lillith's private entrance, he signals his presence, and the door slides open. Dr. Gaust stands there to greet him.

Moto only takes a brief glance. It's enough. His bladder releases.

CHAPTER 7

TOPSIDE TURBULENCE

RL's bedroom comment to Jayderay was correct: Frankie had opened up their antiques shop. Since he lived below it with a connecting spiral staircase, this was no great hardship. However, RL was also right about Frankie's greed, so he would've opened up if gliding down from the moon was required. And the boy was sometimes that high. But never enough to affect his business acumen. Never.

Many things naturally go together. There's burger and fries, fish and chips, chili and toilet paper, just lots of things. And then there is Frankie and RL. They too, go together, like dollars grown inside a corkscrew. Mr. Greed and Mr. Avarice. They each do have good qualities, and keep them well hidden.

Franklin Delano Cornay, was referred to by many (including himself) as "the silly bastard." And he was silly... in some ways. He was also extremely good at buying and selling. And he excelled at cheating and lying. These are requirements here at NEAT STUFF, as they are in many a business. Politics, Law, Religion and Whoring, to name a few. And they're particularly beneficial in the antiques trade.

And Frankie, like RL, was also a murderer. Neither partner knew this about the other. It wouldn't have made a gnat's butt of difference. In fact, Frankie's stature would probably increase greatly in RL's view, since he often did think of the boy as... well... a silly bastard.

But such a revelation of Frankie being a killer had to be avoided for RL's sake. Because the silly bastard had gleefully and delightedly murdered the man who had brutally raped Jayderay. A rape RL mercifully knew nothing of. And she was determined he would never find out. Men can be a little odd about things pertaining to those they love.

And the silly bastard will soon kill again. He's a bit like that. This is Texas after all, and if some two-legged blight needs killing, well... why burden the courts. Frankie is quite civic minded about not bothering the law. So is RL.

Swishing about, futzing with this and that, the silly bastard limps a bit. He's dusting; arranging rare and exquisite items. The same items that he had called cheap crap while giving an appraisal... *before* buying. Now they're exquisite. And expensive.

He checks to be sure the halogen spots are angled just right in the jewelry case. Gimping about, he removes the $75 dollar tag off a foot stool that's been hanging around too long. Making a new price tag of $175, he immediately marks a huge red X through that, and then writes in a sale price of $95. Such artful marketing ploys are rarely discussed between the partners, there's no need, the two are as one where money is concerned. Besides, the thing *is* on sale, and *is* at a considerable discount. Just look at the tag.

What Frankie doesn't do, is worry about RL's whereabouts. Usually, he prefers it when the boss isn't around. Sometimes that man can be a tad prissy about certain things. Like shop attire for example. Frankie has some darling outfits that have absolutely been forbidden. Really now! What's wrong with a hot pink shirt and matching pants with a white velvet belt? And the boss also objects to the silly bastard's *Showtime*. Even though he sometimes joins in.

Showtime is occasionally used to get rid of undesirables. Like pretend customers who aren't buying, but have been there so long the stink of decay has set in. Or some ass who wants a refund, after realizing he's been tenderly... fucked. The nerve of some people.

Now leaning on the jewelry case and easing his limp causing foot, Frankie plays with his newest toy. A very deadly toy when in the wrong hands. And it's certainly in the wrong hands at the moment. He'd acquired this little device on a harrowing rescue of Jayderay from the Waydowns. When the Elvis/Proby mutant had clubbed the Egg Foo out of Dr. Moto, the doctor had lost interest and dropped this little trinket. A baseball bat upside the head can cause just about anyone to lose interest in... just about everything.

Frankie had quietly pocketed the item, and later he'd gotten Elvis to show him its many wonders. It was a ship-issued V-Prod, and besides shooting a body-frying electrical arc several feet, it also had lesser settings. This was fortunate for the silly bastard, who accidentally activated it on one of the lower calibrations. He'd only blackened the toenails of one foot. At its lowest setting the Prod also produced an intensely unpleasant tingling itch. A deep burning prickle that screamed for immediate relief. Discovery of this setting made Frankie giggle. Gleefully. It had so, so many possible applications.

Gimping over to an ornately framed mirror, he checks his all-white attire (RL calls it the ice-cream suit) The boy preens a bit, fluffing up the ever-present cowlick, knowing this adds mightily to his wholesome innocent look.

As the front door opens, Frankie immediately goes on point. A fresh fleecing to start the day!

Except it isn't. What it is, is a semi-regular, rectal pain. Teresa Ann Penny billows in, flashing a blinding smile. And she's wearing an all-white pantsuit! *You blond weed of a twat,* thinks the seething Frankie.

"Hi, Tap! It's always so good to see you." Frankie gushes out the lie effortlessly, exhibiting his boy scout grin complete with chipped front tooth. The woman thinks the silly bastard calls her Tap because of her initials. She's a little mistaken. It stands for tits, ass & pussy. And not much of those items, as she's got the figure of a bamboo pole, with a matching brain. To Frankie, that's all she is, T. A. & P. She isn't capable of being anything else.

"We're a matched set today!" she chirps, pointing at her outfit. "Why isn't that just the cute jingles, we should do lunch at the mall, so everyone could see." Teresa doesn't want to go anywhere with this silly bastard, and would go to great lengths not to be seen with him. Tap is after information.

Frankie would rather take a mallet to his tender parts, than accompany this stupid bitch anywhere. Teresa, like many women, thinks all gay men have an affinity to women. That they all wanted to BE a woman. That they envy and covet every wonderful thing about females. And most especially that oh, so precious, vagina.

Frankie is aware of this and thinks it's an enormous crock of buzzard vomit. With the exception of Jayderay, whom he loves like a mother, and Shadow, whom he's in awe of... the silly bastard didn't even *like* most women. And as far as wanting one of those mysterious and scary orifices instead of his weenie... not ever. Never! He loves that appendage. Quite often.

However, Frankie has a shop to run, so he does have to play up to this type of mind set. After all, this stupid excuse for a woman might actually buy something.

As the woman flits about, posing as she handles various pieces, she chatters away. Never using any foul, unladylike, dirty birdy words. She's just sure that Frankie is taking it all in. Just positive that the boy is taking note of all her gestures and stances; just knowing that he will soon practice and mimic all her moves.

Well, Frankie will indeed *just* do something. He's getting very close to doing it. It's a hard, vexatious world, and the lovely Tap is about to learn just how distressing it can be.

"Oh, my! Frankie, isn't this vase the cute jingles?" and blah, and blah, and "Oh, you darling boy, this lovely figurine is the total cute jingles." and blah, and blah, and "Why this entire little shop is the cute jingles," she titters on endearingly. Tap is quite sure she's endearing.

Time crawls, stars are born, stars die... and Tap... is still in the shop.

What Frankie is quite sure of, is that he's been *cute jingled* about all he can stand. His hand slides causally into his pants pocket. He fondles the Prod. Lovingly fondles.

Teresa continues to cute jingle her way throughout the store, and Frankie dutifully follows. He makes the right comments and answers, complimenting her on what a good eye and fine taste she has. He still fondles the Prod. He's now holding it more than fondling.

"Frankie, honey, I just know I can be personal with you; we're so, so much like each other. Welllll... RL... you and he... you both do take, um... *precautions*, don't you? Of course, I know there are new treatments for that terrible... Aids thing; but you people still really need to be careful." She has affected a look of deep concern... while trolling mightily for information about RL.

This insult to women has the hots for RL. She can't understand how he, or any *real* man, could possibly resist her demure overtures. Her repeated demure overtures. Her everything but unzip his jeans, demure overtures. And she refuses to even think that RL could possibly be interested in the nigger woman that chases after him. Could he be flat-kneed? What a perverted waste that would be.

"Oh, absolutely; we are very careful," Frankie answers, totally deadpan. "Of course, I do so worry about RL; he's so promiscuous. He can barely keep his hands off any damn man that comes in here," he giggles, and his hand now firmly grips the Prod. It's about to be Showtime.

Teresa is currently turned away from him, bending over looking at a chest. She gets a sick look on her face. There are no cute jingles in this bit of news. *I fucking knew it; it's not the nigger bitch. RL is a fag! Both him and this silly bastard.*

From within his pocket Frankie aims the Prod.

"Well, that's very good to hear. I certainly wouldn't wan— OOOOOYA, EOOOOO, NAOOOO," she wails out, both hands flying to her rear as an intense prickling, burning itch drills in and upward. Deep in and deep upward. The feel of a cactus being rammed deep up and in wouldn't be this bad.

"Oh, my goodness," cries Frankie, releasing the Prod's button. "Whatever is the matter?" he asks with great concern, fighting off a fit of the giggles. Within his pocket he slightly lowers the Prod's aim.

"I, I don't know, I suddenly got a terrible pain in my... my back. I can't imag—OOOOYAH-OOOOOWOOHOO," she shrieks, bending over and clawing at her shoes. "My feet, my feet! Oh, fucking Christ my feet!" Bending over was not currently a good move for Tap to make.

"Oh, what can I do, what ever can I do?" yelps Frankie in dismay. What he does do is raise the Prod to its former elevation. And activates it.

"YAHOOOO, WANOOOOOOO! My ass, my fucking ass," Tap screams, straightening up and trying to thrust both hands down the back of those billowy white pants.

Keeping the Prod depressed, Frankie lowers it back to her feet.

"YI-YIEEE, FOOOO! My feet, my cock sucking feet! OOOOHIYOOO, my feet!" screeches the ladylike Teresa as she jigs about trying to get the shoes off. Hopping through the shop, knocking crap everywhere, grabbing one foot, then the other.

Frankie, repeatedly asking what he can do to help, follows closely. He also alternates the aim of the Prod: Feet to butt, butt to feet, feet to butt. And Tap responds with great liveliness. A bucket of frogs fucking couldn't beat her.

As the yodeling, dancing, gyrating woman falls to her knees, Frankie keeps the aim on the white clad buttocks. Sending the Prod's itching, prickling voltage... deep and up. Again, the woman rams both hands down the back of her pants, clawing and digging as she staggers to her feet and gyrates toward the restroom.

Frankie dutifully follows. So does that deep penetrating voltage. He keeps asking if there's any way he can help. She keeps strenuously yodeling. He purposefully stomps on his own injured toes to keep from giggling hysterically. He's such a silly bastard.

Standing outside the slammed restroom door; he solicitously waits. He also kicks the base of a marble pedestal with his sore foot, trying to keep those giggles down. Not knowing if the voltage can penetrate wood, he courteously keeps pressing the Prod. On, off, on, off, and so on. He quits from fear of running its charge down. The throbbing foot isn't working; he giggles. Gleefully.

Inside the restroom, Teresa bends over and rests her face against the room's tiny window sill. Those billowing white pants and her shredded panties are around her ankles. Both of her hands are busy... scratching and digging. Deeply scratching and digging.

Quite some time later, Teresa Ann Penny leaves. She leaves quickly, quietly, and walking awkwardly. She doesn't speak, nor make eye contact. Before getting in her car, she spits something onto the asphalt.

Frankie is pretty sure she won't be back. Ever. He manages to contain his grief. Checking the restroom, he finds some odd damage. The window sill has teeth marks and a chunk bitten out of it. He giggles. Of course he does.

When RL arrives, coming in the back way, he yells out to let the silly bastard know he's in the building. This is best for all concerned; Frankie does tend to get up to things. And RL definitely does not want another repeat of catching Frankie naked and making love to a marble statue. It had been a decidedly male statue, naturally.

"How's the till this morning, Frankie?"

"Empty as a pimp's heart, Boss," he giggles out. He wants badly to tell about the Tap episode, knowing RL would howl with glee. But RL doesn't know about the Prod, and Frankie's wants to keep this secret for a while longer. No need to burden his business partner needlessly about silly little details. Like having a deadly space age weapon about. He might worry. And besides, the thing was only deadly if it was in the wrong hands. Oh, dear.

From long experience, RL doesn't ask about the giggling.

"Are you going out to the Roaton place, Boss? Or are you going to be underfoot all day?"

"And just why is it you're asking?" RL responds, giving Frankie's ice cream suit an up and down look while raising his eyebrows.

"Mon Capitaine! Surely, you're not suggesting that I might get up to something. I'm hurt. I'm devastated. I'm mortified. I'm—"

"Oh, shut up, Frankie; what you are is a silly bastard. And the thought of you getting up to something never entered my mind— mainly because it's always there. But, yeah, I am going out there; hell, I've kinda got to go. It's sort of my home now or is about to be. And that is a plate full that's gonna take some chewing."

"I'll bet on that! So Jayderay still wants to live there? And what about that basement—"

"I asked her to marry me this morning," interrupts RL, in a rather dazed tone. He's learned there's quite a lot of dazes involved with love.

"Well, it's about fucking time, Boss. Congratulations!"

"Um... she said no, but then gave it a maybe."

Frankie is shocked into a rare silence, but it doesn't last long. Only death could bring lasting silence to that boy. Perhaps.

"So," says Frankie thoughtfully. "It's a maybe. Huh! Sounds like a good escape clause option. That woman's even smarter than I thought."

"Thanks a lot, you traitorous asshole," laughs RL.

"To tell the truth, I was stunned at the no; but a maybe will do. I'll take her any way I can get her."

"Okay, so you're *kinda almost* engaged, and I'm guessing you two will live in that house of horrors. So, what about Elvis, Shadow and that Hell's Door in the basement closet?"

"Frankie, the home *is not* haunted, and it was Jayderay's idea to buy the place, BECAUSE of Elvis and Shadow, to protect them. She and I owe that couple more than we can ever pay. As to that damn Waydowns door... I think, I think... I think I don't know."

"How intelligent of you."

"Oh, shut up, Frankie. And while I'm gone, try and make some money."

The house isn't haunted, RL? Really? Ignorance can indeed be bliss... but bliss has a bad habit of betraying those who are afflicted with it.

———•··•———

A few miles away, beneath a hot Texas sun, the Roaton house waits. In its basement, there is *that* door. One step out of it is the Waydowns, where it could not possibly be. The Waydowns, that sealed off portion of a long-buried spaceship. A ship that's beneath a white building in New Mexico.

The door is a hiccup of science. A glitch of math

during an experiment gone badly wrong. An experiment by humans fiddling with a science not of their world. A science that folds and nullifies distance. And that glitch is in RL's un-haunted, normal house.

Inside this home, a mutant shithead, called Proby by some, and Elvis by others, starts happily up the curving staircase. Having crept from Shadow's dusty bed as she dreamed darkly, he'd slipped outside... and gathered flowers for her. He knows from lonely years of watching old movies, women love getting bouquets.

As he inexpertly tries to arrange his offering, a heavy mist forms on the landing. From the cloud, three vague forms slither out. Bringing arctic cold, they flow down the steps like thick, deadly gruel. They remember flowers.

In her bedroom, Shadow's eyes fly open like violet starbursts in the ash-colored face, scars darken, and poorly healed bones ache. *NO! I shall not allow this... he is mine... you no longer live.*

On the stairs, the mist rolls down toward Elvis. Step by step the reaching tendrils curl across the oaken wood, ever lower, lower, lower.

Elvis switches flowers about, tweaks at petals and leaves, totally oblivious to the creeping spectral vapors.

Outside, RL slowly drives his van down the weedy drive; wearing the gooey, sappy smile of the newly engaged. The grin doesn't sag a bit as he surveys the two- storied pile of doom that is to be their home. The gingerbread laden house actually seems to be somehow softer; the garden lush, rather than overgrown, the riotous vines picturesque instead of invasive. The Roaton house looks melancholy rather than menacing, and certainly not haunted. Absolutely not. Love can indeed be miraculous.

Exiting the vehicle, RL stands contemplating his and Jayderay's new home, still smiling sappily. *Absolutely one of the first things to do is get a landscaping crew in here. No doubt, Jayderay will have some instructions to give them... she's pretty good at giving direction.*

Inside the house, cold writhing death strikes.

CHAPTER 8

MEANWHILE, BACK IN THE SHIP

Moto stands before Dr. Lillith Sally Gaust, unaware that he's wet himself. Unaware of the sweat beading on his face, unaware of the gorge rising in his gullet, unaware of the unconscious ape at his feet. All caused by one quick glance... and the stench of her dying part.

He is totally aware of Lillith, and totally aware that he had been very curious as to why she hadn't been showing herself. And quite puzzled about the change in her voice, and to what extent her shoulder growth had enlarged. Now he knows. All has been revealed. Beware of what you wish for.

Dr. Moto has spent decades viewing and causing horror. From the rich opportunities the WW2 Japanese Military had provided him, continuing on after his defection, by way of the U.S. Government and Dr.

Gaust. At this moment, Moto is discovering there can be... too much viewing.

Because this horror is so much different. Causing a deep revulsion, a deep terror for having known this woman for long decades. She is still vaguely human... but utterly repellent.

"Well, well, the esteemed *Doctor* Moto has arrived, bearing a feast. You do at least make a good house boy. Orientals are rather known for that. Aren't they?" Her voice is like rough silk; like sand with oil. Her tongue shows too much.

Moto remains silent, his eyes fixed firmly on the trussed ape at his feet. It moves slightly, giving out a low moan. Moto wants to do more than moan.

"I asked you a question; I'll not ask again."

"Yes, Dr. Gaust; we make very good servants."

"Ah, so! Velly, velly glad you aglee. Now, this Orang you can't seem to tear your eyes away from; it has had no injections, correct?"

"No, Dr. Gaust, only a Prod has been used."

"Good boy, good Moto. And you and this Ho Chi Huong are ready to enter the Waydowns?

"Yes, Dr. Gaust.

"Once again, the Moto performs well. Perhaps I'll not have to send this ape in your place to do a better job. Now... look long at me this time. I SAID LOOK! MIND ME, MAN, MIND ME!"

Making a low strangling sound, Dr. Moto slowly raises his eyes.

———•·•———

Directly below them in the Waydowns, a lonely and lovesick Almost waits for Dr. Moto. Staring at the melted controls of Deck 19's elevator door, he knows only too well they've been disabled to keep monsters out. Monsters like him. From inside, the lift is quite operational... for humans. Humans like Moto.

Seevee sits, waits, and thinks of how proud he had been when he'd been awarded the set of khaki security clothes. He had made it; he was an Almost! He'd developed into almost human with so many of their privileges. Then came the gift, the woman. Tanya—Ton. And then there had come love. But with love came... defection, betrayal, and murder. Love had destroyed the Almosts. And now... now he was a monster; nothing but a Spill.

With his multi- jointed arms wrapping about knobby knees and most of his back, Seevee rocks back and forth, trying to tear his mind away from the past. *Must not back think, much no good. Think Ton, think her, only Ton matter. Maybe much find food and clothes in never before place... never finded before place... place with dead arm.*

Seevee has made a discovery. In the blended decks and convoluted halls of the Waydowns, there were endless unknowns. Abandoned regions filled with drifting haze, rooms with flickering lights and blinking readouts from dusty workstations. There were often human staff lockers, storage rooms, and even the occasional larder. And occasionally weapons, which would be a huge Tanya pleaser.

On his way to rendezvous with Moto, Seevee had taken a wrong turn. While finding his way back, he'd come across an unknown hatch. Frozen in a nearly closed position when that long-ago holocaust had hit. The sleeve of a lab coat dangled from the top of the narrow opening

Seevee will soon learn more about that sleeve. He will find that knowledge requires payment.

The deck directly below the Waydowns belongs to Lakker and his people. The last, the lowest deck of the ship. They escaped the holocaust that created the Waydowns, but not the ravages of time.

Descended from the original human staff, they're a people that've been totally sealed off from contact with the rest of the ship and the topside world... *for over eighty years*. At first, scouts had been sent out periodically, venturing into the Waydowns. The few who returned brought tales of such horror, all explorations were stopped. No one would go. These are a people that slowly devolved into a frontier society. A culture of diminishing manners and mores, of speech, of diet... and of gene pool.

Lakker, he of Long Pig ownership, currently has his face buried between Tanya's breasts. She shucks the flapping Lab coat from her shoulders, letting it fall to the floor. Seconds later it's joined by her new panties; their removal didn't require her help. They indulge themselves in ways that Seevee would not approve of. Much, much no approve.

Lakker is with a topside woman, and thinks he's in heaven. Perhaps he is... but it will have a downside. Heaven always does.

Somewhat later, after heaven has receded as heaven always does, Tanya gets to the real reason for her visit. She's an exceedingly practical woman; she hadn't wanted sex at all. But men must be coddled along, and their penis is an excellent leash.

"So, how many of your people are armed? And are they worth a shit?" asks the practical Tanya.

"Godamighty, woman! You do kinda change the pace

sorta quick don't you," says the recently coddled Lakker. "Well, I reckon I numbers them to be around—"

A loud knock interrupts him, and the cabin's hatch swings open immediately.

"Sherrf! They took the Long—"

"Goddammit, how about you wait and give me a second a'fore you come barging in, Deppity Shank!"

Tanya, looking at the female intruder, remains silent. But she's thinking plenty, thinking with the innate charity all women extend to each other. *Is that a female? Jesus Christ! Has he been fucking that? Hell, I swear, men will fuck anything. And what's this Sherrf and Deppity shit?*

With blazing eyes, Deputy Shank glares at the nude Tanya, but speaks to Lakker.

"Well just s'cuze the tarnation out of me, Sherrf! But it's the Long Pig. In the... down in the power place, I was with some hunters and I seed it! I seed them Melts, the Yellow, they come up out of the not-water and they... they taked him, they, they... just taked him!"

"WHAT! The Yellow took Long? Hell, he don't never get even close to—"

"He din't get close! I tolded you, they come out of the danged lake and grabbed him, and that ain't the onliest thing... they was little ones with them!" Deputy

Shank finally rips her eyes from the naked slut on Lakker's bunk and looks directly at him. "This was like they was waitin,' like they was had planned on it, Sherrf."

"Little ones," says a shocked Lakker. "Hell, we ain't never lost no kids to the Yellow, not never. There shouldn't oughta be no little ones."

With her eyes darting back to the nasty, nekkid, filthy whore on Lakker's bunk, Deputy Shank says, "Yeah, that's what I was knowin' Sherrf. I'm afeared we got a terrible problem gettin' ripe on us. So whyn't you... uh, come with me down to there. If you thinks you kin spare the time... and you might want to cover yourself some more better."

"Thanks for that there advice, Deppity. You wait for me... outside. And close the door."

That still silent, still nekkid, still awful whore on Lakker's bunk, watches Deputy Shank exit. What Tanya had first thought was pregnancy had been a mistake. The little bitch has several tits. And the bottom tooth that grew out and on to her upper lip also added to the cow's overall beauty. *God Almighty, I shudder to think what her snatch looks like.*

But the Deputy is young, maybe early teens, maybe very early teens. And youth has a beauty all its own. And youth always has a magical effect on men, who are often swine. It also has an effect on women... somewhat less than magical. Especially on women who are over thirty. Tanya is well over that mark.

"I take it you and Deputy *Skank* have some history," Tanya says. And where did the wild west, Sheriff and Deputy talk come from?"

"Godamighty, the Yellow come out of the not-water and took Long... and there was small ones with'em. Come out of the lake? Bullshit, it cain't be," muses a stunned Lakker, not even paying attention to the naked Tanya. This is not something she can ignore.

"I asked you a question, Lakker, and you haven't answered. I really expect to be treated better than this," she says, giving a verbal yank on his leash.

"What?... Oh... yeah, right. Well, some of them original human staff, like my folks, had liberrys of real paper books. And they had lots of cowboy shoot'em ups and pitchers. And everbody as had their letters read'em, or heard'em read and them stories kept on being re-told. Anyways, some of the lingo just sorta caught on. That's all been long years back; now they ain't none that knows nothing else," he answers, totally ignoring Tanya's Skank and history comment. No fool is this man.

"So, you and *Skank*, huh? 'Hi-Yo – Yippie, You Cow. Ride the Buckin' Sow,' and all that shit. Huh! Wow, you're a regular John Wayne Sheriff, and I'm so impressed."

The Sheriff, once again wisely ignores the comment. Yes, he's a very smart man.

"Well, whatever," says Tanya. "Listen, I'm coming with you to see this power place, and you can fill me in on these Melts and the Yellow as we go." Motioning toward a small burnt patch on the wall, she asks if that had been some of the Yellow.

"Yep, the shit kinda crops up ever wheres. Only thing that kills it sure, is fire. So, you knows and seed it afore?"

"We call it Gunch. Maybe the Yellow is a better name for it. All we know for sure, is the shit's deadly and we don't dare touch it. Come on, let's get moving... *Sherrf*. I imagine the Deputy Sow, I mean Skank, is waiting." Tanya knows there won't be any objections about her coming along. Lakker wants a way to topside and she's it. And Tanya would bet he has no plans to take the comely Deputy topside.

"What's a Johnwayne?" he asks, once again ignoring the danger zone of her Skank and sow remarks. Smart man is this Sheriff... except just maybe for the Tanya angle. Tanya may cost him more than he can pay. She has that effect on men, and her scarred face seems to have increased that. Could be a rescuer kind of thing. Men can be odd.

"Uh, I'll tell you later, but right now, let's just go. I

want to see... some stuff. This cabin of yours is so close to the hatch, I haven't seen much of your... *territory*... Sheriff."

Yes, Lakker's deck and its original human staff had escaped the holocaust, but they couldn't escape the long decades of total isolation. Nor could they escape the proximity of the ship's power source; they were right on top of it. An unknown energy supply installed thousands of years ago, light years away by unknowable beings.

Ragged, inbred, ignorant and diseased summed up the population of Sheriff Lakker's domain. A few children were in evidence, but Tanya felt they should never have been allowed off the birthing table alive.

Tanya's children never made it that far.

She begins to suspect that what she'd first thought to be radiation poisoning was simply acute scurvy. A people fed primarily by the ship's automated delivery of protein cakes, a few make-shift hydroponic planters, and whatever horrors the hunters brought back from the power place. Damned little Vitamin C in that diet. She also noticed there were no elderly or infants and everyone looked sick. Or dying and badly wanting to get on with it. These findings did not sit well.

As she accompanied Lakker and his sulking Deputy, Tanya's assessment of his deck and people was quick, sure, and typically Tanya: *What fucking piles of shit! Even my Spills are better than these walking turds. Christ Almighty, I'm fucking Lakker for THIS?* Always charitable is Tanya.

Waiting for them, a couple of fifty-something men stand on either side of the locked power place entry. Bert and Giney, who both seem to resemble their names in an unfortunate, inexplicable way. Suiting their stitched together rags, both have on what they no doubt think are cowboy hats. Tanya thinks the men are fair specimens compared to the others she's seen. She also thinks the hats look like an animal crawled up on their heads... and died while there. Not very long ago.

They're armed, kind of. One carries an old military issue rifle, the other a revolver, dangling from a string around his neck. Both make no effort to keep from staring at Tanya, who has not bothered to button her lab coat, and the panties are, well... they're panties.

"Dang-Gooley!" says leering Bert to the leering Giney. And continuing in a voice meant to carry, "That there new fuck-hole is wearin' panties! I swear I onliest seed such in pitchers. Dang-Gooley! She's done got my piss wantin' to curdle up thick. I'm thinkin' I—"

A hard backhand across Bert's mouth knocks the man into the wall, interrupting him... and whatever Dang-Gooley he'd been thinking.

"Open that shit trap again if you want more," says Lakker in an almost casual tone. But there is nothing casual about his glittering eyes. "This here lady is a guest of mine, and she will be treated the same as my Deppity. Either of you yahoos got a problem with that? Bert? Giney?"

Shaking his head silently, Bert holds his mouth as blood trickles from the split lip. The no longer leering Giney shakes his as well, staring intently at the deck, while scratching one shin with a foot.

"I'm mighty glad of that, boys, powerful glad, so sees you don't fergit it none."

There is no smoldering resentment from either man. Lakker is the law, and the law is to be obeyed. Without law, there is mutiny, with mutiny comes chaos, with chaos... people end up in a stew. Old women and sickly children first, and then... and then things get really bad. Berts and Gineys end up on the menu.

As Deputy Shank struggles with the release on the power place entrance, a nipple peeks out through her ragged shirt. It's coming from about where her navel should be. Tanya doesn't miss this and thinks what a twat the woman is. Tanya's own bare breasts flashing out of the lab coat are... well, that's different. They're persuasion tools.

The two guards take zero notice of Shank. Tanya

doesn't miss this either. Nor is she worried about the two drooling, but no longer ogling, hicks. With her army hitch served, her time under Dr. Gaust, and surviving the Almosts, these hillbillies are no threat to Tanya. They have delicate parts that can be swiftly and painfully damaged. Or ripped off. Plus, she's the honored guest of the *Sherrf*.

While the Deputy fights with the long ago smashed and often repaired hatch, Tanya watches, taking note of the busted mechanism, and musing on the people she's seen. *I guess I'll have to up my opinion of Deputy Skank... maybe Lakker took the pick of the pigs. I can see why there's so few children, I wouldn't stick a dick in anything down here either.*

"Godamighty, Deppity, get a move on! That thing's been fixed more times than you can count. How hard can it be to open a patched-up lock? Ain't like you never done it afore."

"Well, the danged thing gets worser ever time, Sherrf. It ain't none of my doin.' How 'bout *yore guest...* MISSY Hay-Hair, lendin' me a hand?"

"Tanya is my name... Deputy *Skank*. If you can pronounce it past that tooth of yours."

Hay-Hair, is it? Just you shut up, Hoglet. Stick that nasty tit back inside your rags and get the fucking door open. Good Christ, I hope I see something I can use down here.

Ignoring this bit of normal women banter, Lakker gives Tanya an offhand warning.

"If we *finally* ever gets to goes in, you be mighty careful of anything that looks like a plant growin' out of the floor plates. They's a forest of'em, and don't touch none 'cause some are mighty quick."

"You sure right about that, Sherff," says his Deputy. "Speshly them there real pale ones. Them is more faster than rats."

Tanya doesn't speak but thinks plenty. Thoughts like maybe she should just get the fuck out here. Her hopes of seeing anything useful has rapidly dwindled from small to nothing.

But Tanya will see things.

And Sheriff Lakker is right about those plants. They are quick.

CHAPTER 9

AND UP TOPSIDE...

RL, the newly engaged, the consumed by love, the sappily smiling fool, stands beside his van. Viewing his new home to be, the Roaton house. What he's seeing is *not* a menacing, dark, hulking, life consuming, vine draped Victorian horror with a basement door into hell. No, not at all. What he's seeing in his mind could easily grace the covers of *Better Homes & Gardens* or *Southern Living*. And it's certainly not haunted. Yes indeed, the brain of someone in love can be a very self-deceiving organ.

Thinking of landscaping, he dreamily ambles toward this prize residence.

A piercing scream from inside shatters his illusions. Ordinarily, RL is an exceedingly cautious man. The unkind call this being a coward. But he is also remark-ably protective of his money... and he's just bought this fucking place.

So, catching himself before totally getting back in the

van, he turns back toward the house. *This is my home... besides that, there's Shadow and Elvis in there...*

Another scream rips out of the house, ending as if cut off by sharp teeth. RL takes off running... toward the front door. *That was Elvis!... gotten through that basement door and grabbed him... not in my home, God damn it!*

Bursting through the door, RL's flash of indignant bravery freezes. So does he.

A spectral knot of writhing vapor hovers above the curved staircase. Bright colored flowers lay scattered on the steps, and standing among them, Elvis fights for his life.

Ropes of the swirling mist wrap around him. As he struggles, another wraith of vapor darts from the cloud, coiling around his neck. They lift him high above and over the stair railing.

Far below, RL watches in horror as Elvis is swung back, crashing his body into the wall. Jerking him away, the vapor again slams him back. And again, as blood sprays from his mouth, while clouds of dust and bits of plaster billow out with each brutal impact.

RL starts up the stairs, scared spitless and shaking, but he owes this lavender man. He must, he has to help... with no idea of what he's fighting. Or how.

Elvis is blasted back into the wall a fourth time.

Totally limp now, he's flopping like a rag doll, both eyes wide open, pupils rolled back, showing red. Framed portraits jar loose and fall, dragging cobwebs with them. Their bubble glass bursting as they hit the oak treads, scattering shards of sparkling glass among the wilting flowers.

As RL nears, a twist of vapor detaches from the dangling body, floating slowly toward him. Grabbing for the misty rope, it dodges quickly, coiling about him.

Again, they lift Elvis; ramming his face into the skylight, smearing it with blood... and the wraiths drop him. Falling, he lands hard, sprawling, rolling across the steps, stopping when one arm flops through the balusters. He lays broken, utterly broken, amid the splinters of glass, and the sad, blackened remnants of a scattered bouquet.

All the tendrils start moving toward RL, gaining speed. And the one already tightening about him begins lifting.

From the landing comes the sound of a door being thrown open. And like the Wrath of God in some black and white film, Shadow swirls into view. Her violet eyes are now all glistening, throbbing white, the ebony lips a gash, peeled back from barred teeth. Her voice fills the house, eating all other sound.

"LEAVE THEM BE! I WILL SEE YOU DO THIS. I WILL SEE THIS DONE, NOW. YOU DO NOT BELONG HERE."

This charcoal sketched woman does not slow her advance as she speaks, seeming to glide down the steps. Facial scars stand out darker against the ashen skin as tar black hair frames those bulging white eyes.

As the misty ropes drop RL, retreating, the gray woman kneels beside Elvis, gathering his head and shoulders in her arms.

Between RL and the woman, the snakes of vapor have once again congealed into a pulsing, knotted mass, silently floating in the air. When Shadow speaks, bits of mist uncurl, darting at her like tongues, but quickly pulling back into their ever-roiling cloud. RL feels their bone aching coldness, something far beyond the chill of death. Far beyond.

Holding his limp body to her, she rocks Elvis, and looking directly at the vaporous cloud she speaks with venom dripping from each word. As before, her voice more than fills the house; words that hang and echo.

"PRAY TO WHAT EVER GOD CLAIMS YOU. PRAY MY MAN DOES NOT DIE, OR I SHALL FOLLOW YOU. THERE WILL BE NO ESCAPE."

The writhing mass disappears as if it had never been. RL rises slowly and takes a couple steps toward the couple. He doesn't fear Shadow, but he'd once been the recipient of the anger that can take her. It's not something he wants to repeat. Not ever.

"Shadow... is he... is he alive?"

"Yes, he lives. My husband lives. But I can feel that he is no longer here. Not here with me." Tears spill, trailing down the ash grey skin. "I know he must not return to those who created him, nor can he be taken to any place of medicine. Can you please use your telephone device to call, to call Frankie? Please."

Fishing his cell out, he asks, "Do you want me to—" he breaks off as a sob wracks Shadow. She's seen the scattered flowers.

"He picked those for me. Elv-is picked those for me. For me... for me. I have never before received flowers. Not even upon my cursed wedding day." The tears drip off her cheeks onto the lavender colored, bloody face of the man who loves her. He had picked flowers for her. Never before in her long, lonely years, flowers.

She's spoken in the toneless manner of a lost child, which scares RL nearly as bad as her GOD voice. Looking at her guardedly, he softly asks, "Shadow, what were those... what were they?"

"They once were my daughters. They will return."

Back in town, the silly bastard is leaning on the jewelry counter idly polishing a few of the better pieces. He's also having to field questions and comments from an elderly couple, who are just too precious for words. And he knows they won't spend a dime, even if threatened with a Nursing Home.

Blue walking shorts support the man's matching tee, along with suspenders and hat; a dainty, narrow brimmed thing with a tiny blue feather stuck in the band. A hat that just begs to be shit in. Completing the ensemble are tube socks sagging into brown leather clodhoppers. He looks like a Hummel figurine. A really old one, with knobby walnut knees. The Mr. Hummel is acting a bit huffy, giving Frankie sullen, foul looks as if smelling something really nasty... like his own denture breath.

Frankie knows from long experience exactly what's wrong with the wizened old fool: The Hummel thinks Frankie is a silly bastard queer. This isn't a problem for Frankie. Frankie thinks Frankie is a silly bastard queer. He revels in it.

Mrs. Hummel's floral pantsuit compliments her hubby's attire. Frankie is puke sure they have match-ing denture jars with cavorting cupids on them. She, of course, thinks Frankie is just an absolute darling. So does Frankie.

Coming mostly from the woman, the inane conversation continues, as Mr. Hummel makes occasional grunts and snorts of contempt. Frankie has heard all this verbal diarrhea countless times. He's exceptionally good at dealing with it... IF the fuckers are buying. These two ain't, and ain't gonna; they're at a free museum. Whee. The crap flow continues:

"Where on earth do you find all these interesting things? Do people bring these wonderful pieces in to sell? Do you ever take things on consignment? Oh, my! This is just fabulous... what is it? My grandmother had one of these, exactly the same. I wonder what ever became of it? I'll just bet that awful sister of yours took it. Don't you think so, Hubert? You know how she is." (Mr. Hummel grunts) "Oh how wonderful it must be to work around all these beautiful items every day!" And on it goes.

Frankie smiles his beaming smile, flashing his chipped front tooth, making all the appropriate responses. He could do this in his sleep. The jewelry has been put away. It hadn't needed polishing anyway; he just loves touching it.

And finally the woman says it. That inevitable, nausea inducing, testicular cancer causing statement:

"Oh, how I wish we could afford to buy some of these beautiful things. Don't we, Hubert? Why, we will think about all this, and be sure to come back." Hubert grunts.

Frankie smiles, nodding, his cowlick gleaming. His hand slips into his pocket. He grips the Prod. He's been wanting to use it pretty much since the pair walked in.

God damn how I'd love to send an itching bolt from this lovely Prod. Drill it into both of them... but the codger would probably swallow his teeth, choke, have a heart attack and die... then the wife would start screeching and wailing... and THEN... why then RL would show back up...and he'd know I'd gotten up to something. The Boss does get so prissy about some things. Maybe I should up the voltage and just kill these two no-buying wastes of floor space; that'd be quick... but then I'd have to drag'em into the back and bag them. I wouldn't bother frisking them, they're not carrying anything but lint and pennies... But I'd still have to wait for RL to help me lift the geezers up into the dumpster... and he'd naturally want to know what the hell we were throwing away.

Yes, RL definitely would get all whiney about customers dying in the shop. He has before. It's so blasted inconvenient, and plays absolute hell with sales. Frankie's right; RL is just too, too prissy.

As Frankie struggles with his attack of "want to real bad," the matching pair of pains continue their way about the shop. He keeps his hand on the Prod. He's beginning to think that just a light dose of the penetrating itch, surely, surely wouldn't give either one heart failure. He watches these *customers*. He takes a firmer grip on his new toy.

The shop's land line buzzes and he answers with his cheery, predatory, "Neat Stuff!"

Straight to the point, RL says, "Elvis has been hurt bad; he's been beaten unconscious. Don't ask, just get here."

"I'm on my way, Boss." *All right! now I have an excuse for... Showtime!* And the Prod is activated.

So are the customers. They suddenly shriek, yodel, and dance about yowing. Frankie releases the button and they stop just as abruptly, hands clutching their butts.

"Here now, you two! We don't tolerate such behavior in this establishment. You'll have to leave," lectures Frankie sternly. His serious tone is ruined when he giggles. To make up for that, he pushes the Prod button again, briefly.

"Yowee-Yowee-Fooo-Uooo," harmonize the customers as they jig about, clawing away with intense zeal.

"Now I said that's enough nonsense! You can have fun and dance in your own home; this is mine, and I won't have it! Out! Right now, I want you out of my store!" says a fiercely scowling Frankie, pointing at the entrance. "Now!" He gives the pair another slight blast and is gratified by more chorusing, springing about, and clawing... with intense zeal.

Muttering in bewilderment, they squirm and scratch toward the exit. Frankie gives them a final jolt... a courtesy extended to help the aged along. They respond with more intense zeal. And he giggles. He's such a gay and silly bastard.

Locking the door behind Itchy & Scratchy, Frankie flips the sign to CLOSED. He grabs the shop pistol from beneath the counter. It could be needed, this is Texas, after all. Killing the shop lights, he checks to be sure the two seniors have gone. He doesn't want to come back and find them squirming about on the asphalt... and mining in themselves with intense zeal. That would take up valuable parking space. And if stuffy RL saw them, there'd be some tiresome explaining needed.

But they're gone... and then so is Frankie. Giggling with intense zeal.

Tearing his mind away from the joy of dealing with his customers, Frankie heads to the Roaton house. RL and Jayderay's new home. The one that isn't haunted.

In his, not haunted house, RL kneels next to Shadow. He's trying to get grip on what she's just told him: that the murderous, eldritch glowing, vaporous things were her children.

"They're your... they were your daughters?"

"Yes, they once were my children in a life long ago. They are of no consequence at this time! My husband drifts from me. I will not allow this. Elv-is must not pass into the beyond. He cannot yet go there."

"But, but you said, you said... they'll come back! What are we—"

"Hear me, hear me now," Shadow pleads, cradling Elvis, her tears glistening. "My husband, my all, fades from me." The white flecks in her violet eyes are beginning to pulse larger, shooting outward, the scars on her face darkening. "Must I manage on my own? Will you not help, will you not lend aid?"

"Yes, at once," RL answers shamefully. The woman and Elvis should have been his first concern, not some damn ghost ropes that were gone. He owed these two, they had saved Jayderay from worse than death. He owed them everything, and besides; he actually, truly, really likes the pair. This is not typical for RL. Toward most of the population, he tends to be... well... a bit of... a fucking asshole.

"Frankie will be here soon, but we need to get Elvis off the stairs, and into the ground floor bedroom. If I take his shoulders, can you—"

Shadow interrupts him by effortlessly rising with Elvis in her long-ago broken arms; his head lolling against her breasts. This charcoal cast woman holding her dying, lavender skinned man; it's a scene screaming from some graphic novel.

"Carrying him is not the help I need, RL. I can easily bear that which I love."

RL hurries down the steps to the bedroom where Frankie had recently nursed Jayderay. Shadow silently follows.

Pulling back the bedspread, RL stands there holding it ready, feeling totally useless. And wishing mightily he was somewhere else.

"No, let us not cover him; he feels so very hot," she says, "I wish to lay him on top of the bedclothes, so that I may examine him."

Shadow gently lays her man onto the bed; her husband, her battered, dying husband. Wiping the blood away from his nose and mouth, feeling his skull, his neck, arranging and checking his limbs, she kisses him softly.

"I cannot detect damage, but I am so ignorant of such things. I know not what else to do," she says kneeling beside the bed. Her hands rub at the badly mended breaks in her arms. "I do not know what to do," she repeats, quietly weeping. "Please help him."

RL goes to his knees beside her, placing a hand on her shoulder. "Frankie will know. That boy is a good medic, he will know what to do."

She reaches up, gripping his hand so tightly he winces, speaking again in that toneless, lost voice that worries him.

"Yes, he will know, he must know, he has to know. And Jaderay? Will she also come? I badly need her with me."

"She will be here for you. As you were for her, she will be here."

And so they kneel there together, this gray, heartbroken woman and her dodgy friend. She turns into him, burying her face into the hollow of his neck. RL hasn't many good qualities, but deep compassion for women is among them; to him they are all special. He holds her as she quietly cries, stroking the ebony waves and curling locks of hair. He doesn't say anything, knowing words can sound hollow. They wait for Frankie.

RL is wrong, very wrong about something.

Shadow's man is out of luck. Frankie will not know what to do.

CHAPTER 10

BACK IN THE SHIP

Beneath the wretched decks of the Waydowns, at the very bottom of this huge, ancient starship, Tanya and the group step through the hatch. They're now in the area which has supplied power to the entire ship for thousands of years.

There is no visible machinery, reactors, or cooling towers. There isn't any big glowing read outs set in massive, bolted structures. No steam, no vapor, no heat. There is only the low thrumming that can *almost* be heard and felt throughout the ship. It's never heard, but always heard.

A large circular body of dark water can be seen far off in the distance. An awesome power source made by extinct beings who were far, far more advanced than humans. There's an oppressive, brooding quiet, humbling eeriness about this alien place.

"Hell... this ain't shit," says Tanya, looking around

disdainfully. Tanya has never felt humble; it's not in her.

"Just listen to Missy Uppy Ass blowin' her hot airs! Whyn't you go on back up to them there Waydowns, where you was borned, if'n you don't like—"

"Tanya is my name, and I was born topside, *Skank*. And you really need to watch that snaggle toothed mou—"

"They ain't no such place! Shank interrupts. "Such like talk is Hersy, and we don't allow no Hersy talk in these parts. I don't wanna be hearin' no such talk from the likes of you, *Missy*. I'll—"

"Enough, Deppity! Tanya is here on my invites, you need to remembers that. Now, get goin' and show me where the Melts took Long. Now!"

"Yessir, Sherrf. But you might warn yore... *guest,* agin, these parts ain't safe like what she's used to. And... she oughtn' talk no Hersy! She oughtn' talk nothin'—"

"Godamighty, that's enough, Deppity!" barks Lakker. "I done warned you afore about sayin' Topside is Hersy. Topside is real!"

Burt and Giney have stood silently by, scratching, listening, grinning... and scratching. There seems to be quite a lot of that. At a nod from Shank, they reluctantly tear their eyes from Tanya, and lead the group toward the distant lake. Both keep turning back to look at the topside woman; Lakker hadn't said they couldn't look. And they keep scratching.

The area is deceptively immense, with a gradual slope toward the lake, which had seemed close by. It had also appeared fairly small. Neither observation was even close to accurate.

And there were plants. Sort of. Some bushy, some almost tree tall, all in varying shades of green. A forest of them, yet none were close enough to touch the other. And none looked as if they actually grew out of the deck. It was more an appearance of having been placed in position, like in the yard of a dollhouse. Or like they had... walked there.

Tanya begins to suspect they are not really plants. The circulatory system that moved air on all decks was also present here, and she could feel occasional breeze across her face, lightly ruffling her hair. But the leaves never moved. *Lakker said the trees could be quick.*

As they walked, Lakker rambled out an abbreviated, hand me down history: While mutiny and madness continued to consume the decks above, it became apparent to the Originals, the human staff, that they were... in the shit. Their isolation from the rest of the ship above the Waydowns was indefinite.

To supplement the ghastly, ship-made protein bars, they'd tried to develop the power area. While not a total failure, they were forced to abandon the effort. The lake water was not water. Their lab animals drank from it, seemed to thrive on it, but ultimately vanished. As did some of the staff. And there were the plants... these did not bear experimentation well.

And it was down here that the Yellow first appeared. Emerging in small splotches without any apparent design. It seemed to magically spread, and it just loved humans. There was no cure; once taken was forever... forever Yellow. The power place became locked and off-limits to all but hunters, desperate for food.

Burt and Giney led the way, taking a winding trail that avoided getting too close to the unnatural looking trees. Lakker and Tanya were in the middle, as sulking Deputy Shank brought up the rear. Pouty mad, that upward jutting tooth nearly spearing her upper lip with every step.

Both hunters continually glance back over their shoulders. They're being sloppy guards, but Tanya is quite an eyeful. Those looks are always complete with gap toothed smiles... and drool.

No one knew *how* quickly Burt died. Or *when* he eventually would die. But everyone knew *what* killed him. Burt was murdered by a lab coat.

On one of Burt's increasingly frequent looks back, both halves of Tanya's unbuttoned coat fell completely open. And there was all of nekkid breasted Tanya at once… in skimpy panties. It was too much for the brave frontiersman. He kept looking backward as he kept on walking forward. As Giney turned on the winding trail, Burt did not.

The plant moved like lightening. The second that moon-eyed Burt brushed against its leaves, they enveloped him. Wrapped him up like sausage in cabbage. There was no sound, no thrashing, or unpleasant leakage. Just a green cocoon, standing there calm and quiet. The leaves wrapping him had been a light yellowish green. They immediately began turning darker.

The group stands in frozen silence for a few seconds.

"And he din't even have no time to says Dang-Gooley," remarks Giney rather wistfully.

"Tarnation, why couldn't he been thoughty enough to flanged his pistol out as he got et up? We ain't got us many guns left."

"Well, they ain't no sense whinin' about it, Deppity. It's as gone as he is. And when we gets back, don't you fergit to go tell his woman."

"Oh, Sherrf! How come I gots to be the one to tells her?"

"Fucking hell! Aren't any of you even going to try to get that bastard out of there?" demands an exasperated Tanya, pointing at the trussed-up Bert. Not only was there the loss of a gun, but the leering doofus was one of the few she'd seen that might have known which end of a pistol the bullet came out of. Maybe.

"Well, whyn't you gives that a try, Missy Perfume Panties? I'd really loves to see you all tucked up in—"

"Oh, do shut it up, Deppity," Lakker breaks in with a weary sigh. "Listen Tanya, we cain't help him. As soon as anybody touches that there leaf wrap, they'd be right up alongside of Ol' Bert. And it'd be just as quick too. It's been tried more'n once, so now we let'em alone. Okay Giney, let's get goin' and keep your damn lookballs on the trail."

Tanya and Lakker follow, with Shank bringing up the rear. She's muttering to herself. They hear an occasional word. Words of endearment that women often use concerning other women: bitch, tramp, slut, and so on. And on.

A woman describing another woman is often an art form. A thing of kindness, love, and beauty the world over. Shank knows how. And so does Tanya. Most women do not like most women. It's an odd thing; one that men aren't even aware of.

As they trek through the brooding, deadly forest, Tanya catches quick glimpses of dark forms flitting among the green boles and leaves. Fast moving shadows of different sizes that appear and then are gone. None touch the vegetation.

"Them shadders you keep seein' is the offshoots from all them lab animals that got away from the Originals," says Lakker. "Long time back when they tried to farm in here, they had quite a few different kinds. Ain't no tellin' what all they've fucked themselves into bein' through the years. Sometimes them hunters will bring back things that cain't even be described. Ain't no harm in most of'em. Of course that don't mean all, 'cause there's Long Pigs and such."

Tanya's ears prick up on this last casually mentioned "there are Long Pigs and such." She wonders just how often the "and such" make appearances. She damn sure knows what a Long Pig is, and doubts she wants to see any of the *and such*. Tanya begins to realize that her plan for getting help from this deck full of hicks is going from bad to worse.

Tanya is right. Things are indeed going from bad to worse. The worse is just a few trees ahead.

"Sherff," calls out Giney, who has studiously kept his 'look-balls' on the trail. "We's gettin' near the shore, and mighty close to where them Melts come out and grabbed Long."

The trees and shrubs become sparse, then totally stop quite some distance from the lake. It's not gradual; they form a line like soldiers. Just like they had been put in place. Or marched there.

Standing at the tree line brought out the enormity of the lake, and the size of the bowl it was in. Looking across that body of not-water, the distant vegetation was only a green blur. The deck gradually angled up on all sides, and the plants seemed to stretch forever.

"It was 'bout right there that it happened, Sherrf," says Giney, pointing at absolutely nothing. There were no marks on the deck, no tufts of fur, just the ships floor. "Them Melts just come thrashin' out of the water and swarmed all over Long. They was more of'em higher than I can make number."

"There was at least two duzzin'," pipes in the Deputy, who actually could count to ten. "All yellow and drippin', and like I done tole you Sherrf, they had little ones sorta taggin' along."

Lakker stands there looking at the nothing, wondering why he'd wanted to see this. See what?

"Well, Long did put up a helluva fight and squeal, but it din't make no nevermind. He was come a cropper," comments Giney needlessly.

Tanya turns from looking at the spot of nothing they had come all this way to see. No doubt Burt would feel he'd been wasted and likely say something about it, something intelligent like Dang-Gooley.

Gazing out across the lake, she sees movement. Nothing which is very comforting, or likely to be of any help in her quest for 19. The not-water has no real color of its own; it's a murky, slightly phosphorescent swirl, much like a polluted bay. And it isn't totally still; it laps quietly at the deck. Now and again, she sees a stream of bubbles trail a long line across the surface. And further out... she spots what looked like a huge back break through the water.

"What the fuck was that?" Tanya asks the three hicks she's saddled herself with. "What lives in there?"

Naturally the hicks are all still staring stupidly at the space of nothing they'd came to see. The group turns toward her as one, and the Deputy speaks.

"Don't nobody knows fer sure. But peers to me them Melts sure enough live in there. You kin bet them there see through panties you keep flashin' around on that. Well, whyn't you stick yore head in and take a look see? You ain't done nothin' on this trip till yet, 'cept to get Burt killeded... Missy."

"How about you show me how to do that, *Skank*. From your smell it must be about time for the yearly bath."

Lakker, who'd been standing silently looking out at the unstill not-water, interrupts. He knows if he doesn't, the two women could come to blows, and *HE* might end up in the water trying to break them apart. Smarter than he looks is this Sheriff.

"All right you two, shut it up and let's get on the trail back. We done about seed all there—"

"SHERFF!" screams Giney, pointing at the water.

⸺⸺•••⸺⸺

Up on Deck 19, Dr. Moto unsteadily leaves his ghastly meeting with Dr. Gaust. Her private entrance slides shut behind the urine drenched, blankly staring man. Staggering to his station, leaning against it, he mechanically wipes his face. Behind him, the Extender's portal rolls blackly, its frame of pulsing light give him the pallor of someone very sick. He is, and is about to get worse.

Huong, having returned from his preparations, watches with cold silence. He's seen similar looks of terror. He saw it in the faces of his wife and children. Witnessing it first hand before their oh, so unfortunate disappearance. And he has the same degree of solicitude for this old Jap dickhead. With a fleeting smirk, he decides to alert Moto of his presence. With a military, eardrum bursting bellow, he announces himself.

"HUONG REPORTING!"

"AIEEE!" screams the old man, whirling in Huong's

direction, falling back against the work station, and making a sizeable deposit in the seat of his trousers.

"Oh... Huong... you, you startled me. I, I... yes, I see you are ready. Very good. Um, yes, very good," squeaks out Dr. Moto, as the smell of his loaded pants join the miasma of sweat, fear and urine already hanging about him. It is not being a good day for this man of many aromas.

"I understood you wished us to leave with all due speed, Doctor."

"Yes... that is correct. Yes, that is right. Quite correct you are. You are right. However, new... new information has... has been brought ... has come to me," says Moto, raising a shaking hand to his bandaged head, trying desperately to keep from gibbering. Trying with all his might to drive the sight of Gaust from his mind.

"I feel... Huong... I think we should, uh, perhaps we need to... the mission has been postponed. We are to, to go at another time."

"But, Dr. Moto, what of the meeting with the Waydowns woman? Will she wait?" asks Huong, feeling his chance to escape slipping away. He then impales Moto by asking, "I'm surprised Dr. Gaust has decided to delay the mission." Bullseye by Huong!

Moto clenches his hands together as his eyes widen. The thought of another meeting, another *sighting* is unendurable. His age wrinkled face looks like a terrified prune; a prune frightened beyond coherent thought.

Huong, correctly reading the prune, strikes again.

"Doctor, if you need to be elsewhere, I could go in alone. I've fought in there before. And if this Tanya can guide me to the topside house, I will get the Extender. I've seen pics of it. I will bring it back, directly to you." *If I find it or not, I'll already be topside, and I'll never look back.*

"This is, is, is most excellent, Huong." *Most excellent indeed, yes, yes, I'll send this gook in, that should buy me enough time. I have banked much money for many years. I will go. I'll never again have to, to see... to face... to see HER again.*

Betrayal and treachery between these two employees of Dr. Gaust. What could possibly go wrong?

Well... there is Tanya.

CHAPTER 11

TOPSIDE TEEN SCENE

Frankie heads toward the Roaton house, wondering what the devil he can possibly do about Elvis. Being a trained Navy medic is all well and good... for treating humans.

But I'm not even sure what Elvis actually IS. Being man shaped is one thing, but he's also got lavender skin, purple hair, and for all I know, battery acid for blood. And I'm pretty sure I've seen what looks like a scale trying to peep out of his hide. Oh, shit! Maybe I'm worrying about the wrong thing... RL said Elvis had been beaten... well that's just ducky... that probably means RL has killed somebody, and we've got a body to get rid of. No! I AM worrying about the wrong shit... what about Shadow? If I can't fix Elvis... and he dies... what will she do... do to ME!

Life can be hard for a silly bastard. Worry is even harder; he's not used to it. And he certainly is not used to worrying about a woman. But Shadow... they have some brief history. An intense but brief history. A history he can't comprehend. A history he doesn't want to comprehend. A history he does not believe... except he does. Quickies become longies... of regret; this is not gender specific. Frankie doesn't feel like giggling right now.

Driving his vintage VW Beetle, Frankie weaves in and out of slower traffic. He soundly curses the drivers for inconsiderately obeying the speed limits. He's not overly concerned about getting stopped; it would be a remarkably short delay. Once any cop stepped from a patrol car, Frankie is quite sure they would frenziedly scratch back in; he's brought the Prod. It's the boy scout code: Be prepared.

It's not a traffic stop that slows Frankie down. It's a regurgitation of teens; a squalor of teens; a scat of teens; it's several teens. Their yesterdays have slipped away unnoticed, they're squandering their todays, and they're eagerly pissing on their tomorrows. The future shines bright.

Frankie screeches to a halt at a *green* light, as the group languidly strolls the crosswalk. They purposefully slow to a crawl, grinning with stupid insolence at Frankie. They smirk at the geeky, goody-two-shoes sitting in his little bug of a car. They're all absolutely delighted he's in a hurry. At best, they each have the brain pan of a small oyster. And it might take the entire lot of them to manage that much, sort of a collective effort.

Rolling his window down, Frankie rests his arm on the door. He's holding something. He silently mimes saying a few words.

They notice, and oh, my, this is better than free dope. The beetle driving twerp wants to give them some shit. This is going to be so, so good.

The only white guy in the bunch, a frizzy red headed prize with green teeth, is particularly thrilled. And he can speak. Wonders do occur.

"D'jew want sumpin' mutha fucka? D'jew say sumpin' mutha fucka? HUH?" Beneath the foul mouth, a few orange whiskers grow on his chin; they've been twisted into a limp, lovely spiral.

"Well, sir," says Frankie. "I'm in a teensy-weensy bit of a hurry, or otherwise I certainly wouldn't say a word about this."

The rest of the teenage fecal matter began to coalesce around Green Teeth. This is going to be so, so good.

"I really hate to ask this of you, sir" continues an apologetic Frankie, "but would you, could you... please suck my dick now... instead of later, like we agreed?"

And then Frankie uses the Prod. And Frankie has increased the power just a teensy-weensy bit. And

Frankie... fries the living shit out of Green Teeth's crotch. Smoke blossoms, screams erupt, and the smell of fused cloth and pubic hair stirs about. And Green Teeth spiritedly go-go dances. Quickly tiring of this, he collapses into a fetal position on the hot asphalt. No doubt this is comforting, compared to his seared genitalia.

Giggling, Frankie maneuvers his little geeky car around the crotch-fried asshole. Life can be rich with joy. It's all in what a person makes of it. The silly bastard has a lot of experience at making life fun; the Frankie way.

Behind him, a bewildered group of America's bright and shining future, stand looking down at one of their own. One who has fallen in his chosen line of duty: putrefying the population. He'd been quite exemplary at it. This mollusk brained group had been right about one thing. And Frankie would agree... this encounter had been so, so good.

Shortly after the teen entertainment, Frankie arrives at the Roaton place. That un-haunted showplace home that RL has bought. He's no longer giggling.

Carefully examining the comatose Elvis, it becomes apparent to Frankie that his earlier fear had been right. He didn't know a rat's butt from a pickle concerning the mutant's physiology. He doesn't share this revelation with Shadow, who watches, tearful and silent. Frankie tries hard to affect a knowledgeable, competent, and comforting front for the distraught woman. And to hide the fact that as far as his medical knowledge went, things would BE better if a rat's butt or a pickle were here. *They* might know what to do.

Unlike Shadow, RL is definitely not silent. He fidgets about constantly checking the creases in his jeans and asking pointed, asinine questions. This is particularly bad because of Shadow's presence. This is hardly the time for Frankie to make statements like: I don't really have a clue, but I think this fucking lizard is going to die. It's not the time for truth. Truth can be inconvenient.

"Well, at least tell us if... How about the... What about..." and on and on RL goes.

"Okay, Boss. Here's what my vast med training is telling me. It's telling me that you need to be quiet and not ask stupid questions. It's telling me that you need to go somewhere and get really busy doing something else. It's telling me to take the pistol I brought from the shop and run your jabbering butt out of here. So please, either shut up, or go away. Preferably both." While saying this, Frankie's eyebrows dance, and his eyes keep darting toward Shadow.

RL opens and closes his mouth several times. It's

the guppy imitation again. He looks at Frankie, looks at the dying mutant, and then at the quietly crying gray woman. It's Shadow's silent tears that do the job. A woman's tears are a water that can move just about any man... even a guppy-fied one.

"I'm sorry, Shadow. I, I... I'll go wait for Jayderay in the front room."

"An absolutely capital idea, Boss. I'm so impressed. You may close the door as you leave."

"Please, RL," says Shadow, in a strained, desolate voice. "Please send her in when she, when she arrives."

RL leaves without another word. He remembers to close the door. Not bad for a guy who's having one hell of an engagement day.

There's plenty of medical paraphernalia left from Frankie's previous care of Jayderay. And he uses everything he can that will give Shadow the illusion of his competence, trying to give her hope. He moves the stethoscope about, he shines light in both of the eyes, in both of the ears, he moves the stethoscope about some more, he checks the blood pressure several times in several areas. And still more innovative stethoscope use. He wishes he could consult with the rat's butt and pickle.

During all this he keeps up a litany of: Uh- huh, yes indeed, very good, and that great comforter, Hmmm.

All of these lies he delivers in a very up-beat, positive tone. He does avoid saying: I'm sure the patient will be fine, just fine. Which is usually a medico's kiss of death.

After he's almost worn out the stethoscope, and the blood pressure sleeve is nearly in tatters, Frankie assumes the most beaming, boy scout, "I would not lie to you," face he's got. It's a very good one, he deals in antiques after all.

"Shadow, I truly believe he's okay... for the time being. Obviously, he's in a coma, which is the body's way of healing itself. I will continue to monitor—"

A light tapping on the door interrupts him, and Jayderay enters, going directly to Shadow. Without a word, they quietly hold one another. At times such as these, some women can actually care about another. It's rare. The enigmatic, ashen Shadow had once helped Jayderay. Had helped her through a traumatic time of emotional devastation. And Jayderay will never forget that. But repayment is going to be rough. It may be impossible.

Frankie knows a rescue when he sees one, but doesn't quite run from the room. It's more of a fast slither with decorum, and out he goes.

"God damn it, Frankie! What the hell have you been doing in there? Performing brain surgery? So out with it, how is he?"

Frankie looks at RL silently for a few seconds before he speaks. He's thinking mightily about the Prod in his pocket. Thinking of it with great, great longing.

"I've been in there playing with myself, but I had the very devil of a time gettin' off, on account of Shadow standing there, being all inconsiderate and crying. I can't imagine why, just because her husband is laying right there dying. What the fuck, RL? You don't actually think I know anything about diagnosing him, do you? I've been putting on a damned act for her. Elvis is some kind of a... of a test tube spaceman, he's dying, and I know fuck all about helping him."

"Sorry, Frankie. Really, I am. Crap! Can you think of anything we CAN do?"

"Well, yeah... sort of. But you're not gonna like it."

"I could like a lot of anything if it'll save him. Frankie, we can't let that kid die. We're kind of his family, and I don't even want to think about what it'll do to Shadow if he does die."

"Okay, then here it is. I know a surgeon that I do quite a bit of... business with. I'm sure I can get him out here."

"Frankie! Are you out of your mind? So, this surgeon is so much of a friend, he'll keep his mouth shut about what he sees out here. He'll work on an alien that looks like a purple Elvis, and not tell. Bullshit! No matter what he tells us, he'll sell the story. Hell, he will totally broadcast it!"

Once again, Frankie quietly looks at his boss for a few seconds. *Sometimes RL is such a child. Do I have to spell it out for him?* Taking a deep breath, he speaks gently.

"RL... I didn't exactly plan on the guy ever leaving here."

"WHAT! Damn it, that's worse, we sure as hell can't force him to move in with us. What are we gonna do, put a ball and chain on... Oh. I... Oh, I see. And this... this is a friend of yours, is it?"

"Not really. And he probably won't come willingly, but I can, and I will, get him here."

"Jesus Christ, Frankie. Kidnapping and murder. Jesus Holy Christ."

"Okay, RL, okay. Calm down. I know I can get him to come if he thinks he's finally gotten a date with me, so then it won't be kidnapping. And afterwards, if he should *kinda* get lost in the basement and *sorta* wander into that closet and out into the Waydowns, well... you know... shit happens."

"Jesus Christ, Frankie. I mean, Jesus Holy Fucking Christ. We can't, we just can't do this."

"Okay, fine. You the Boss, on your head be it. Let

our friend die, and then you can deal with Shadow and Jayderay."

It's RL's turn to look at Frankie for several long seconds. *And everybody thinks Frankie is silly... a silly, harmless poof... hell, he's a God damn psycho. But... but if this doctor comes willingly, and later, if he does just happen to wander into the basement closet and out into the Waydowns... well, shit does happen. But we can't! We absolutely must not do this!*

He thinks of the dying Elvis. He thinks of Shadow's tear-streaked ashen face. He thinks of Jayderay's trembling bottom lip, her wet brown eyes. *But damn it! It's still kidnapping and it's still murder, no matter how they're wrapped. We absolutely must not do this. We can't. We won't.* RL takes a deep breath and speaks.

"How soon can you get the bastard here?"

So, so easily can some poor, unsuspecting sap's fate be sealed. Desperate times, desperate measures, and needs must. It a phrase that sounds good, but it's still kidnapping and murder.

However, RL and Frankie are... adaptable. If it's for a good cause.

CHAPTER 12

THE DECK DOWN UNDER

At the very bottom of this buried starship, on the shore of a not-water lake... Giney screams.

"SHERRF! Look at the water!"

Several heads have appeared from the neck up; gleaming yellow orbs without faces. The membrane growing across their mouths pulse rapidly, obscenely, silently. Dripping shoulders rise into view, melted lumps that were once hands emerge, reaching. Behind them, more heads show; there are over a dozen now.

"RUN!" yells Sheriff Lakker. To his everlasting credit, he does not. Yanking his pistol out, he faces the Yellow.

Shank and Tanya are first down the trail, with Giney at their heels.

Like diseased surf, the Yellow surges forward, all of them. Chests become visible, then legs. Behind them, smaller heads bob to the surface.

On the trail, the only sounds from the runners are their feet pounding against the deck, the gasping for breath, the flapping of clothes. They do not look back. They run.

At the shore, sweat rolls of Lakker's face, heart hammering his chest. *Godamighty, so many, so fuckin' many! I ain't got near enough shells.*

Shank pounds down the trail, her lungs straining beneath multiple breasts. Tanya is right behind her, and closing. Older than the women, Giney's breath is giving out. His chest heaving like a bellows, legs going weak, he falls further behind. Only terror keeps him going.

Behind them several shots ring out, sounding flat, sounding final as the noise recoils among the green forest. Those waiting quick plants.

Looking back toward the noise, Shank can see the slow running Giney behind, and realizes the Sheriff stayed at the shore. *I cain't deserts the Sherrf!* And as she tries to about-face, stumbles, falling hard, bouncing and tumbling. Bawling a cry as a bone in her leg snaps with a wet branch sound.

Far behind the runners, Lakker backs slowly away from the advancing Yellow. Only one of his shots scored a hit, but the thing had only staggered back a step, then continued lurching forward. He fires again managing to hit the creature a second time. Once again it falls back a step, but on it comes. *Godamighty, they cain't be stopped!*

Trying desperately to miss the fallen Shank, Tanya leaps but fails, landing on top of her. The girl shrieks as broken bones grind together. Tanya struggles to her knees, and then sees the deputy's crooked shin through the rags.

"God damn it!" Tanya spits out. "This is just fucking peachy. *You* would break a leg."

"I din't do it on no purp—"

"Oh, shut the fuck up." Turning her back to the girl, Tanya says, "Here, put your arms around my neck, and climb on my back."

"No, I ain't ridin' you none, I'll just get you kilt, and I din't know the Sherrf stayed back theres. I ain't leavin' the Sherrf, I got—"

"Well, you sure as fuck can't help him now. Lakker's doing his job, and he ordered you to run. He's no slouch, he can make it. Now get you're stinking ass on! Or I'll slit your throat myself," says Tanya, whipping the scalpel out of her coat. "I don't leave the wounded bchind."

"Danged if you ain't got some sand, Missy. But you right, I'd onliest slow him down. Okay, then hunker down lower and I'll try to hitch me on."

Shank grunts with pain as she climbs on but doesn't cry out. Tanya rises and manages a jouncing, fast walk. She doesn't get far.

Giney, his eyes rolling wildly, spit and snot streaming into his beard, sees the women... and never slows. Plowing into the pair, knocking them flat. Stumbling over them, he lands sprawling, dropping his rifle. Scrambling up, he keeps right on running.

"You bastard!" screams Tanya, as she struggles toward the gun. Everyone hates a coward, especially a man. On her knees she grabs the abandoned rifle and manages a shot at the retreating back as he makes a turn. "I'll kill you for this, you cocksucker!"

"Dang it, you missed," grunts Shank from the ground beside her.

"I won't miss the next time; I'll have the barrel up his ass. Come on, let's go get that son of a bitch!"

"Danged if you ain't gots sand, but I cain't goes no more. You go get him; my leg's too bad busted to ride pigga-back. I cain't takes it. Don't you let that coward make it to the hatch, he'll lock us in sure. I'll wait for the Sherrf. Go!"

"Sherrif Lakker may not *BE* coming, you idiot! But I bet those yellow shits are. Just shut up and gimmie your arms again, or I'll grab that busted leg and drag you."

At the not-water, backing away from the advancing Yellow, Lakker stuffs his pistol back into the tote. *Ain't no sense wastin' bullets... I hope to hell they're slower when they get out of the water.*

The Yellow are definitely slower when they reach the deck as they slouch and shamble out on clumps of feet. But they keep coming, and it's quicker than it looks.

Godamighty, if they make it to the hatch… they'll take my whole deck. Sheriff Lakker whirls around and runs.

Adding to their speed, the Yellow aren't taking the hunter's winding trail, nor do they fear the plants. Brushing against them, slapping them aside, without any retaliation from the greenery, on the Yellow comes.

"Christ you're heavy," grunts Tanya, trying to manage a dog trot with Shank on her back. "How many damn tits you got anyway? Feels like a fucking dozen."

"I din't axe you to carry me none," snaps the injured girl through gritted teeth. Every jog explodes pain in her splintered shin and the rifle strapped across her back digs in with each bump.

"And my tits ain't none of yore bidness!" she adds, as her snaggle tooth jabs up and down like a sewing machine needle. "Dang this leg's killin' me," she says, craning her neck around to look back down the trail. "And I only gots three, not no duzzin."

"Shut up and quit squirming back there damn you! You're hard enough to carry without that twisting around shit," wheezes Tanya. "I don't know how much more—"

"I sees the Sherrf! And he ain't foolin' around none about gettin' here neither. Hump a gourd! The Yellow is tryin' to flank him, they comin' through the trees!"

"Shit on this," Tanya gasps, staggering to a stop. "I'm blown."

———•••———

Above Lakker's deck, a lonely Seevee sits watching the elevator door. Waiting for Dr. Moto, who might just ignore any agreement with Tanya, and haul him back to 19. Take him to Dr. Gaust and certain death... after long, long experimentation.

From the door outward, the walls have patches of burnt areas. Dark, flaking spots against the slick white walls, peeling with the remains of fire-bombed mold. It had once gotten this far.

Hugging his knees with knobby arms, Seevee rocks back and forth on his boots. Inside them, his trimmed-to-fit feet ache dully, as they always did. But he never removes the military footwear; they help him appear human. He thinks they do, and being human is of upmost importance to him. For Ton.

Gazing at the motionless elevator door, its melted controls mock him. They had been ruined long ago to keep monsters out. Monsters like Seevee.

Seevee who once had the freedom of Deck 19. He and the rest of the Almosts had been treated like human staff. Well, *almost.* They got to wear security khakis! And combat boots! And cooked food!

But then came Tanya. And the collective shit flew.

She'd been tossed away, Tanya had. Given to the Almosts by Dr. Gaust. For their amusement, for their pleasure. And they took her, and took her, and took her.

But there was Seevee, their straw boss. And Seevee fell in love. Trotting chummily along with love came the Almost's desertion. They all fled into the Waydowns. With Tanya's whispered insinuations softly drilling into Seevee's brain.

The murders came shortly after the desertion, very shortly after. Leaving only Seevee and Tanya. And it had all started with love. Love for Ton. Seevee sighs. There are a lot of sighs connected to love.

Moto much no come. Sneak snake Moto... Seevee much, much no trust. Much more trust even, even Coilers. Seevee hungry, thirsty. Must wait, Ton say. Must do for Ton. Seevee much luff Ton.

Seevee waits patiently, like a much beaten, yet still loyal dog. His trimmed feet ache.

"I'm blown," pants Tanya for a second time, sinking to her knees. "Slide off and I'll help you sit. Let's shoot some of those Yellow fuckers."

"Best let me, Missy, least ways till you breathe easy. I done seen yore shootin', you tends to miss."

"That bastard was moving, and the name is Tanya. Now get off me, Three Tits."

"Well, them there Yellow ain't gonna stand still none for you."

"Get fucking down, Shank."

After a painful, grunting dismount, Shank sits splay legged, checking the rifle. Snorting in disgust, she says, "It don't matter none, there ain't no more bullets. That shot you took was the onliest one... and you missed."

"He was moving, damn it!"

"Well, he sure weren't goin' fast."

"I think I'm gonna break your other fucking leg."

This exchange continues as Tanya none too gently splints the leg using the worthless rifle. She cuts part of the bloody pants leg off for binding. She doesn't even think about using Shank's shirt... she's afraid there might be more than three breasts. The woman and girl resemble a pair of cranky owls with their heads continually swiveling about, looking for the Yellow to burst from the trees.

Sherrif Lakker finally arrives huffing but not totally

winded. Not bad for an older man. But he's constantly rubbing his chest, which Tanya takes note of.

"Godamighty, Deppity! Them Melts are near up our ass, and you goes and breaks a leg!"

"Yeah, she's like that," says Tanya.

"Listen, Missy, I ain't—"

"Cut it, you two. We ain't got no time for women shit; the Yellow are a'comin'!"

They frantically get Shank across his back, and jog for the hatch. She's white faced, jaws clenched, that wayward tooth jabbing at her nose, but the girl doesn't cry out. Screw the pain, to hell with the Yellow, she's more interested in telling Lakker about that bastard Giney's treachery. She tells, finishing with:

"And Missy here shot at that coward devil, but a'course she missed."

"I *AM* gonna break your other fucking leg," spits Tanya.

"Both of you shut up," pants Lakker. "I'll cut Giney's nuts off when we catch him, whilst you two holds him down." This is not just talk, he fully intends on doing it. The Sheriff hates a coward, and particularly if it's one of his own men.

Behind them, the Yellow lurches through the trees and onto the trail. What once were feet make a sludgy sucking noise against the deck with each step. It is their only sound. They're filled with hunger, with want, with need. With anger and thought.

Trees and plants thin as the group nears the entrance. Up ahead, Giney struggles with opening the hatch. Hearing the three, he spins around. Seeing Lakker, his eyes become saucers.

"Sherrf! Sherrf Lakker... I, I, I thought you was done come a cropper, or, or, or I'd have stayed and hep'd you fight 'em off. Where'd you find these two? I, I, I was a'lookin' but never seed'em on the trail."

Tanya is in the lead as they walk closer to Giney. Her hand flashes from the lab coat.

Blood gushes from Giney's slashed belly. Both hands slap loudly against the gaping wound, as life spurts red through his fingers. Lips move silently as intestines spill around the futile grip. Uncoiling like purple snakes they splatter to the deck. Mouth still working, he slowly sinks to his knees, looking in horror at the bowels, thinking they can't possibly belong to him. And topples face down into his offal.

"That was a mite too quick fer the likes of him, Missy, but you gots sand. And seems yore aim's alot more better with a knife," Shank painfully grits out from Lakkers shoulders.

"He wasn't moving," says Tanya, wiping the scalpel's blade on Giney's back.

"Godamighty, you two girls quit jawin', the Yellow's still a'comin! Slide off, Deppity and get the damn hatch open, whilst I gets my breath."

Shank staggers about opening the repaired lock, and pulls the hatch shut behind them. In pain and haste, she makes a mistake. A terrible mistake. A mistake she will pay dearly for.

So will others.

Quite some time later, with Shank stretched out on Lakker's bunk, her leg stripped of the splint, he takes a deep breath.

"Deppity, I'm shit for sorry... but that there leg is just too bent too bad. They ain't no way 'round it; it's got to come off somewheres around the knee."

"NO, SHERRF, NO! I, I cain't, I cain't live no cripple... *I won't.*" Shank's bottom lip quivers against the jutting tooth, her eyes glisten with held back tears. But they're close. The maimed do not fair well in a frontier village.

"Godamighty, Shank, I don't *wants* to do no sawin', but they just ain't no—"

"What the hell are you talking about, Lakker!" snaps Tanya. "Her leg's nowhere near bad enough for amputation."

"But they ain't nobody left that's got this here kinda doctorin,' maybe if the bones weren't so outta lined up ...

maybe I could. But not this here. It'll go green for sure."

"I've had emergency field training; I can do this. Jesus Christ, Shank, you really are a pain in my ass."

"Well, I hopes you can doctor more better'n you can shoot... and... and... I thankee."

"He was running, damn you. I think I'll pull that tusk and cut a few tits off you while I'm at this... and you're welcome."

"You leave them tits alone, Missy Sure Shot. But this here tooth might'n be bad to lose... *IF* you can aims good enough to gets it." The sweat has washed enough dirt from the girl's face to reveal a sprinkle of freckles across the nose. She's just a kid, maybe not *even* fourteen. Lakker is a pig. A caring pig, but a pig.

"Lakker, you want me to knock this mouthy Deputy out with a club? Or you got any type of anesthetic, anything that'll numb her?"

"I gots a batch of corn likker that'll melt her throat."

"Get it. Get a lot. And I hope to hell you got some kind of needle and thread. I'm gonna have to cut to set."

Much later, a drunk but pain free Shank snores away peacefully. While a pale and drawn Tanya takes another swallow of the anesthetic, grimacing as the fire goes down.

"Jesus Christ, this stuff is awful! I don't think you could smooth this shit out with a hammer."

Lakker nods. "Yeah, it ain't 'zactly known for goin' down easy. Some batches is better'n others, but this here ain't one of'em."

"I noticed. Well, things didn't go as easy as I wanted, but she'll keep the leg," Tanya says, nodding toward the passed-out Shank. "But it's gonna be a rough mother fucker when she wakes. You got plenty of this crap?" she asks, lifting her glass.

"They's plenty, and I'll keep pourin' it down her and on where you had to cut. I thankee, even if she dies, I thankee. She means special to me... somethin' fierce she does. And you done real good takin' that there tooth out; it was mighty thoughty of you. That thing was always bothersome to her."

"I'll just bet it was a little *bothersome* to you as well," Tanya chuckles. "Anyway, it was easy pulling it after she passed out. And now, *I* don't have to see it. She certainly won't die, but she might want to when she wakes. That leg's gonna hurt so bad she won't even know the tusk is gone."

"How long you figger she'll be laid up?"

"She's a tough little bi—she's a tough kid, so if you can find her a crutch, I bet she could manage a bit of hopping around by tomorrow. Of course, that depends on how much of this fucking Drano you keep pouring down her."

"If you mean the corn, I plan on given her every drop she can get down. I don't want her hurtin' no more than can be helped. She's powerful special to me. So... tell me why you back packed her when she broke that leg? You two sure ain't been no buddies... women usually ain't."

"I don't leave the wounded behind, ever. I'll dump a fuck-up or a coward, but I won't abandon anyone that's bad hurt. Especially a fighter, and she's damn sure that. I'll kill them myself before I leave one."

Looking directly at her, he nods, saying, "It's the only right way they is. I done it more'n once. Okay, now let's talk about us takin' that there Deck 19... and gettin' up to Topside. You done seen some of us, so what do you think?" In Lakker's speech, the word topside always sounds capitalized.

"Nothing good, Lakker. I was hoping for more guns and some people who know which end the bullets come out. And that don't piss themselves when they sneeze."

"How about with me, the Deppity, all our guns, and whatever peoples and such as you already got?

"Maybe. But I don't intend to risk my own ass taking 19. I plan to lead from the rear."

"Godamighty, woman! I'd risk anything, risk everything to get Topside."

Lakker's statement should've set warning bells off for Tanya. But she's been drinking moonshine, and plenty of it. So.

"Topside!? Mother fuck topside, Lakker! I could get there today; I mean right now from the Waydowns if I wanted. Shit on God damn topside. I want Deck 19. I WILL have it!"

"WHAT? You mean you can gets to Topside right now? From them there Waydowns?" he asks, jerking his thumb toward the corridor.

"Hell, yes. There's a door out there that leads into a topside house. Big fucking deal. 19 is the way; 19 is where control is! We take 19, and the entire ship is ours."

There can be moments when a person knows immediately, they've made a bad move. Knows instantly they've made a dangerous blunder. Tanya has just stepped in a huge, dangerous pile of shit and she realizes it.

The big man's face changes, his eyes become feral. And Tanya understands all at once. Topside is as much heaven to this man as heaven is to a Fundamentalist Christian. Never seen it, only read and been told about it, but must, must, must go there. Must go to the place where everything is always plentiful, always wonderful, always full of never-ending ecstasy. And she's just told this hick that his heaven is literally next door.

Lakker leans forward, saying, "Topside!" Saying the word, his eyes glow with reverence, with rapture, with madness.

Tanya slips a hand into her coat pocket. She grips the scalpel. *I've got to get out of here. If I give this crazy bumpkin any time to think, he'll force me at gun point to take him. I see it in him.*

Yes, Tanya should see the insanity in Lakker. She should recognize it. It is a mirror image of her own. Her own madness is Deck 19, and it is certainly no less than his.

"Tell you what, Sheriff. I'll take you there today and you can see for yourself. But first I've got to find my guide, that Spill I've told you about. He's the one that can actually find it. I couldn't get there by myself."

"Let's go! I'm comin' with you," he says, jumping up, knocking his chair over. "Topside," he says again with wonder, his eyes huge and shimmering.

"No, you won't, Sheriff! You've got to keep Shank dosed up. We're sure not gonna leave her behind. I don't leave the wounded, and neither do you. When we get her up there, those people can fix that break in minutes. I'll bring a stretcher back and we'll carry her easy."

The light of madness fades a bit as he looks over at the unconscious Shank. "Yeah... right, Shank. She means to me... means to me fierce. And sure, they can fix her right! Of course they will... it's, it's Topside... they can do anything. Yes, yes, I will see to her while you're gone. Yes... and then, and then Topside...yes."

Tanya never releases the scalpel till the hatch to Lakker's deck closes behind her. And then she runs.

Tanya knows quite well that women are devious; she has vast personal knowledge of this valuable asset. She rarely thinks men are devious; they don't have the fucking brains for it.

But there are exceptions, and Lakker is smart. The enraptured hick could decide to go looking on his own... and might actually find the door. He could get through the house, and somebody topside just might listen to his ravings. That will not work for her. She wants no possible topside interference to Deck 19. That is hers. She will have it. And she intends to use Lakker, Shank, and any other stumble bum cannon fodder they can muster.

No, Lakker must not reach that door. Tanya will not let this happen.

Stopping at her cabin long enough to pick up the Uzi, Tanya notes that the always loyal Seevee hasn't returned. Since her trip below, (the deck down under, as she's begun to think of it) Seevee's overall status has risen greatly. *Maybe I'll let him lick my feet when I get back. Might even let him move his pallet in from the corridor... for one night.*

As Tanya thinks of ways to stop Lakker... and be generous to Seevee, as Lakker cares for his Deputy, as Shank blissfully sleeps, below them all: the Yellow are busy. Yes, the Melts are at the busted-lock hatch, and they are very busy. Those that still have fingers left are trying hard.

They are working very hard... working at Deputy Shank's mistake.

CHAPTER 13

MANY EVENTS, MANY PLACES

As Elvis lays dying in the bedroom, RL watches Frankie head for the front door. On his way to kidnap some extremely unlucky and unsuspecting surgeon.

"Wait, Frankie! Hold on... what the hell are we thinking? What is this—"

"Damn it, RL, this is no time for any of your prissy shit. We don't have a choice!"

"But Frankie... what will this surgeon *know*? Hell, man, he won't have a clue any more than you do! Then we'll be right back in this same fix... AND then we'll have some idiot doctor on our hands that needs... uh, placating."

"That's good, Boss... 'placating'... I'll remember that one, I might need it. But yeah, I guess you're right. He wouldn't know anything either... the ignorant bastard. Okay, so now what?"

"Hell, how am I supposed to—"

"RL! Frankie!" yells Jayderay as she opens the bedroom door. "Shadow says Elvis, he goin' and she don't know if, if…" she chokes back a sob. "You GOT to, to do *something* RL, and do it now."

To RL, this is the double-whammy, to be implored with tears by the woman he loves to do the impossible. Frankie feels an identical inadequacy, and they both turn and look at each other.

"Please help… he fades from me," says Shadow quietly from the bedroom. "I can feel him slipping further into the void, even as I speak. If he goes, I do not know that I can follow. But I will not live without him." She kneels on the floor beside Elvis, leaning over, stroking his face and hair. This woman without color, this woman of shifting gray shadows, this broken woman, this woman who loves. Her tears are spent, and she repeats softly that one lonely word: "Please."

"Yes, we will," says Jayderay firmly. And she says it looking directly at RL and Frankie. She says it with brimming eyes and conviction, looking directly at RL and Frankie. She says it with total faith… looking directly at RL and Frankie.

RL and Frankie are looking directly at each other. And they're not seeing much. They're just two very bent businessmen who are thinking: What the fuck now? And if there was a pit of bubbling lava close by, they'd trample each other to dive in.

"Boss," says Frankie, motioning with his chin toward the living room.

"No," Jayderay says, seeing the furtive chin pointing "Whatever you two decide will be with all of us knowin.' Right now, you hear?" It was said in that voice often associated with married women. The voice that won't allow an argument. She doesn't get one.

"Listen RL, what if we go back into the Waydowns, do you think we could find our way to that elevator? You know, where Elvis smacked the dog shit out of Moto. If we could get there, maybe we can find him. And then we'll drag his ass back here, he'll know what to do for Elvis."

"Frankie, listen to yourself! IF we can find our way, IF we can find Moto. Hell, man, we won't LIVE to get there and back, we'll be something's dinner."

"Maybe. But we've lived through it before... and Elvis told me Moto was one of the top shits back in that lab he came from. Let's go get the bastard." Frankie looks over at Jayderay and Shadow, then back to RL, saying, "We've got to."

RL stares at him a second, nodding slowly. "Yeah," he sighs, "I guess we do. But God damn it, we're charging into those Waydowns with one pipsqueak pistol, and, and, and what? A death wish and winning smiles to get us to wherever we're going?"

"There may be another way into the ship," says Shadow, holding her husband's hand. "I know not why, but my touch—"

A shuddering gasp from Elvis, interrupts her.

Meanwhile, back in the ship on Deck 19: Huong has suggested that he alone could go to meet Tanya.

The brave, highly honored, greatly esteemed Doctor Moto latches onto this idea. He does so with fear-produced incontinence satchled in his pants. This is salvation!

"Yes, that is a most excellent idea, Huong! Most excellent indeed. There is no need for my presence at this meeting with Tanya." Moto's eyes continually take furtive looks in the direction of Dr. Gaust's door. *Yes, you little sweet- butted gook, you go, you get eaten in the Waydowns. While I vanish.*

Wiping sweat from his face as it trickles from beneath the bandage-turban, Moto continues. "By arrangement, the woman Tanya will be waiting and escort you to the door. You will enter the topside house, and I authorize you to use any means necessary to search for and find the Extender."

Huong listens, silently watching. *The old Jap is terrified... and keeps rolling his eyes toward Gaust's office. What did this bastard prune see in there? I have no intention of ever finding out. Damn, will he never get through running his fucking mouth?*

"Understood, Dr. Moto, Huong says, in an attempt to speed things up. "If I find the Extender I will bring it directly to you. If I do not locate it, I am to return and prepare a squad for a more thorough search."

"Very good, yes, most excellent. However, in the unlikely event that I am not present upon your return, you must check in with Dr. Gaust," says Moto, still blotting sweat from his face, as his eyes constantly bounce between Huong and the dreaded door. *Yes, do check in with the Honored Horror, you little pink flower. My only regret will be that it is not I who get to... sample your tenderness. You would oh, so much prefer my gentle ministrations.*

"Understood, Dr. Moto. I will depart at once." *Yes, I do understand, you old baboon...I understand what lies beyond that door has scared the living shit out of you, and you've no intention of being here when I get back. Well, that makes us a good match... because I'm not coming back.*

"Excellent! Yes, most excellent, Huong. I wish you good fortune on your mission. You may go now."

With a final look toward Dr. Gaust's closed door, Moto heads to his quarters. Time is not on his side, but he desperately needs the showering cycle of his Groomer… and fresh clothes. *At last, after all these decades… I'll never wear a lab coat again. And never to speak with the Honored Tarantula again. I cannot. I must push the sight from my mind.*

Exiting the Groomer without waiting for the drying jets, Moto throws on some hastily grabbed clothes. There was no choosing, so he now wears that sartorial abomination known as a leisure suit; from the 70s. Picking up the hated lab coat long enough to get his Prod, he discards the garment for the last time. He's leaving this cursed ship and Deck 19 forever. Freedom is a mere elevator ride up to the outside world.

Taking a quick glance in a mirror, his blackened eyes look back from beneath the white bandage. Dr. Moto looks like a hunted raccoon with a jaunty little cap. A terrified rodent that hasn't yet escaped. He rips off the dressing with much wincing and uttering curses about the treacherous Proby.

That ripping off should've included the suit. Talk about horror.

Yes, Dr. Moto will leave the ship. But there will be a detour. A detour of long duration. He will wish he had remained on Deck 19. He will wish this for a long time. An incredibly long time.

———·••·———

Beneath Deck 19, in the Waydowns: Tanya leaves her cabin with the Uzi lovingly clasped to her bosom, headed for the door that leads into the Roaton house. This is a very determined Tanya.

Not far from the determined Tanya, the waiting Seevee hears the elevator hum and sees the melted controls flicker. Scrambling to his throbbing feet, he watches the door slowly open. Revealing Huong. Revealing Huong with an Uzi pointed directly at Seevee.

"You! You're Stevie... the Almost... and you're wanted for desertion. Bringing you back to Dr. Gaust would be well rewarded," says Huong, nodding thoughtfully. *But I must not let greed trap me... and I damn sure don't want to face Gaust, or whatever made the old Jap shit himself.*

"But if you obey me, maybe I won't haul your ugly ass back. So, where is the woman? Where is this Tanya? Answer me, Spill!"

Huong's gun does not waver; the stubby barrel doesn't even twitch, and his poisonous eyes do not blink. And Seevee feels this meeting is not starting off well. But being called a Spill fires up his dignity. The dignity that Tanya has kept beneath her little bare feet... kept there along with Seevee.

"Seevee not Spill! Seevee much, much not Spill. Seevee belong all for Ton. Where Moto?"

Moving for the first time, Huong steps out of the elevator as his Uzi makes an ominous metallic click.

"Seevee needs to watch his big mouth or he'll find himself back on 19. And that's *Doctor* Moto to you, *Spill*. His actions are not your concern, I AM. Now... where is Tanya?" The gun issues another deadly tick.

Seevee is right; this meeting is not off to a good start. And it's not likely to improve any. Because the absent Tanya has acted like... well... she's acted like Tanya.

Below the Waydowns, on the ships last deck: Lakker supports Deputy Shank's head as she swallows another mouthful of hellfire.

"Oh, Sherrf! I don't knows what hurts more badder, drinkin' this here burnin' crap, or my busted leg."

"Believe me, Deppity, you need to keep drinkin'. That there leg's likely to flare up mighty fierce for a spell and—"

"*Likely* to flare up? *Likely* my tits, Sherff! It's throbbin' so bad I cain't reckon why it ain't jumped off this bunk and runned around by its ownself."

"Well," chuckles Lakker, "I'm proud you ain't lost that fun mouth of yours." He reaches over, brushing the sweaty hair back from her forehead, and caresses her cheek.

"Instead of ponderin' on the leg, how 'bout you study on how you're even more purty now that Tanya got rid of that there wrong tooth of yours."

"No foolin' Sherff? You really think so?" she asks, grabbing his hand with both of hers. "Don't sweet talk me none 'bout such as that. Do you really think… do you true reckon that I'm, I'm… that I'm pur— I'm that way?"

"I ain't sweet talkin' you none, girl. You knows I always thought about you that ways," he says, meaning every word. Leaning over, he kisses her lightly on the lips. "And don't you talk no more 'bout them there tits right now; my old ticker just cain't stand it."

She giggles. Love can be a great anesthetic.

"But… whilst you was conked out," he adds, "I did tells Tanya to cuts that there lower one off—"

"WHAT!"

"Just funnin' you, girl," he laughs. "Ain't no way I'd want any of'em gone, and I think that there bottom one's my favorite."

She looks at him a few seconds, her face drunkenly serious. "The bottom one? No funnin'? Really?"

"Godamighty, girl! We cain't keep talkin' tits with you havin' a busted leg… it's hellish bad on me. But yeah, that there bottom one is my most grabby ever time."

"Well, Sherff, I, uh, I cain't get up to no sparkin' right now, but... uh, well...would... uh... does you wanna sees it?" And she blushes... real purty like.

Love can also be truly wonderful. Truly.

———————

Not very far from the Sheriff and his Deputy, the Yellow are busy. With remnants of fingers that fumble and slip, the Melts try to open a hatch. A door that the Deputy did not lock properly. An entry that will lead them out of the power place and into Lakker's area. They still have their brains. They still have their memories. They still know things. They still want.

And Shank's big screw up, that awful mistake... just might give them everything.

Behind these struggling, diligent Melts, at the very bottom of the ship, the metal floor angles gently downward. It slopes beneath the odd forest of often deadly plants and all the flitting, strangely shaped shadows. On it goes, under the hunter's trail, where the unfortunate Burt stands in trussed repose. And finally, the deck disappears under the not-water lake.

Far across those murky, unknown depths, the opposite shoreline faintly shows a blur of green. Out in the middle an enormous, glistening back breaks and roils the surface. It could be part of a long, sinuous neck.

Whatever it is, the wetly shining segment slowly glides back into the water, sending small waves radiating out. And all is silent.

Yes, on the surface all is now calm, but beneath, down in the endless dark, in the deep... things are never still.

In those depths, along with many others, the Long Pig drifts. The not-water moves him about, in a slow, rotting, porcine dance. Long is not dead.

And back at the power place hatch leading on to Lakker's deck, the Yellow work. One or two at a time, those with fingers are diligently trying.

At the Roaton House, a shuddering gasp from Elvis interrupts Shadow, and she cries out softly.

"He fades. He drifts from me. I feel it; he will soon be beyond all hope of return. Please, please, you must do something. Please." She holds one of the lavender hands in both of her own. The charcoal skin flexing as black tipped fingers clutch his hand to her face. The ebony lips kiss, and tears start again, rolling down her gray cheeks.

"We ARE going to help," says Jayderay, putting her arm around the woman's shoulders. She's talking to

Shadow but she's glaring at RL and Frankie. "RL, you do something, and you do it now. You hear?"

RL has heard. So has Frankie. Both men would jump through their own buttholes on a pogo stick if it would help. And they feel that such a feat would be much easier and eminently more possible than what's being asked.

Frankie looks at RL, who's looking back, and just standing there, mute as a dead mime. *Well thanks a lot, Boss, you fucking stump. How did you ever guess that I was so eager to take this little minor problem in hand. You prick.*

Under Jayderay's baking stare, Frankie makes a needed dry-throat clearing sound. RL continues to imitate a dead muskrat, so Frankie makes the throat clearing noise again. He has to start somewhere.

"Shadow, you were saying there might be another way into the ship, or into where Elvis came from?"

"Yes, Elv-is thinks my touch will enable the Ex-tender to open. Much like I can open the basement door into the Way-downs. I know not how nor why, but when once I touched it, the Ex-tender began to glow. That frightened him, and he told me I must not come into contact with it... that the device might open. Open and enable passage into and from the place of his origin."

"Whoa! So that *is* how he got here, through that breastplate gizmo. The Extender *is* a portal. I knew it! I told you so, RL. Boss? Damn it, are you hearing this... or did you die?"

RL has indeed been hearing and this dead muskrat mime snaps back to life. Slowly kneeling before her, he asks, "You can open it, Shadow? The Extender?"

"That is what Elv-is told me. He thought this to such an extent that he kept it covered, to guard against my forgetting and touching it."

"Is it upstairs?"

"Yes, in my... in our bedroom. You would be unable to locate the room; I will go... and then... and then you will be able to aid my husband? Please."

"Absolutely we will," breaks in Frankie. "Me and the Boss will go and fetch back just the right person. And I have very persuasive means to *placate* them, to encourage their willingness to help. In fact, they'll be positively eager to." And he giggles. Of course he does.

Shadow kisses the unconscious Elvis quickly, laying his hand gently across his chest. Turning to Jayderay, she says simply, "He is my life, my all."

"I know that, honey; more than you realize," replies Jaderay. "I won't leave him, now you go on and get that breastplate thing."

As Shadow swirls away, Jayderay turns to RL and

Frankie. "It don't matter who or what you got to bring back. Just do it! You hear?"

"If she can open up a way for us, we *will* bring help. That I can promise you," answers RL. "But as far as—"

"They ain't no 'buts' about this, RL. You two go and you get."

"Hot Damn, RL! We're going into a spaceship. Man, oh, man! I always knew I was a Han Solo kinda guy!"

"No you're not, you're a silly bastard, who got to use a new word. As to going into a spaceship, we've both been in the Waydowns, and that's part of the ship," says RL, feeling like the day has turned to shit... and he's standing in it neck deep... and sinking. On this, his engagement day. Such happiness.

"Oh, don't get all prissy-wissy and technical, Boss! And while Shadow's gone, just what the hell *did* happen to Elvis?"

Glancing over at Jayderay, RL says, "I think Shadow's daughters attacked him, at least that's —"

"Her daughters!" interrupts Jayderay, "Her daughters are dead, RL."

"I know."

"Ghosts," says Frankie calmly. "I told you this place was haunted, O Noble Leader of mine. Man, oh, man! Things keep on gettin' better and better around—"

"Better? Better!" Jayderay spits the words at him.

"You havin' fun, Frankie? We got a dyin' friend layin' here, and you wanna play haunted house? Just you both shut up and shut up now. She gonna be back and I don't want her hearin' nothin' 'bout nothin' except helpin' her husband. You hear?"

Both men look at each other. Obeying a woman is usually the best thing a smart man can do... cowardice being the better part of intelligence. Immediately their lips look stitched together. A shrunken head couldn't do any better.

***

While in the Waydowns: On their way to the secret door that leads into the Roaton basement, Huong has to help Seevee along. Aiding him with occasional jabs from the Uzi. Seevee is being slow, trying to locate the hatch with the lab coat sleeve dangling out. He wants to make sure he can remember the location; to impress Ton. Perhaps she might even explore the new, un-plundered area with him.

"Much no push Seevee!"

"Then Seevee needs to get his ass in gear," says the increasingly impatient Huong. "Are you sure you know the way, or has this Tanya just fed you some bullshit to get rid of you?"

"Seevee know way. Ton tell, much tell Seevee way."

"Then fucking get on with it! If Seevee doesn't get me there pretty damn quick, I'm going to *much* put a bullet up Seevee's *Spill* ass, and find it on my own."

"Huong no find, Waydowns much, much big. Seevee know. Seevee not Spill!"

"And I think Seevee is full of shit," snorts Huong, looking at his watch. I'm going to give you another—"

"There!" cries Seevee, pointing down another corridor toward the jammed hatch and white sleeve. Huong is forced into a fast trot to keep up. Seevee slides to a stop and begins carefully examining the partial opening, not touching. This is the Waydowns, death is always everywhere.

"What the fuck is this, Spill? It sure as hell isn't the door I was told about. This is just another hatch into more fucking Waydowns!"

"Is mark... mark for way... mark by lab coat," Seevee lies quickly. "Much know way!"

Huong's dead eyes look at Seevee, not blinking. He slowly nods, but the Uzi remains on Seevee. "Maybe. Maybe you do, the coat sleeve would make a good marker. Okay, I'll buy it for now, but how much further, Spill?"

"Much not far... Seevee much not Spill."

"You listen up, if it looks, walks and quacks like a fucking duck, then I call it a duck. A much fucking duck. Now move, *Spill*... before I put a bullet in your tail feathers."

With a look of utter confusion on his face, Seevee heads off in what he hopes is the right direction. *Duck? Quacks? Tail feathers? Huong much, much crazy.*

They continue on, with Seevee desperately hoping he *can* find the Roaton door and pondering the meaning of tail feathers.

Behind them, the empty sleeve slowly moves sideways a couple of inches, and then back. It jiggles up and down for a few seconds and then becomes still.

It's a fishing line.

Several long minutes pass, as the two walk through the perpetual haze and gloom of the Waydowns. They both keep a watch for the slithering tentacles of a Coiler but see no signs. Stepping over or around the detritus of past mayhem and carnage, and kicking aside broken lab equipment is always necessary. An occasional well gnawed bone splinters beneath their feet. Now and then they hear the scurrying or screech of things better not seen.

Huong is not overly spooked by any of this. He's fought in the Waydowns and seen its devastation before. But he's not easy with it; he's a soldier.

As they turn down yet another of the countless hallways, Huong's already thin patience gets thinner, and Seevee's already worried brain gets more worried. Seevee suspects Huong is about to leave Seevee's bullet riddled ass behind in a pool of blood and continue looking on his own. Seevee is pretty smart.

"God damn it, you lost Spill son of a bitch, I've had all of—"

"Wait, wait," quails the smart and prescient Seevee. "Much there soon, much, much soon!"

"And you're gonna be much, much fucking dead." The Uzi emits an ominous sounding click. And Seevee's bowels join in, making an equally ominous sound.

"You've got five more minutes, you mutated fuck."

They continue on, as Seevee peers ahead, looking desperately for the door, and wondering what his chances are if he should dart into some side chamber. And run like death was after him. It would be. For the first time ever, he wishes one of the hideous Coilers would make an appearance. That would give this crazy, duck-feathers Huong something to apply his murderous tendencies to. And Seevee could bravely disappear.

"Hold up," says Huong tersely. And Seevee the Almost... almost shits himself.

"What... what wrong?" he quavers.

"Look ahead, you blind piece of shit. Someone's coming toward us."

Squinting through the drifting haze with the frantic

hope of the condemned, Seevee looks. And deliverance is at hand.

"Ton! Much, much Ton!" Seevee squeals with joy... and *much, much* relief.

After a quick who's who and where's Moto, Tanya and Huong get down to the purpose of their meeting. And a very relieved Seevee breathes easily. It won't last.

"Yeah, Seevee was taking you in the right direction, but let me save you the trouble. The door controls have been ruined," says the well-informed Tanya. She should know, she's the one who recently put a couple of bullets through them.

"What! How?" This is not news the deserting Huong wants to hear. "Damn it, how in the fuck did that happen?"

"I've no idea, but that's no longer a way to get topside." *He's without Moto, and wearing security khakis... I can use this little shit... and he's kinda pretty... if I have to fuck him at least I won't puke afterward.*

"Show me! Maybe it can be repaired," demands Huong. Who has zero interest in screwing the one-eyed Tanya.

"Well," answers Tanya, shifting her own Uzi to point directly at his face. "I might do that, but first let's be clear on who gives the fucking orders around here."

Seevee immediately scuttles a few steps to one side, pulling his knife. He'd have no trouble at all killing this insulting human duck's butt. *Call Seevee Spill... much no like tail feathers Huong... Seevee kill for Ton.*

Huong's dead eyes look into Tanya's. His eyes flick to her gun, then to Seevee, and then back to Tanya. *I misjudged this scar faced cunt and her Spill; she's had training and the Spill is totally hers. But I can't go back, I shut the damn Elevator. Fuck.*

Huong is pragmatic and smart enough to know he's got a losing hand. Chancing a wry grin, he shoves his gun barrel toward the deck.

"Okay, I apologize, and you're in charge. I'm sorta stranded, so how do I get out of this mess."

"You get out of this mess by joining me. You never intended to go back, anyway. I was assigned to 19, and I've seen your look in grunts before. The smart ones realize they're never leaving alive. You're deserting."

Huong stares at her a few seconds, and then nods. "You're right. And so, I have no choice, do I." It wasn't a question.

"Sure you do, Deserter. You're free to head out on your own, but there is no way out, fella, no way out except with me."

"Yeah, I've been in this Waydowns shit before, and I believe you. I'd use up my ammo and wind up in something's belly. What's your game, what are you after?"

"My game, as you call it, is to take 19. I want that deck and I want the Gaust bitch. I know how their system works. The rest of the ship takes orders from 19, all the way up to topside. And after I deal with Gaust, I intend to be the one giving orders."

Huong's face show's no emotion, other than a slow blink of those terrible eyes.

"Christ, you want the entire ship," he says slowly. "What about that building on top? Isn't that military or government crap of some kind?"

"Yeah, in some classified, long forgotten file it is. There hasn't been an on-site inspection for decades; the top brass are afraid of Dr. Cunt Gaust. Every deck and all staff take orders from 19 and have for years. I worked it, I know it, and I'm gonna fucking have it," answers Tanya, her good eye glowing as the other revolves faster.

Huong slowly nods. *She's a certifiable fucking nut case, but it'll be a way out. From what I've seen, she's right; Deck 19 is the hub. Hell, she's my only way out.*

"Okay, I'm in. But I've got questions," he says finally.

"Good choice," she says with a knowing smirk. "I'll fill you in as we walk; I've got a couple of hillbillies I want you to meet. They're not much, but they're definitely not short on guts."

"No go, Ton!" yelps Seevee. "Seevee much find new area, much need show! Maybe—"

"Not now, Seevee. I need to get to Lakker's deck, and start—"

"Ton! Much new place, maybe real food... maybe much... maybe guns," the Almost whines, seeing yet another bastard taking his place with Tanya.

"Seevee! I *said* not now! You can go, scout it out, and we'll come—"

"Ton much no find... get lost—"

"Are you jabbering about that hatch with the sleeve marker?" barks Huong. "I can find it again, Spill. I'll get her there."

"Seevee not Spill! Seevee much not—"

"Be quiet, Seevee, and get moving," commands Tanya. "We'll join you soon. Huong, are you sure you can find it? This is a fucked up, easy place to get lost in. And he's right, there could be guns, it needs checking out."

"Yeah, yeah, I'm sure I can find the place. Did you say we're going to meet 'Hillbillies'? Tell me I heard wrong."

"Nope, you didn't" she chuckles. "You're just gonna love meeting the Sherriff... *and* the lovely Deputy Shank."

"Sheriff and Deputy? Why am I not surprised."

"You probably will be. So be a good boy, Huong, and

maybe I'll fix you up with the Deputy. She has quite an aroma. And three tits."

"Oh, fuck."

"That's the idea, Huong," laughs Tanya.

Below the Waydowns, on the ship's last deck, Lakker strokes his deputy's hair as she softly whistles out an inebriated snore. And he thinks it's quite a cute little snore as he adjusts the worn blankets.

Gazing down at her, he smiles a bit sadly. *Got feelings for you, girl... fierce feelings. Me pokin' Tanya was just bidness. Just bidness for gettin' to Topside. It's powerful bothersome that something might happen to me, and what would become of you. I'm on in my years, and they ain't no help for that. But Topside, that there's the answer... I can be more young there and you and me won't never have no more miseries.*

Quietly searching the cabin, he's shocked to find the crutch where he thought it was. All inanimate objects scamper off and hide just when they're needed most. They're sneaky, treacherous bastards.

Pulling that oddly obliging crutch from under the bunk, he quietly wipes it down, and places it within easy reach of his patient. The deck's infirmary had long been emptied of anything usable, and this particular crutch he had once found propping up some sickly-looking tomato vines. Propping them up for some gardener who wasn't around. The tomatoes hadn't looked any better after Lakker appropriated the crutch, leaving them sinking in the slush of homemade dirt.

Appropriate is a good, quasi legal term that sounds so much better than steal. Lakker was the law after all, and at the time, he'd had a sprained ankle. To his credit he only took two of the four tomatoes... and the crutch of course.

Giving Deputy Shank another check and finding her still deeply tanked, Lakker smiles knowingly at the moonshine's effectiveness. With a sigh, he heads out for a tour of his deck. He'd much rather stay, gently stroke her hair and think of topside. But duty is duty, and often the sight of the Sheriff making his rounds can stop all sorts of mischief before it becomes mischief. Mischief like stealing tomatoes.

Good sheriffs come to care for their people. Even if the salary is only sad veggies and mystery meat. And Lakker was a good lawman, albeit a reluctant one. He hadn't wanted the thankless job. It was like a constant, throbbing hemorrhoid. But somebody absolutely had to do it.

Someone always has to lock up the dangerous drunk, put knots on the heads of thieves and troublemakers, settle arguments over which wife or husband belongs to which wife or husband, and so on.

And sometimes, just sometimes, the law has to take some sniveling ass who refuses to learn... and *remove* him from society. In Lakker's world, removal does not mean to house, care, feed and entertain the shithook for years... or even a day. No, Lakker doesn't fool around; he's good at his job.

Certain plants in the power place were well fed and deeply appreciative of the Sheriff's law keeping diligence. Especially the dark green ones.

Keeping his very anesthetized Deputy in mind, Lakker intends to make this a quick tour. It will be. It will be extremely quick.

Striding from his corridor into one of the larger areas, he immediately recognizes trouble. There are no people. There are no sounds. At the very least there should be the voice of some woman telling her man to get his lazy ass moving. There is nothing. Unconsciously, he starts rubbing his chest.

Stopping, Lakker fishes the pistol out of his leather tote. When a gun is needed, it's needed; time for fiddling around is gone. Slowly he walks among slush filled planters, their meager offerings, and the constant stench.

All Groomers and other large basins had long ago

been ripped out and used by hopeful, salivating gardeners. Their gardens also served well for soil manufacturing... as in where the slop buckets were emptied. Feces makes powerful good dirt.

Every cabin door he can see is closed, and this isn't normal either. Usually, the larger areas are busy with the comings, goings, and commerce of any village. Bartering, borrowing, gossiping, and occasional whoring... with the ensuing argument over payment. Clothing was the much-preferred coin of the realm with the play for pay girls... as opposed to shriveled, shit-grown tomatoes.

Quietly moving further in, the Sheriff checks to be sure the gun is fully loaded. *Godamighty, what the hell happened here? It sure ain't nothin' good, I'd bet all my likker on it...they sure as hell ain't all sleepin'... hell, some of 'em won't shut up even then... or at gunpoint neither. What the hell is goin' on?*

As if on a single command, all the cabin doors slowly swing open, and the Sheriff gets his answer.

The Yellow have indeed been busy. They found Shank's mistake; the hatch from the power place has been opened. And pestilence issued forth.

In the Roaton House:

Shadow glides back into the room, cradling the Extender, still wrapped in a dusty sheet. The grays of her face seem darker, the scar across her nose appears pasted on. Ebony tipped fingers repeatedly grip and release the Extender through the cloth. This piece of extraterrestrial metal is the best hope of saving Elvis. And herself. If he should die, she will walk outside. She will cease to exist.

"Set it on the floor, Shadow,' says RL. "Let's take a good look before we find out if it will actually open for you. None of us knows a damn thing about the process, and we don't need any outer space monsters popping in for dinner."

"You're right, Boss. We wouldn't get lucky and have Dr. Moto fall out at our feet. It'd likely be '*The Shite-ater From Saturn*' with big gnawin' teeth and lots of clutchy arms, and—"

"Oh, do shut up, Frankie," RL says absently, pulling off the sheet. "If such a creature did show up, you'd be the first to get eaten."

So there, sitting before them is the Extender. Look-ing remarkably like the breastplate from a medieval suit of armor. Which is exactly what RL had thought when he first got it. Bought it from a perpetually drunken junk dealer, who'd been totally convinced the thing had turned his wife into raging, craving, demanding nympho. Of course, the breastplate hadn't been responsible, it was what had crept out of it. And that had been Elvis, during a brief escape and frolic from the ship's lab.

That exceedingly happy wife still thought it had been her husband. Her vastly improved husband. There isn't much left of that man anymore. He's been savagely used. Repeatedly used. Used hourly. Only Viagra has saved him. So far.

Soon after purchasing that deceitful piece of *armor*, an unsuspecting RL also began experiencing all manner of pleasantries. From vanishing pizza, to a kidnapping and an explosion. Pleasantries indeed.

All this mysterious fun continued until Jayderay insisted he take the devil cursed thing out to the Roaton place. Her church had placed the house in her care, during probate proceedings. He'd obeyed, still thinking it was a just a breastplate. And then... well... and then there had been more Elvis. And Evis met Shadow. Shadow who'd been in the house decades before RL was born. Then came love and with it... complications. Love always comes with complications. It wouldn't be love without those.

Shadow and Jayderay watch from the bedside, as the men examine the Extender. Something they've both done several times before. Men are odd creatures.

"You two done fooled plenty with that thing before

today, and still don't know nothin' about it. Now's the time to *do* something," says Jayderay in dangerously gentle tones.

RL recognizes those tones. They're not bedroom gentle. They're not holding and cuddling gentle. They're the tones a woman uses just before gently tearing someone's butt off. Usually her husbands.

"Okay, fine. Frankie, you've got the pistol, right?"

"Yeah... but here, you take it. I've got my razor," answers Frankie with an air of great sacrifice. He doesn't mention the Prod tucked in his pocket.

"That razor. Yes... I'm sure you do," says RL, taking the proffered automatic. He's a little bothered by Frankie's ease at giving up the pistol. A razor wielding Frankie might get a bit too zealous. No doubt the doctor can be herded with a gun... but probably not with a throat slashed down to his scrotum. "Well, when we get in there, don't be too... eager."

"Not to worry, Boss, it's me; I know we need the bastard alive."

Sighing heavily, RL says, "Shadow... let's see what this contraption will do."

Kneeling gracefully before the Extender, Shadow leans forward. Her alabaster breasts pushing out against the low-cut gown. RL winces at the sight of scars crisscrossing the chest. Placing her hands on the Extender, a spider web of blue light immediately begins pulsing across its front. And a faint smell like overheated wiring rises from the piece.

"I know not how, nor in what manner I'm affecting this device," Shadow says, looking over at RL. "Nor do I know if this will continue after I remove my hands."

"None of us really knows crap about it, only what Elvis has said." answers RL. "You're doing fine, just keep your hands on it and we'll see."

Beneath her fingers the light continues its rhythmic throb as the electrical odor increases. "I believe I feel a vibration each time the blue—"

A humming from inside the thing interrupts her, and vapor seeps from within. Pushing out, surrounding the Extender, the fog slowly spreads.

"You back away now, honey, and come sit here with me and Elvis," whispers Jayderay. "Let the two men deal with whatever it doin'."

"Oh, yeah, you bet," says Frankie. "We're total, absolute, bony-fidy experts at this. And it's probably about time for something real toothy to jump out—"

"Be quiet," snaps RL, gripping the pistol as he backs away from the growing cloud.

"Frankie," says Jayderay with a withering look, "do you need my remindin' on why we doin' this?"

Frankie withers, and his lips assume the shrunken head look.

As they watch, the cloud rises while spreading further out on the floor. And the droning sound stops. The blue light fades, vapor thins, and an opening appears. The group looks directly at Dr. Moto's work station. The ship's Extender screen has become a two-way passage.

"And we can just walk in... I knew it," breathes Frankie with delight.

"Yeah, and whatever horrors are over there can stroll in here," whispers RL.

"Oh, my Lor— I think I'm gonna take up prayin' again, RL. I told you that thing was devil's work," says the wide eyed Jayderay.

"My husband... please, my husband."

"Yes, Shadow, this is all for Elvis, but we can't just charge in there," says RL. "We've no idea who *or what* might be out of our view from here.

As if answering a prayer, Dr. Moto strides into view. Stopping at his desk, he begins hurriedly searching. His haste and blackened eyes give him the look of a worried, furtive raccoon. Well, this raccoon can just forget about whatever he's looking for. He's not going to need it.

As Moto appears, RL quickly turns to Frankie with a finger to his lips, and a look of castration in his eyes.

Now is not the time for any Frankie-ness. He gives Jay-deray an almost as serious look. They both nod simultaneously.

With his back to the portal alcove, Moto continues to root about at the console. RL steps into the room with all the noise of a dust mote, pistol pointed at Moto's back. Frankie follows with the stealth of a flu germ, his razor lovingly gripped.

Several soft steps bring them within touching distance of the still rummaging Moto. Frankie gives RL a beseeching look, a look of please let me. RL nods, and Frankie clears his throat.

"Dr. Moto."

Without turning the doctor replies, "Not now! Return to your work station at once."

"No, I won't, Doctor... I think I'll aim a stream of piss at you, *sir*."

Moto freezes. None of the staff would dare speak to him like that. Slowly turning, he starts slipping his hand into a pocket.

Frankie moves with dazzling speed, and the glinting razor presses into Moto's scrawny neck. Blood immediately seeps out in a bright red trickle.

"Don't, Frankie! We've got to—"

"Not to worry, Mon Capitaine. I'm only encouraging this asshole to keep his hands where we can see them; he thinks he's tricky. Now, dear Doctor... slowly, slowly... catch'ee monkey... pull your fucking hand out of that pocket. I almost hope you try something so I can give you another mouth to smile with."

Moto obeys, and Frankie slips his own hand into the pocket, and fishes out a Prod. "Why just look at this, RL... it was only a fob for his keys," Frankie giggles, as Moto's blood continues to dribble onto the razor. And another Prod goes into Frankie's pocket.

"What do you want?" whimpers Moto, speaking without even moving his lips. "I can offer—"

"You can shut up is what you can do, Dr. Sayonara," says Frankie flashing his All-American boy scout smile.

"All right," says RL, "we've got the son of a bitch, now let's get the hell out of here before we're discovered."

As they push Moto through the portal, a question dawns on RL... can Shadow close it? The best laid plans of mice, men, and dipshits often have a flaw. And sometimes these flaws can be serious. Serious as in fatal.

RL and Frankie have no way of knowing that Dr. Lillith Sally Gaust receives automatic notification whenever the Extender is activated. Yes, indeed; the best laid plans can be... problematic. As in fatal.

Down in the lower bowel of the ship:

Sheriff Lakker stands in the ominous quiet of a large deserted area wondering where the hell all his people are.

The answer comes as every cabin door silently opens. The Yellow have been busy. Very successfully busy.

Slouching from each opening comes a glistening, suppurating Yellow Melt. The only sounds made are the mush-suck of each dissolving foot as it walks on the metal deck. The membrane covering what had once been their mouths pulses in and out. Eyes roll blindly beneath a wet coating, and arms reach out with slowly fading hands. And within the wet, yellow coated skulls of all... are brains. Minds that must accept that which cannot be accepted, minds that desperately try to deny that which cannot be denied, minds that crave and need.

They move as one, but never touching each other. Shambling toward Lakker, they form a horseshoe of sentient blight. A corral of fungal rot and growth. Their touch is much worse than any death; bestowing a nightmare of horrid, filthy life. Always and forever.

Blind, yet seeing, mouthless, yet communicating, they slump and droop toward Sherrif Lakker. A relentless tide which only a flamethrower could stop.

"Godamighty, the Yellow done took all my people...

took every fuckin' one," mutters Lakker as he stuffs the useless gun back into his pouch. "It ain't possible... how'd they get in?... how'd they take'em in such a short time," he says with the voice of someone stunned by a brutal punch.

Slowly he backs away from the wave of advancing mold. And remembering their pursuit at the lake... some of them can move with a degree of speed. *Shank... I cain't leave her, it don't matter what... I won't. Gots to moves fast... fetch her, get us into them Waydowns.*

Still backing, Lakker takes a few deep breaths. And abruptly spinning about, runs, in a pouch bouncing, hat flying, full out, deck pounding flight.

Behind him the line of Yellow halts; blind eyes stare, mouth skins pulse. Within seconds they surge forward en masse. Not one of the Melts ever brushes against another.

Already gasping, the old lungs straining for more air, Lakker reaches his cabin door. Frantically jerking at the lock and looking back down the corridor. A sharp pain pierces his chest for a second, and then is gone. It's not his first. *Not now, not now... I cain't, I gots to get Shank out afore my ticker goes.*

That hallway is filling with the Yellow. Filling with an ambulant, thinking, murderous mold in the shape of human. The wet, floor sucking sounds of their stumps flow over him as on they come. A few are faster than the rest. They're close, so close he smells the decaying, suffocating odor of the rot eating and transforming their bodies. And on they come.

For centuries Earth has had a name for this disease. It is Leprosy. And this extraterrestrial strain is much deadlier; it is hive sentient.

The door lock releases, throwing Lakker into the cabin as he screams for Shank. Leaping to the bunk, he slaps and shakes the girl, jerking her upright by the arms, and heaves her across his shoulders.

"SHERFF!" yells the shocked awake girl, "WHAT IN TARN—"

"The Yellow's a'comin' and there ain't no time, girl! Godamighty, they a'comin' down our hall!" Grabbing her crutch, he lunges for the open door... just as a diseased yellow arm and head thrusts into view.

Back at the Roaton house, the good Dr. Moto is shoved through the portal into the bedroom, holding his bleeding throat. Frankie has a helpful hand clenching the back of the doctor's skinny neck, softly whispering tender promises of ghastly things.

RL immediately calls for Shadow; desperately hoping that her touch can turn the Extender off, closing the portal. If not, then they'll all end up in very large petri dishes... with Moto attending.

Shadow swiftly kneels, placing both hands on the spacesuit piece, and instantly the opening is gone. Not just closed... but gone. And the Extender remains, which is of great importance to Frankie. He has plans. He's going to get up to something. He's known for that.

"Sakes, RL! There ain— there are just no words for it. It's like voodoo, 'cept it's a machine."

"Just like in the movies," giggles Frankie. "I've been saying all along—"

"MY HUSBAND," interrupts Shadow in her awful, room filling voice. A voice from a place that does not know light. Black eyebrows arch higher, meeting the midnight ringlets of hair laying on her brow. Ebony lips tremble against star-white teeth, as the eyes fill.

"HELP HIM, I BESEECH YOU. WITH MY LIFE I BEG."

Only the labored breathing of Elvis can be heard for several long seconds. All look with pity and fear at this woman of roiling grays. A living, charcoal rendering of a female from an ethereal world. From an existence far beyond any of this groups knowing.

Frankie is the first to break the spell. Only he has intimate knowledge of how truly human and broken this woman is. He drags Moto to her.

"This is Doctor Moto, who has much knowledge of Elvis. He will examine your husband. He will determine what is needed. He *will* heal your man."

"But I... but, but I cannot! I, I must have proper equipment!" sputters Moto. "I will return to the ship, and then—"

Frankie casually slaps him, and with the same hand, grabs a hank of hair from the swollen head wound. Yanking Moto down to his knees, twisting the hair until the doctor's face is turned upward, Frankie leans down and speaks quietly.

"Listen to me, Rice-A-Roni, and hear me well. That man" he says, motioning with his chin toward Elvis, "is a friend of mine. A very good friend, and he's told me quite a bit about you. Do not fuck with me. You will be provided with whatever you need for the examination. I can obtain any accoutrements, medication or drug that you deem necessary, prescription or otherwise." Frankie's words make a soft sound, like a sprayed mist for prize flowers... from a mister filled with piss.

"You will not need to return to the ship," continues Frankie's deadly words. "And dearest, dearest Doctor Moto... I beg of you... I beseech you... I implore you... do not let my friend die. If that exceedingly regrettable thing should occur, then I will be forced to give you to Shadow. And then I strongly suspect your life would never end. Think of it, sir, just think of it." Frankie finishes with a merry twinkle in his eyes, while giving his best, most wholesome, cutest, chipmunk smile.

From his knees, Moto glances over at Shadow, then back to Frankie. *I have seen horrors that would shrivel your tiny American soul. This spectral gray bitch you threaten me with is nothing compared to what I've seen... But I must tread these waters carefully... this boy-girl is dangerous... it likes its razor.*

"Yes," replies Moto. "I hear you. And Proby, um, Elvis, will not die under my care. In return for this—"

"In return," Frankie interrupts, "in return, I won't peel you like a fucking onion. Isn't that just dandy?"

"Uh, yes, that is most... uh, most dandy."

"Oh, very good, Doctor, I'm just ever so glad we agree. Now get your God damn ass up, and go to work."

Shadow watches as Moto rises. With her violet eyes pulsing to near white, she reaches out and grips his wrist. He flinches at the touch, his face a grimace.

"I feel you, man, I know of you from my Elv-is. You belong on another plane, one not connected to this world. Should he die, I will take you there. I will stay with you in that place."

Jerking from her grasp, Moto's face is awash with sweat and he visibly struggles for command of himself. Grabbing his burning wrist he finds it coated with frost. *What is this creature? I was wrong... this, this one... she is the one to fear... the boy/girl can only kill me.*

Dr. Moto does something he's not done in decades. He bows. He bows low, saying, "I am humbled in your presence; I will not fail you."

Moto is not humbled... he is terrified. He needs to be.

⁓ ✦ ⁓

Sheriff Lakker, with Shank across his shoulders and gripping her crutch, lurches for the open cabin door. And it fills with one of the Melts. Another Yellow immediately appears behind it.

"Dump me, Sherrf! Dump me and runs," screams the girl.

Lakker does neither, he doesn't even think. Charging with the crutch thrust forward as a battering ram, he hits the fungal human directly in the chest, forcing it back into the one behind, just as a third slouches up to join them. The Melts fall back into the corridor, one against the other like dominos going down.

Unknown to Lakker, the glistening skin of one Melt is very adhesive to the skin of another. Their hide is a mindless mold and tries to meld like with like. As the fallen three struggle to get up, each fight against the other trying to break free. They're like glue coated frogs in a trough.

Taking the narrow opening left by the struggling, gummy Yellow, Lakker runs for the hatch leading into the Waydowns. Shank bounces on his back, silently clenching her teeth.

The horde filling the corridor behind the stuck together trio come to an immediate halt. They're sticky, but not stupid. They stand there not touching, their mouth membranes pulse rapidly. No doubt calling the three blocking the hall idiots.

As a badly winded Lakker reaches the Waydowns hatch, he collapses against the crutch he'd unconsciously kept. Shank speaks, sounding almost apologetic.

"Sherff, I hates to tell it, but the dang Yellow done got past them stuck ones, they comin' and they bein' mighty spry about it. Sherff?"

Clutching his chest Lakker silently drops to his knees as the crutch clatters to the deck.

Rolling off his back, she lands badly, shrieking with pain, but scrambles to him.

"Sherrf! Sherrf! What's wrong, what's—"

"Hatch," he gasps, pointing needlessly.

The herd of Melts are near enough to hear the

squelching sounds of their ankle stumps hitting the deck.

Fighting against the splinted leg, pulling herself up by the door's locking system, she claws at the bolts and levers. Totally different from the power place hatch, the girl has never used this exit. Only Lakker had ever gone through this forbidden and feared entrance to the Waydowns.

The sucking, wet stomping sounds of the Yellow drill into her as they slouch forward. Closing in, the melting remains of their feet eating up the last few yards of distance.

"I CAIN'T OPENS IT, I CAIN'T!" shrieks the girl.

Sliding on his knees, one hand clawing at his exploding chest, the other dragging her crutch, his face white and streaming with sweat, the big man falls against the hatch.

Now only a few feet away, the Melts begin reaching out with the thick syrup of dissolving hands.

Straining for breath against invisible steel bands crushing his chest, Lakker throws the door open. Shoving the crippled girl sprawling through, her crutch clattering beside her. Gasping, he falls forward onto his face. Laying halfway across the threshold, his hands scrabble uselessly trying to pull himself into the Waydowns. "Grab the crutch girl, RUN!"

Sobbing, nearing hysteria, Shank grabs his hands; yanking, jerking, straining. Her broken leg shrieks, keeping her from getting traction. Dropping to the good knee, she grabs Lakker's belt. Lifting as she pulls, aided by terror, she drags him further, but not enough to clear the opening. With pain gritted teeth, she takes another grip on the belt.

Realizing he's still not clear of the hatch, Lakker weakly pushes himself up as she pulls. Their combined efforts work; his feet slide past the opening.

And a melting yellow hand grabs his ankle. More reaching arms are coming right behind it.

Seeing the hand slap onto Lakker's ankle, the girl screams in rage, seizes the hatch, and slams it into the glistening forearm. Throwing her weight against the door, crushing fungal meat and bone between metal jamb and metal door.

With rupturing heart, Lakker pushes on the hatch with his free foot, adding pressure to Shank's weight against the door. Their joined strength pinches and finally severs the rotting yellow flesh and softened bones. Snapping shut, the hatch automatically locks.

And that melting hand still grips his ankle.

"I kin cuts it, Sherrf," she screams, "I kin cuts it off!"

No. She can't. But she will try.

———•••———

Far above on Deck 19 an office door glides silently open. Dr. Lillith Sally Gaust glares unhappily about. That orangutan lunch is not sitting well with her new, still evolving digestive tract. She intends to correct her diet very soon.

This incarnation of Dr. Gaust has a slight resemblance to the old one: it's human shaped. Sort of. The similarity stops there. No other likeness remains of the once pretty young doctor who had long ago gained control of Deck 19 and the lab experiments.

That same doctor who had once gotten caught up in the 1950s rock and roll craze and developed a panty-liquifying crush on the hip swiveling Elvis Presley. Her case of bra vaporizing hots became unendurable. Even her pubic hair vibrated. Laying hands on the real item was impossible, but a solution *HAD* to be found.

So... she had the power and the lab to incubate her very own Elvis. But experiments often go awry. What hatched was... Proby. A lavender skinned, eggplant haired, (sort of) Elvis lookalike. And it was an immense, perpetually in trouble, pain in the butt. It was also hung and oversexed. She kept it.

But what now stands in Lillith Sally's open door is no longer Dr. Gaust. It's no longer really human. A few months back she'd been bitten on the shoulder by a fellow scientist, who was *certainly* no longer human. It was another failed experiment, another Lab Spill. But this one had been a bit different.

That biting Spill had once been a Deck 19 scientist, one who had developed some badly aching morals and terribly enlarged ethics. These were painful... to Dr. Gaust. So, the esteemed sister scientist found herself donated to the altar of science. And the accompanying innovative experimentation. Life can be difficult for a scientist with a conscience. And long; very, very long.

That shoulder bite became infected. Or became what Gaust initially *thought* was infected. She had been wrong. The wound was not infected. It was developing. It continued to do so. Becoming emergent within weeks... it took her.

The new, improved, industrial strength Dr. Gaust steps forward. A brave new world indeed.

Very close by, inside Proby's Bowl-A-Rama game, something else is also being active. It wants out.

⁕

At the Roaton house, Dr. Moto busies himself carefully examining the unconscious Elvis. Aka, that mutant shithead Proby. Most of this is nothing more than an act designed to gain Moto more time. The doctor had quickly and silently diagnosed Elvis. After monitoring the troublesome shit for over 60 years Moto knew this creature. And he remained silent, knowing the prognosis might end the need for the doctor's presence. In fact, it would probably end... Moto. That blood thirsty boy-girl would see to that.

I must have more time. I must be ready before the change. The demon-eyed gray woman will not leave the bedside, but perhaps the others can be sent on errands. With luck, Proby's transformation will happen while they're gone. The witch woman will be so shocked, she will never know I'm gone.

The degree of care and scrutiny that Dr. Moto exhibits in going over this lavender pain in the butt is quite admirable. The doctor's high level of care is being greatly encouraged by Frankie. The silly bastard who stands close by silently polishing his straight razor. And smiling. The blade is not a comfort to Moto, and that smile... considerably less so.

Jayderay and Shadow are also standing back out of the way. Shadow rubs her badly healed arms constantly, the lips a black slash across her face. Occasionally speaking softly, Jayderay tries to comfort her, knowing words can't help, but needing to try. She owes and loves this gray enigma of a woman.

RL flits between the living area and the bedroom like an expectant father ping-pong ball. He fidgets, frets, and has finger combed his hair so often it looks like a disease. The creases in his ironed jeans have been repeatedly checked till they're limp from the eye pressure.

Having been warned by both Jayderay and Frankie to quit asking stupid questions, RL has kept quiet for all of maybe ten minutes. His concern is genuine; he truly likes and feels for this odd, not quite human couple, but more... he's indebted to them. RL doesn't take his debts lightly. But.

But there is also a wee tad of selfishness mixed in with RL's anxiety. He's been thinking that if Elvis should die, it's inevitable Shadow will... and then Jayderay will remove RL's ass. And there's the small matter of the ghosts... if that's even what they are. Without Shadow to drive or keep them away, this place will be untenable. This *not haunted* house. This house he's just bought. This house he plans to live in... with Jayderay. Money is often at the bottom of even the most noble of concerns, and RL had plunked down a considerable wad of cash for this property.

"God damn it, Moto, you've had long enough. What's wrong with him?" demands RL, unable to keep quiet any longer.

"I agree, Boss, he's had plenty of time. So, my good precious doctor, surely you've had sufficient opportunity to form some idea." Frankie steps closer to Moto, whispering.

"Maybe you need that Prod I took rammed up your withered, oriental ass. Having your shit electrified might clear your brain."

"YES! Yes, I have, I have a prognosis," bleats Moto. The thought of Frankie lovingly inserting the Prod has indeed cleared his brain. Its clarity is now quite astounding. He has an absolutely, positively, amazingly clear brain.

"Very good, my dear Sir Doctor! I'm sure you want to share those findings with us. NOW."

"YES! I do, I do. I WANT to share," says Doctor Moto, once again responding with great speed. He's also frantically thinking of ways to get rid of this Prod shoving round-eye. Moto needs time, but he's unsure of how much. *I must be careful, the boy-girl has medical knowledge, he will know if I try and send him after nonexistent medications or equipment.* Bracing himself for the coming protests of disbelief, he speaks:

"Only my direct superior, Dr. Gaust, knows all of how Proby was... formulated. She is currently... out of the ship. However, through my many years of, of nurturing him, I've gained a great deal of knowledge concerning his physiology. That being said—"

"Quit stalling," interrupts RL. "What can be done?"

"Certainly...yes, of course. I will require some unusual items. I need a blender with an excellent puree capability, a feeding tube with funnel attachment, pomegranates, two unpeeled whole pineapples, and... and... and bovine blood along with the animal's urine."

There are a few seconds of stunned, motionless silence, which breaks as RL lunges forward, ramming the pistol into Moto's gut and Jayderay yells.

"WHAT? He talkin' hoodoo! RL, you do whatev—"

"Hold up," interrupts Frankie. "Don't kill him just yet. I've read of similar concoctions, but not in any textbook."

"No. Do not kill him," Shadow says softly, her eyes beginning to boil. "Should he fail, he is mine and I will take him with me. My... the man I was forced to marry long ago, had an old journal passed from his family. Within the pages could be found ancient remedies, and some did call for ingesting various urines. He had occasion to force some of them... on me. We must try whatever Dr. Moto recommends. Please."

RL sighs, pulls the gun away from the quivering Dr. Moto, and looks at Frankie.

"Well, we've got to do something. What do you think?"

"I think Sushi-Breath here," answers Frankie, motioning with his razor, "might be playing us for time,

Boss. But the bastard does know Elvis, and he's obviously terrified of Shadow, so... maybe he's telling the truth. Like you said, we've got to do something."

"Hell, I'm not even sure what a pomegranate is, Frankie. Much less where to look, and as far as the ... the cow stuff, maybe a vet?"

"Well, United usually got pomegranates, and always got pineapple," says Jayderay. "But I don't even want to think about gettin' the... that other stuff."

"I can get the urine, blood and feeding tube, Boss. I know someone who keeps a few cows as cover for certain other... activities. Jaderay can get the fruit while you keep watch over the good Dr. Do Little."

"There is no need to be concerned about my actions," mutters Moto, looking over at Shadow. "I will obey."

"Shut the fuck up," says Frankie amiably... with a smile.

Frankie is right. Dr. Moto is playing them for time. And Moto certainly does know Elvis. He knows him inside and out. The doctor definitely doesn't want to be around for this aggravating mutant's coming... *change*.

———•◆•———

Back in the Waydowns, Seevee shuffles dejectedly off to explore the sleeve marked area, while Tanya leads Huong to meet Lakker. And the deputy.

"I think Lakker's area is the ship's very last deck, Huong. It leads to the ship's power source, and that's probably the very bottom of this hulk. Unless there's more under the lake," says Tanya.

"Lake? There's a fucking lake down here?"

"Yep, but don't get your hopes up," she laughs, "you won't be skinny dipping with the deputy in it."

"Hopes? My only hope is getting the hell back up to Deck 19. This damn Waydowns is going from shit to worse all the time."

"You said it, Wonder Gook, you said it. With all that hoping of yours, you better include not meeting up with any Melts," Tanya says as she turns down another hallway

"Melts? Plural? What in hell are... never mind, I don't want to hear any more—"

"No, you don't," interrupts Tanya, chuckling. "But just so you'll know, Melts are Gunch in human shape, they're people that got taken by it... The Yellow."

"Jesus. It's even worse than I thought. Don't tell me this Yellow has something to do with your plan to take 19 and— WHAT THE FUCK IS THAT?" he yells, pointing ahead at a huge carcass.

"It's a Coiler... good Christ... what could do this?"

"I've only seen their tentacles reaching through a

hatchway. I had no idea of their size," Huong mumbles to himself.

In front of them lies an enormous, orange and green body. Deflated eye-stalks dangle sightlessly, and protruding from a slit in the torso, its giant parrot beak of a mouth yawns permanently in death. Several, nearly black, scaled tentacles are strewn about in loops. They've been ripped off.

"I don't think even another Coiler could do this," Tanya breathes out the words, her fear sounding in each one. She looks upwards into the haze clouded heights. White support stanchions glow slightly as they disappear into the fog, as beads of condensate drip down their sides.

"This wasn't here earlier, this is recent," she continues. "We have a truce and sort of an alliance with them, I hope to fuck they won't think I'm somehow responsible."

"God damn it, Tanya, let's don't just stand here waiting on, on whatever did this. Let's move!"

"You're right, but I'm—"

A wailing cry interrupts her, as it comes echoing from further down the corridor. A human cry.

"That sounds like Shank! Damn that, that girl, what the fuck now? C'mon let's go," says Tanya starting off in a wary trot, skirting the massive tentacles.

"WHAT? You're gonna charge toward that scream? How fucking smart is that? Whatever did this," says Huong gesturing at the dead Coiler, "is probably doing more of it."

"Then stay," she yells over her shoulder, "but you better keep looking up, that's where they live."

Cursing fluently, an exasperated Huong follows. Repeatedly, nervously glancing upward... and in all directions. He's smart and knows there is no getting topside without her. But he thinks longingly of killing the scar faced blond bitch... while he feverishly looks up. And looks to the left. And to the right. And over his shoulder. And so on.

Ultimately, surviving in the Waydowns was luck. If any living creature lived for long within these twisted, foul decks, it was just plain old luck. The bad kind. Death can often be a preference in the Waydowns. And elsewhere.

On Deck 19, the new and improved Dr. Gaust lurches a bit as she walks into Moto's work area. Her legs are not yet accustomed to the brain signals that now come from an altered source.

As always a flickering blue surrounds the currently blank Extender screen and portal. (The one Moto has recently been encouraged through.) That light casts the shadow of Gaust on the opposite wall. It's a somewhat different outline than would've been displayed a few weeks ago. It is not a comforting silhouette. It's taller, and seems to undulate, to bob, dart, and weave. Moto had seen what made this new shadow. And Moto... had richly disgraced himself.

Looking about, she strokes her smooth, newly grown and somewhat triangular head. The old one still flops about, and is beginning to smell. Gaust sees the blinking lights of the Christmas arch leading into Proby's nursery/play pen/ prison. A giant cardboard Santa stands faithfully beside it, offering everyone a bottled Coke. Both stolen decades past on one of the little bastard's topside forays. Back before the Extender had been taken from the ship by some top brass idiot. Dr. Gaust thinks idly of the little lavender troublemaker; her very own Elvis. She almost smiles at the memories of raising him. And fucking him.

But, Lillith is not here looking for her Proby/Elvis creation, those type of desires are in the past. Nor is she searching for Dr. Moto, knowing he's off to get the long lost Extender. She also knows he will be back. He better... or he will die quickly of old age. As she would.

This ancient starship continues to sporadically emit a time treatment originally intended for an alien crew during intergalactic flights. Presumably due to some extraterrestrial geek's fuck-up, the effects seemed limited to certain areas of Deck 19. Since she, Moto, and Proby had lived for years in those spaces, their aging was remarkably slowed... while they remained in the ship. The time-treats may have been permanent for the extraterrestrials. Not so for humans. A bit of experimentation on a strenuously objecting *volunteer* had proved that. Humorously so to Dr. Gaust, but the volunteer had not been amused. He died. Moto was unaware of her findings.

Staggering toward and through the Christmas arch, Gaust's mobility steadily improves. She wanders the aisles and passages made by all of Proby's games, toys, and general crap, occasionally recognizing items from her college days. Stopping before a bubbling jukebox, she peers briefly at the displayed records. *I remember those being larger... I wonder if my recall has been altered?* Further on, a stop at a 5 cent Coca-Cola machine with a hand crank and tiny, square delivery door: *Yes, good, my memories are intact... those God damn little bottles could get jammed up inside... then I'd get no coke and lose my fucking nickel. Yes, memories... the switch, yes, I do remember the switch... not something to forget... I will use it... if boarded.*

Moving deeper into the maze she spots an arcade

game she remembers well from some long ago midway: the Bowl-a-Rama. Dr. Lillith Sally Gaust stops before it. She reaches out.

Something inside the game has become very aware of Gaust. Eagerly aware.

***

Below Deck 19 in the Waydowns, Tanya slows and then stops as she hears another anguished bawl. In her time on these twisted and forsaken decks, she's heard plenty of screeching. But this is different. *Damn, that's definitely Shank, but it doesn't sound like she's getting her butt chewed off… it sounds more like… more like… what?*

Huong comes pounding up from behind, breathing heavily, frowning and still trying to look in all directions at once. Wiping sweat from his face with an already sodden khaki sleeve, he looks longingly at the back of Tanya's imminently wringable neck. *That idiot pet Spill of hers isn't around, it would be so easy… feel so good… so satisfying… like my wife was… like the brats when they squealed.* He shakes his head and manages to rid himself of this temptation, at least for the present. He speaks.

"Sounds like what or whoever that is, hasn't died yet, and ain't that a shame. Since you've stopped, can

I hope you've found your brain and we're not going to look for something that'll fucking eat us?"

"Well, Huong-y, you can always hope, even here in the Waydowns there's that. But no, we're going on. And besides, this is the direction we'd be taking anyway. You heard that last scream… did that sound like somebody getting mauled?"

"What the hell are you talking about? It was a scream. I don't give a shit if it was some Spill being eaten or gettin' butt fucked."

"I kinda suspect you'd know how that last one would sound. And how to make it. But I'm serious, to me it sounded like… I don't know… like… oh, fuck it… it sounded awful."

"And I still don't give a shit."

"Well, feel free to stay behind. And then maybe I'll get to hear *you* scream," says Tanya, as she takes off again.

A disgusted Huong looks up, all around and everywhere; he ponders not following the bitch, knowing that being afraid is a natural product of the brain. But being afraid and alone can become terror, which bypasses that organ. And being alone in the Waydowns leads to mindless quivering-gibbering… and being had for lunch. He follows her.

Not too far from Tanya and the pondering Huong, Seevee trudges sadly along, hoping mightily he can find that partially open hatch with the dangling coat sleeve. He can't bear the envisioned scene of having to tell Ton that he couldn't find the damned place. No doubt in the presence of a smirking Huong, who would then lead them directly to it. Unerringly, without so much as a pause, right to it.

This thought brings others. Other torturing, bedeviling, penis shriveling feelings about that crazy, duck feathers man. Thinking of the bastard with Tanya. *Seevee luff Ton... much luff... Duck feathers man no good for Ton... Huong much sneaky snake... much no good.*

Cautiously peering around a corner, looking down one of the endless hallways, Seevee spots the slightly open hatch and that tantalizing sleeve. Hanging limply from the door, it draws him forward. Eagerly touching it, caressing it, fondling it. *Seevee find, Seevee find! Ton be so proud... much, much proud. Ton hug Seevee... Ton KISS Seevee. Ton see Quack Huong much no good... much, much no good. KISS Seevee... move Seevee to Ton bed, let Seevee all time Ton bed!*

With vastly inflated and euphoric visions of Tanya's reaction to his find, Seevee pulls at the hatch entry. It doesn't budge an inch, not even a fraction. Of course it doesn't. He's an Almost, he's nearly human, so presumably he's got the same God... why should his luck be any different than theirs?

Looking through the miserly space provided by that crack of an opening, his luck continues... and he can see very little. Muttering to himself, he places a foot against the wall, wedges his fingers into the crevice, grips the hatch, and with a muscle rupturing, back splintering pull, manages to widen the crack a couple more inches. Enough to see a bit more of the area beyond. And maybe enough to push a knobby arm through to get additional leverage to finish opening the door.

Crouching now, and slowly sliding his hands along the door's edge, his eyes move with them, greedily looking in for some Tanya pleasing loot. With his multiple elbows bent out from his sides, he looks like a roach who just discovered a tear in the refrigerator's seal.

Rising further, straining to see through the flickering dim lights and haze within, he reaches up to pull the dangling empty sleeve out of the way.

A thick fingered hand explodes out of it, grabbing Seevee's wrist, brutally jerking his arm into the opening. Another powerful wrench pulls the arm through the narrow crack, peeling the flesh off his bones like skin from a banana. Seevee's shoulder rams into the door, preventing him from being pulled in further.

But that doesn't stop what has him.

———··———

As Tanya nears the entry to Lakker's deck, that terrible, obviously human scream diminishes. It trails down into a constant keening moan. Making a turn, she stops running. And then starts a slow walk toward Shank. *Oh, damn this... just fucking damn this.*

Realizing that she cares, shocks Tanya more than what she sees.

The girl sits in the middle of the corridor. Rocking back and forth, crying in a high, endless, desolate whine; holding Lakker's head and shoulders to her chest. Holding all she had ever known since childhood, holding the man who had taken her in when no one else would, holding the man who had loved her.

As Huong jogs up behind Tanya, she turns to face him, speaking in a low emotionless voice.

"If I hear one wrong word from you, to or about, this girl, or the man, I will kill you. Is there anything about this you fail to understand?" Her blind eye darts wildly, as the other steadily drills into him.

Breathing hard, Huong stares at her for a few seconds before nodding. He doesn't much fear death, but he doesn't want it, and damn sure knows when he sees it. This blond woman is insane, but she's his only hope of getting out of this hell. He nods again.

"Do you want me to stay back, or try and help?"

"Stay until I call you," she answers, turning abruptly, walking toward Shank and Lakker.

The man's leg is a few feet away from the couple. Laying near the locked hatch, it has been brutally hacked off at the knee. Savagely, hysterically cut by a sobbing young girl trying desperately to save Lakker's life. To keep the Yellow from spreading, from taking him. From horribly consuming the only good thing in her life.

The Melt's hand still clutches the amputated leg. The surrounding skin is turning yellow as the mold gradually creeps up from the ankle. Still creeping, undying, still consuming.

Continuing her high-pitched wail, the girl is unaware of any presence until Tanya stands beside her, placing a hand on her shoulder. Shank looks up at her blankly, with her red face awash in tears, snot, and saliva. And she explodes.

Throwing one arm around Tanya's legs, still holding Lakker's head with the other, the girl screams.

"TANYA! I'M SO REAL SORRY! I DIN'T MEAN IT, TOPSIDE AINT NO HERSY, TOPSIDE IS REAL, PLEASE, PLEASE TAKE HIM TO TOPSIDE. HE

WON'T BE SICK IN TOPSIDE, YOU AIN'T GOTS TO TAKE ME, I AIN'T—"

Tanya drops to both knees, wraps her arms around Shank, pulling the screeching, blubbering face into the hollow of her neck.

"Hush, Shank. You be quiet and listen to me. We must be silent, or bad things will come. They would take the Sheriff. You're his Deputy, you must protect him."

Lakker is dead. He had been a good man. That can't be said of many, not anywhere. And in this swirling pit being a good anything was almost impossible.

As the man and girl had forced the hatch closed, severing the Melts wrist, his laboring heart had quit. Not realizing, she had tried to save him, tried to keep the mold from moving up the leg, from taking all of him. Hacking, sawing, screaming.

Stunned by the religious hysterics of Shank's outburst, and her own actions toward the unhinged girl, Tanya continues holding her. *What the hell am I doing? Cuddling this filthy ignorant girl, here in the middle of a shit hole. Damn this! I need to grab Lakker's gun and just leave this squalling kid. Her and her fucking dead sheriff... and her broke leg.*

What Tanya does is continue holding that, filthy, ignorant girl. And begins lightly stroking the matted hair.

Life can be messy for someone like Tanya, who discovers for the first time... that she might just give a shit about someone.

Standing where Tanya had left him, Huong still wears the disgusted look, but he hasn't said anything. Not a word. Why bother. But gripping his Uzi, he thinks plenty. Life is not messy for Huong. Life is for doing and getting.

Still hugging and petting the softly crying Shank, Tanya looks at Lakker's body stretching out from the girl's lap. He's the color of slate. The bloody stump of his knee, the butchered off limb with its yellowing skin, the crude knife lying beside it, tell an awful story.

So... the Yellow came. How did the fucking Melts get out of the power place? Christ, they're smarter than we thought. Almighty God... this girl had to cut, trying to save—

A small voice with hitching breath breaks into her thoughts.

"He... he's... he's dead, gone, ain't he? Not even no Topside doctorin' can fix that. I knowed that. All along I, I knowed it... in my guts, deep where the hurtin' stays, I knowed. I, I, I knowed it when I cut."

Taking a deep breath, Tanya keeps the girl's head cradled in the hollow of her neck. *Christ she smells.*

"I am sorry, Shank. Really, I'm truly sorry. Yes, he's gone. No doctor or place can fix that."

Shank turns her face and looks down into Lakker's. "If I could onliest hear him, hear him once more time."

"Oh, chil— Shank. I'd give you that if I could. You hold him a bit longer, tell him goodbye as best you can. Then we've got to get moving."

As if she hadn't heard, the girl continued tonelessly, looking down at the loved, dead face. "He, he carried me. When them Melts come and they taked the village, he carried me. He runned and toted me when his ticker was bustin' and I din't even know. He gots me through the hatch when I couldn't open it. I never even got no chance to say thankee."

"Thank him now," Tanya says softly, "and then we must go. There's something on the prowl in this area. Something huge that we couldn't fight off."

"Go? Tanya... I cain't go no wheres," she answers looking up at her. The tears have cleaned more dirt away, allowing the dim freckles to show, making her look even younger. "I ain't got no place no more anyhow. The Yellow done taked it. I knows the Sherrf is gone and dead, and I, I, I made my peace. I'll just sits and stays here with him. I don't care none what comes."

"Shank, I've told you before, I don't leave the wounded behind, and I certainly won't leave you."

"I don't need nobody sorryin' for me," she says with a hint of fire in her voice. "You tolded me afore, that you'd kill me your ownself instead of leavin' me wounded. Then, then… then you do that for me now."

Tanya pulls back, placing her hands on the girl's shoulders, looking directly into her eyes. "I'm not feeling sorry for you, I need you with me. I have plans and I need your help."

"Don't nobody need me no more, Tanya. I knows that. I gots a bad busted leg and don't knows nothin' about anythings."

Tanya takes a deep breath, looking at this misbegotten spawn of an abandoned people. A lost, bereaved and broken child, for whom death would truly be a mercy. She stands.

"You listen to me you snot nosed brat. Lakker was a good man, and I don't say that about many. I'm not gonna let you shit on him by turning into a whining tit-baby. A spoiled little bitch, who wants to sit on her nasty ass till something eats her. You're coming with me, even if I have to knock you out and drag you."

Shank's eyes widen as she continues to stare up at Tanya, her jaw muscles knotting, chin lifting. Sitting up straighter, she lowers Lakker's head onto her lap.

"I always did say you gots sand… *MISSY!* And I ain't nasty neither."

CHAPTER 14

SHOPPING, DEATH, AND A SOAP OPERA

At the Roaton house, RL is being RL; a hard and thankless job no doubt. He's fretting, fidgeting, and repeatedly finger combing his hair. He also adjusts the rolled-up sleeves of his chambray shirt, checks the ironed pant leg creases in his jeans, and polishes his loafers against his calves. Managing all this while constantly pacing from the bedroom into the living area, and back again. Glaring at Moto with each circuit.

Dr. Moto sits quietly, hands in full view, resting on his knees. His eyes are closed in gentle contemplation. A small, kindly, harmless little fellow who has been vastly wronged, yet endures with acceptance all that this cruel world doth bestow. And the bastard is plotting like a prick.

Nearby, a scarred, charcoal portrait of a woman, tends her husband. Whom everyone but Moto thinks is dying. Moto knows the lavender skinned trouble maker well. Knows him too well, as he was involved in its… brewing. And for several decades afterwards had to babysit the oversexed, eternally teenaged, terminally inquisitive turd. Moto knows Elvis is not dying. It may be something a lot worse than that.

As her ashen, ebony nailed fingers lovingly caress Elvis, Shadow also keeps a watch on Moto. She's not fooled by his current saintly demeanor, not a bit taken in by this oriental navel-gazing act. She knows him from the stories Elvis has told, she knows from touching him, she knows Moto is a monster. And she knows… he's plotting like a prick.

Pacing back into the bedroom, RL gives Moto another searing look, and then speaks quietly to the woman.

"Shadow, all this waiting is driving me batty. Will you be okay with this pile of manure," he says gesturing at the doctor, "if I step outside for a few minutes?"

"Yes. All will be well. I have no fear of that evil man. Perhaps taking the air will calm you."

"Thanks, I won't be long." And with another glare at the manure pile, RL heads to the front door.

That manure pile remains silent and motionless, but it is plotting. While maintaining his "I'm so good I'm never even flatulent" act, Moto thinks hard, thinks feverishly hard, thinks because his life depends on it.

Yes, go for a walk you weak man. This will be my best chance to escape with you gone. And I must be gone from here before Proby's change. This grey thing of a wife will think I've caused it. There is no weakness to this witch, and I feel great horror about her. But she is consumed and distracted by Proby... her precious Elvis. Yes, it will be best to be gone before the other round-eyes get back. Especially the boy-girl, he of the eager razor and blood lust. I very much suspect he will insist I sample Bovine urine. Yes, I will try with this un-alive female.

But before the Moto Manure can even excrete a word, Shadow snaps her head toward him. Her black lips ripple against her teeth as if she's tasting the air. Sable brows arch over violet eyes that have specks of white beginning to appear.

"I feel there is a growing deception within you, Doctor. I feel it well. The poison of it fills you. This is an occurrence that is most unwise. Most unwise for you."

Moto visibly flinches, his eyes flying open. He does not look in the direction of Shadow's voice, he feels such an action might also be unwise.

"Let me assure you, uh, Madam... Shadow, that I have no idea as to what you mean. There is no deceit in me." Hearing her take a step, Moto cannot keep from looking. He looks. It is not a comfort to him, and he blows his goody two-shoes act... he streams flatulence.

"Fouling yourself will avail you not, Doctor. You no doubt feel that with RL gone, you can easily escape. I think not. I deem it best that until the return of he and my other friends, you should be kept away from my husband."

Reaching out to him, she quietly adds, "You will now accompany me to another room." This definitely does not sound like a cordial request. It isn't.

"Yes, yes I will, yes!" squeaks Moto, quickly shrinking back from her. He remembers the frost that had formed on his wrist when this ghastly woman had grabbed him. He fears her touch, sensing that it could go deeper than mere flesh and bone. Much deeper, into another world deeper. And besides his terror, he will go because he needs to be somewhere alone. Alone to manage his getaway before the shit hits the Elvis fan.

Shadow directs him by pointing and a few one-word directions. Moto is most cooperative. Even eager. Motioning him into a small room with a window, she speaks.

"Wait in this place, Doctor. Frankie shall come for you when all is in readiness." After she closes the door, he hears the key turn and the ancient lock click into place.

"Thank you, so much," says Moto softly, making a slight bow in the door's direction. And he smiles, looking over at the convenient window. *The horrid ghost woman has made my flight the proverbial piece of cake.* Stepping to the window, he fastidiously brushes away some cobwebs. Pushing aside the curtain, it tears apart as easily as the webs, dropping to the floor in rags.

Waving the dust away he intently examines the window. Its brass latch is encrusted with blue-green verdigris, and obviously hasn't been touched since Moto tortured WW2 prisoners. A smile flickers at the thought of those Americans who had nicknamed him Mr. Moto. Named him after a movie character; a Japanese agent played by some Hungarian Jew. How putrid; how American.

Doctor Moto, no Mister to it, continues his examination of the easy-escape window. *No doubt the wood frame will be stuck fast to the casing, but my strength is that of the young... and twice that of those with a pure heart.* As is often, he's so impressed with his own wit, he has to stifle laughter. *Mustn't alarm that dreadful witch woman.*

Hanging on an adjacent wall is an oil portrait of a stern man with a chin like an elephant's ass. From the over-carved frame, it seems to extrude from the painting, as if that elephant needs the toilet. Moto glances at it, wondering idly why the fool hadn't hired a liar to paint.

That chin, with its man, look back at him out of their Victorian frame. And idly wonders what an oriental prune is doing to their window.

As Dr. Moto enjoys his own humor while preparing to escape, he fails to notice the temperature dropping. Moisture with an oily sheen forms on the window glass.

Three tendrils of cold, dark mist silently creep under the door. They undulate and entwine while rising from the wooden floor. Forming a pulsing, throbbing spectral cloud, they drift slowly toward that window. These daughters are deeply pissed about having their playtime with Elvis interrupted. They intend to make up for that, with Moto.

Yes, Doctor Moto, you will escape this room, but it will not be that often spoke of piece of cake. And the taste of this particular confection will be... unique. Even for your exotic appetites.

Shopping in town for the requested fruit, Jaderay continues to have severe misgivings about the entire Roaton house mess. And she's certainly aware of who started that ball rolling. She did. Practically whored herself to get RL to buy the place. This self-knowledge is less than comforting; introspection often yields that result.

This is just down right voodoo-hoodoo, and we got no call to be trustin' that old Jap man... he up to something. If this don't work, what then? Is he gonna have us dancin' to bongos and killin' chickens? I'd like to make him do a little dancin'.

Jayderay would be shocked to realize what a funny, progressive old world it is. In the United States, sacrificing chickens in a religious ceremony is legal. As is slaughtering whales in the name of some tribal heritage. To forbid either of these shameful acts has been termed discrimination, racist even. But a Mormon goes to jail... for marrying too many Mormons. How funny and progressive indeed. Even... Woke.

Picking up a whole pineapple and wondering if there's an uglier fruit, she places it in her cart. *Sakes they prickly things! And I can't believe any of this is gonna work... and with cow's blood... AND its wcc. I'm glad Frankie's doin' that part...and I'm sure not gonna ask him questions about how he got it. Fact is, if it weren't for what Shadow and Evis done for me, I'd shuck all this, grab RL, and go home... MY old home, and be done with the Roaton house. And now, RL says we got ghosts! It's enough to make me get religion...*

again. Oh, Gramma! I can almost see you shakin' your head and sayin', "What's my baby girl got herself into? She foolin' with voodoo, and haints, and space-mens... and ALL on account of lovin' a man crooked as bed springs!"

Pushing the cart with its ugly fruit while muttering to her dead granny, Jayderay forges ahead. Suspecting the future holds bad things.

Jayderay is right. The future does hold bad things; it's like that, and should never be trusted. It offers much, like a presidential candidate, and delivers... like a president.

—————

While not too many miles away, in a lovely pastoral, bucolic setting, Frankie is buying... cow piss. This is a bit unusual, even for the silly bastard, not to mention he also wants a smallish amount of the same animal's blood.

However, the owner of this hard-to-find dairy farm, knows the boy and knows he tends to get up to things. More to the point, the owner does considerable herbal and chemical business with Frankie. So as usual, there are few questions asked.

But the lumbering ox of a farmer isn't too keen about having to draw blood from one of his darlings. They're not really worked as dairy cattle, that's just for show. In reality, they're spoiled pets for him and Mable, the wife.

Standing outside their farm house, the ox pushes his John Deere cap to the back of his head, hooks his thumbs through overall suspenders. Rocking back and forth on boots that have each pant leg carefully caught on their tops, he speaks.

"Blood? Ummm... I dunno about the blood, Frankie. I really don't like pricking any of my moo-ers, except when they're sick and need medication. Does it have to be cow blood? Couldn't you use some other kind? How about some of Mable's? She's pretty much a cow."

"No, this has to be genuine, Hank. Besides, don't you think Mable might object just a little?"

"Well, yeah, now that you mention it, she probably would. She can be a bit ornery over the least little thing. You know how it is with wimmin; there's no pleasing them most of the time. Well... I guess mebbe you *don't* know, I forget tha—"

Just then the large butted, huge breasted Mable steps out of the house, heading towards their barn. Seeing Frankie, she smiles, waves, and starts ambling toward them. Hips roll, breasts sway, and cows stare in awe.

Immediately Hank agrees to drawing cow blood. Eagerly, frantically agrees, and in the same breath, says there's no need to mention the proposed blood substitution to Mabel.

But just one syringe full is all, and Frankie is to put a little extra something in the next delivery of herbs and medicines. It's odd how the looming presence of a wife can speed up a husband. Men need wives. They are often bewildered *when* they have one, and of just *how* they got one. But they definitely need one.

Mable exchanges a few pleasantries with Frankie, and then *helpfully advises* Hank.

"Pull your pant legs down over those boot tops, Henry. Will you ever learn to dress? Do you want to look like some hayseed in front of Frankie? He always dresses so nice when he visits." She also mentions that Hank is stretching his suspenders out of shape. "They're not thumb pockets, you know. And pull your cap down, wear it properly." Mable often improves mightily on Hank's appearance. Quite often.

Yes, men need wives. They make life so interesting.

With a box containing an old-style Mason jar of amber colored liquid, funnel with attached feeding tube, and a full, bovine specific syringe, Frankie departs. He chuckles over the "practically a cow," comment about the amply endowed Mable.

And then he erupts with a fit of giggles, thinking

about the good Dr. Moto. This concoction may work, but Moto... is going to have the first taste.

Moto may have given us a legitimate cure for Elvis, and I really do hope so, with all my little thumping gizzard, I do. But regardless of this noxious mixture's efficacy, I'm going to have the doctor sample some of the ingredients. Particularly the urine... yes, he must taste test for proper salinity. And if this proscribed treatment of Elvis should fail... up his oriental ass goes at least one of those pineapples... at least one.

Frankie giggles some more. Delighted with both images he's conjured up. This silly bastard is often delighted with himself.

On ship's Deck 19, the former Dr. Gaust places both hands against the Bowl-A-Rama. Leaning forward, she fixes her gaze down the 5-foot-long alley at the game's opening. Above that dark space, garish lights display a ball knocking pins in all directions. Lightning bolts, flying pins, and words blink continually, proclaiming: STRIKE! PLAY! STRIKE!

The new and improved Dr. Gaust stretches towards those flashing words. But something feels wrong; feels in the way. Straightening, she takes hold of her imped-ing body part. Her renewed body has the strength of youth, and she pulls. Tissues stretch, muscles part, and tendons snap; there is very little blood. Having removed the minor obstacle, she drops it. As it rolls away, she again braces herself against the game, leaning forward.

Inside that amusement machine from a by-gone era, something has become very aware of the reconstituted Doctor. Something that was a heartfelt gift from Tanya. A yellow gift of esteem placed there by Seevee at her direction. A gift meant to keep on giving.

It's also a gift that will backfire. Backfire dreadfully, and Tanya... will pay.

Tragically pay.

Decks below Dr. Gaust and the gift: Seevee's arm is brutally yanked through the partially opened hatch. His meat scraped from the bone between door's edge and frame; the flesh rolling to the shoulder like a bloody donut.

Another wrenching pull slams Seevee harder into the crevice as his free arm pushes on the adjoining wall. Desperation takes over thought and Seevee draws both knees up against the hatch. He's pulling at his trapped arm, yet the force of his knees is increasing the door's pressure holding it.

"TON!" he screams, as blood gushes down the white

metal. "HELP SEEVEE, MUCH HELP! TON, TON, HELP!"

A final twisting jerk from whatever has him... tears Seevee's arm from shoulder.

The limb's sudden rip from its socket, and Seevee's terrified pushing, throws him to the deck, slamming the door.

Clamping his remaining hand over the spurting, mortal wound, too weak to stand, Seevee scoots frantically away from the closed hatch. The effort is needless; what maimed him cannot open it. Seevee hears it pound and shriek on the other side. It wants more.

"Ton, Ton help, help Seevee, Ton..." he tries to scream again, but the loss of blood is too much. Toppling over, still holding the gaping, spewing hole in his shoulder, his eyes begin to glaze. *Must rest, small rest, no sleep... much keep eyes open... Ton come... Ton much come.*

Far from the dying Seevee, but still within the Waydowns, Tanya has pushed, bullied, and insulted Shank out of the debilitating grief.

"Don't try and get up on your own, just wait while I talk to Huong," she tells the girl, pointing toward that sullen asshole.

"Who? Oh! I din't even know they was anyone else," Shank says, looking over. "Dang, he sure is quietsome, ain't he."

"Yeah, right now he is, because I told him to be, or I'd put a few bullets in his ass. But believe me, he can get mouthy. And Shank... don't trust him."

"You tolded him that? And you don't trust him none? But you lefts him holdin' a gun? Well, you gots sand, and I knows you ain't dumb none... so why?"

"Well, that's a good question, and it deserves an answer. But this isn't the time for it. For now, let's just say he needs me to get out of here. And I need... *we* need him so *we* can take Deck... never mind, I'll tell you about that later. But don't you ever trust him."

"Yeah, Mis— uh, Tanya, I heard that part the firstest time, real clear like."

"Good, remember it. I'm—"

"I saw you pointing, and figured you wanted me," interrupts a frowning Huong, walking up.

"This is Shank, and she's coming with us. I want you to help get her up and on—"

"For fucks sake, Tanya! Is this another damn Spill of yours? I can smell it, and it's a cripple on top of... gak-yak-gak," says Huong, finishing oddly... due to Tanya's gun barrel pushed against his teeth.

"It's really good that you remembered I told you to

watch your mouth, Houng-y."

"Yeah, he is a mite mouthy, ain't he," comments Shank from the floor. "I don't know the meanin' of that there word he called me, but I don't want no help from the likes of him."

Slightly easing the barrel away from Huong's delicate lips, Tanya speaks quietly, almost amiably.

"Listen to me... Grunt. I want you to fetch that crutch laying over there, hold it stable, and I will help the girl up and onto it. Do not let her fall, or *you* might get hurt. And keep in mind, I can get out of this place without you, but you will never make it without me."

Nearly whispering, he says, "I'm about to puke from the thing's smell, and I do—"

"And the sight of you gags me... DESERTER! That girl's worth ten of you. Now get your ass moving!"

As the disgusted Huong stalks off for the crutch, Tanya kneels beside Shank, but before she can speak, the girl does.

"Ain't nothing wrong with my ear holes. I cain't help it 'cause I stinks. I never knowed I did till I... till I... smellded you," she says blushing. "But I ain't sorry none, there weren't never no good ways to wash up. And I ain't no *thing*," she spits out, cutting her eyes toward Huong. "But I, uh, I thankee for what you said to him about me."

"I meant it, girl. And when we get to my cabin, I'll teach you about the Groomer. That'll get you so clean you'll sparkle. But it's a long walk to get there, so how's the leg?"

"It's painin' me powerful fierce, but I kin dang sure one-leg it right smart with that crutch," she answers, just as Huong stabs the crutch down beside her. "And *you*," she says glaring up at him, "kin just suck up all my sweet-hole smell you wants."

Huong swallows convulsively, but manages to retain the mostly stoic appearance. But his breathing becomes exceedingly shallow, as he tries mightily to draw in air from his toenails.

Grinning, Tanya says, "Shank, I always did think that you got sand." *But I've got to admit he's right, child... you are rank.*

"You've got to leave him, girl," Tanya continues, glancing at Lakker's body. "We can't make any arrangements for him. Do you understand?"

"Well... 'course we're gonna leave him," responds Shank with a puzzled look. "We never et the ones we had knowed, we always gived them to—"

"Okay, okay, okay," quickly breaks in Tanya. This was something she had suspected, but absolutely did not want to hear about. "What I meant is that we... we can't... there's no way to—"

"Oh! You talkin' about a, a... fyoonrul and sayin' words. The Sherff tolded be about them kinda silly things. He's dead, he's gone and I done feel my peace with it. Let's git on to the walkin'." A harsh frontier raising has made this girl practical... if not very hygienic.

Tanya simply nods, admiring the girl's ability to "git on." It's something Tanya has a shitload of. She thinks most women do. She figures most men... do not. A man would be trying not to cry, refuse to leave the body, and other dithering bullshit. Tanya has a low opinion of men, and, being Tanya, only a slightly higher one about females. *Except* for this dirty, busted leg, nuisance girl sprawled in front of her.

And somehow, Tanya is okay with this. Maybe a little more than just okay. Tanya has never had a friend, not really. She never wanted one. That's what she always told herself. It's what lonely people tell themselves. It's their armor against hurt, their wall against rejection, against life. But that armor can become their life, can become all there is, all they have.

Tanya is in danger... her shield has developed a crack. A malodorous one.

Huong listens to the two, not saying a word. *Jesus fucking Christ... this stinking little pig IS a Spill... an eater of her own dead... I've got to get out of this mess.* His frown deepens, but he keeps the crutch ready.

This man is dangerous and treachery runs deep in him. He will not forget this demeaning treatment. Payback will come soon. Very soon.

But Huong is a man that can be bought. For the right price. Most people can. Value given for value received, it makes the world go around. All worlds, everywhere.

She's not coming. It's too late anyway. Seevee lays watching his life pour out from the bloody pit where his arm once grew. Too weak to keep his hand over the wound, he looks at the shiny red pool spreading out over the deck plates. He listens to the creature scream, hears it pounding and tearing at the hatch cover. The arm wasn't enough. It wants the rest of him.

His eyes open and shut, flickering rapidly at first, but now slowing. Seevee strains to keep the light, strains to keep life, strains to keep love... but it is not enough to stem the outgoing red tide. *Ton not come... Ton not hear Seevee... much want Ton... much show new place... much things for Ton... Seevee much luff... much luff for Ton.*

At the Roaton home, RL is outside, doing his pacing and fretting on the weedy, graveled drive. Taking the air as Shadow had termed it. Noticing there's been enough recent traffic to flatten the plants, creating tire paths from the main road. As he mentally adds 'weed the drive' to his things-to-do list, he spots movement in the gravel.

It's a Roly-Poly, an innocuous little pill bug, silently going about whatever bug business it has. RL drops to a knee, and lays his hand in front of it. It stops, twitching its feelers, and then crawls on board. He'd read somewhere they're not really an insect or a bug. They're a crustacean, related to shrimp, and have a plated shell that completely encases them when they roll up. RL marvels at this tidbit of information, and thinks it's piss poor protection from a shoe. And damned ineffective against a tire.

"You guys are just like chickens, always crossing a road without any idea of why," RL says... to the bug. Standing, walking to the grass, he shakes the tiny creature into the growth, and says... to the bug, "Now, stay off the drive, you little *shrimp*. You'll live a lot longer."

As Jayderay's Taurus turns in, RL says... to the bug, "See! I just saved your life, you owe me, and don't you forget it."

This is a man who registers a severe negative on any ethics scale. Yet he tends to be a sap where women, children or animal life is concerned, even bugs. But not for spiders and male humans of course. Those are for stepping on. Or cheating in business. Or both.

"Sakes RL!" yells Jayderay as she climbs from her car. "What you doin' piddling around out here? You can't be leavin' Shadow alone with that Moto. Do I have—"

"How nice it is to see you, fiancé of mine," he butts in before she gets really wound up. "And Shadow said it was okay for me to *piddle* around outside. Hell, that doctor is so terrified of her, he's nearly a statue. Besides, by piddling out here, I just saved a pill bug's life."

Jayderay can't keep from grinning. "I don't doubt you did, you softy. And it's good to see you too, honey," she says, giving him a hug. Looking over at the house... at their house, she adds, "But she shouldn't be alone in there, don't matter what she say. Something bad wrong with that place, RL."

"Good Lord, woman; don't talk about our new home like that. I... *we*, just laid out some serious cash for this... this exquisite house, so don—"

"EXQUISITE HOUSE! Exquisite, RL? Let me tell you just how exquisite this all is. We got a mad scientist in there 'bout to perform Hoodoo on our *not 'zactly human* friend, who's likely dyin' on account of being attacked by ghosts... and *they* the ghosts of his *not 'zactly alive* wife's children. We got a soap opera from hell goin' on, and we ain't even moved in. Did I leave anything out?"

RL doesn't point out that she failed to include the UFO beneath this exquisite home. Or the Waydowns in that spaceship. He feels it might not be helpful. So, he says:

"You didn't mention that I think your gorgeous."

"Oh, shut up, you," she says, crushing him in her arms. "I also left out the part 'bout me bein' in love... and that it was *me* who wanted this place."

Holding her, RL wouldn't care if the house suddenly grew fangs and yawned. With his face buried in her hair, he grins wickedly, and murmurs softly.

"I scheduled a séance."

"WHAT!" shoving back from him, "You did wha— Oh. You, you, you donkey butt. Okay, you got me, but you also got yourself a job. Get those sacks out my car, boy, then tote them along with your smiley butt inside that *exquisite* house. Exquisite! Sakes, it sounds like something Frankie would come up with."

"Well, speak of calamity, and here it comes," says RL, seeing Frankie pull into the drive. "Maybe we should ask his opinion about having a séance, and see if—"

"YOU GET IN THAT HOUSE , RL... NOW! You not checking with that boy on any such devilness. He'd think, and then get up to something, like he always do, and then you'd have a real problem... me."

"Yes'm, Miz Scarlett," and he totes away with only a brief wave at the arriving calamity. RL is getting an early handle on how to be a successful husband.

"Everything about the same, Jayderay?" Frankie asks, climbing out of the VW. "RL sure seemed in a hurry to go in."

"I pretty much just got back myself, but I don't think anything else has happened. Did you get that awful voodoo stuff?"

"Every blessed... drop of it," he answers with a grin. "And, um, by the way, did you get *whole* pineapples?"

"Yeah, two big fat ones, and my those are awful prickly things. Why?"

"Oh, I was just making sure," answers Frankie, flashing his most innocent smile. "Whole ones, big and fat! That's just perfect, just super, and yes indeedy, they are quite, quite prickly," he finishes with an explosion of giggles.

Jayderay does not ask what's so funny. She knows the boy far too well, and that fit of giggling will not be good for someone.

Inside that *exquisite* house, Jayderay accompanies RL to check on Elvis. She goes to Shadow immediately.

The storm-cloud woman seems calmer, with some good news. And some that's a little ominous.

"Since I guided Dr. Moto into another room, I'm feeling that Elvis no longer drifts from me. He is stationary on this plane, and his air is smoother, deeper, and the body tremors have ceased."

"We're all truly glad to hear it, Shadow, really we are," RL says, a little shocked by how much he means it. Caring for people, especially voicing it, isn't always a strong brick in his foundation; unless there's money involved for the mortar. "Has there been anything out of that fuc—, uh, that septic tank Moto?"

"No, not a sound, as I did request of him. But I feel something, something that is odd. I know of his presence; he has not moved from that place. I am of this house, and nothing happens here that I do not feel at least some awareness of. Perhaps the depth to which I'm within my husband has dimmed my perceptions; for I cannot feel anything from that room but... a void. My words are not sufficient, but the best which I can do is a, a deep blackness."

"Well, all the windows are warped or painted shut, and I haven't heard any breaking glass. So. Um, Shadow... you did lock the door?"

With one dark eyebrow rising slightly, she answers. "Most assuredly, RL, I did lock that room. I left the key in the door, exactly where I found it. I have felt no exits from that space."

"Then he's in there," RL says firmly. He wouldn't have taken anyone else's word for it, because he well knows the house can be... tricky. He and Jayderay had once gotten lost for hours on just the second floor.

"And he can stay there awhile longer, till we're ready," continues RL. "None of us wants to see or hear him."

"Please do not let us be lulled by my husband's current ease. We must have Dr. Moto administer unto him."

"Then let it be my pleasure to encourage his attendance," says Frankie, thinking of pineapples. Those large pineapples. Those large and prickly pineapples. "I'll put him to work on the, uh, the medications." And he swishes away. Gayly.

The remaining group chats over the bed of an unconscious Elvis. There's nothing that increases the urge to converse inanely, than a hospital or sick room. It's like a disease.

And Frankie walks back in, not swishing or gayly. Going directly to RL, he looks only at him, and speaks quietly. But his eyebrows are flapping; they might lose hair.

"Houston, we have a problem. A very serious problem."

"Don't tell me that bastard's not in there," says RL, in an even lower voice.

"Oh, he's in there all right, Boss. But I don't think he's going to help," answers Frankie, now nearly whispering.

"Like hell he won't. Just you go put a foot up his ass."

"Umm, more likely a pineapple, RL, but even that probably won't work. You better come see for yourself."

"What are you two mumblin' to each other 'bout?" demands Jayderay. "That's never a good thing between you two."

"Just a bit of... reluctance from our doctor on call," answers Frankie. "Not to worry, ladies, we'll sort it out and be back in a jiffy-jiff." He's gives a quick no shake of his head to RL, and they both head out the door.

"Shadow, I'm worried," says Jayderay looking over at her. "Frankie didn't giggle none during all that whisperin', and neither of them even nodded to us as they left. That ain— that's sure not like RL. He always got manners for women."

The grey woman slowly shakes her head, the ebony ringlets brushing scarred cheeks. "A blackness is all I can feel from the room," she says reaching out and taking one of Elvis' lavender skinned hands. "And the cold, it is very cold in there."

At the room, Frankie opens the door with a bow. "Behold our esteemed fucking doctor. The guy that's going to save Elvis."

"Oh, shit," says RL quietly. He doesn't enter.

"Precisely," responds Frankie. He doesn't enter.

Before them, Dr. Moto stands awkwardly, as if somehow his skeleton is no longer the right size for his flesh. Green syrup bubbles slightly from each ear and drips from one lobe. The eyes are bright, clear, and wide, staring straight ahead with intense interest at something only he can see. It is not a sight of his choice.

"Oh, shit," repeats RL, still not entering.

"I think if he could, he would," responds Frankie, still not entering.

With a deep breath, RL takes a few steps toward Moto, Frankie follows without enthusiasm, fishing out his razor. There is no giggling.

"Moto! Can you hear me? Are you in there?" demands RL, waving a hand in front of those terribly alert eyes.

"Boss, I don't believe he's faking, I think the bastard's hotlink has squirted out of his bread. Whatever's left inside of—"

"Yes, Round-Eye," Moto suddenly answers, his eyes swiveling toward RL. "*We* hear you. It is a long time in here... it is forever in here... long time... in here... long time." The voice is without inflection, yet very much alive, ghastly alive, horrifically alive. His bright, knowing eyes snap away from RL, back to looking intently forward.

"Jesus! What the hell was that?" whispers RL with sweat beading his face.

"Well... that just may have *been* hell," Frankie answers, still unconsciously gripping his razor. "Boss, let's get out of here and lock the door on this, this... on *this*. He can't help Elvis now. I think even Shadow would agree."

Both men back out of the room, never taking their eyes off whatever Dr. Moto has become. As Frankie pulls the door shut, his eyes fall on the man with the chin portrait. *If I'd been the one getting painted, that artist would've got a pineapple... a whole one.*

"RL!" yells Jayderay.

CHAPTER 15

BACK IN THE WAYDOWNS

With Lakker's pouch around her neck, the girl's teeth clench as each hop jolts the broken leg. But not one moan, not one complaint, not one sob or tear has come from Shank. Gripping the crutch with both hands, she occasionally reaches over, grabbing Tanya's shoulder to keep balance.

That perpetually frowning Huong has voluntarily taken point, proving himself to be a good soldier, if nothing else. Turning often to peer back through the drifting haze behind them, he's doing double duty as rear guard, since Tanya won't. And he's silently cursing the pair.

God damn both of them... a lunatic helping her filthy cannibal... on a fucking crutch. It's gonna take us forever to get back to the cabin... if we make it at all. And where's that fucking Seevee, when he might actually be useful?... I'd load that hopping stink bomb onto the Spill's back, and double time the shit out of him. I will help Tanya take Deck 19… and then I'll gut her crazy ass on my way topside.

"Tanya," gasps the girl, slapping her hand onto the woman's ever-ready shoulder.

"You need a break, hon— Shank?"

"Huh? No! Well, maybe onliest a little one," she admits, panting. "But what I was wantin' was to ask if maybe, if you gots another of them there coats like you wears… that I could, uh, maybe borry it, like?"

"Christ, girl! Of all things to ask for," Tanya chuckles. "Hell, there's plenty of lab coats still around, mostly in lockers. But I bet Seevee could find you something a lot prettier; how would that be?"

"Uh, well… okay, if you, uh, if you think that's gooder," she answers, her face mirroring the disappointment in her voice.

"Shank? You can *have* a lab coat. If that's what you really want, then it's fine by me."

"Oh, thankee, thankee, Tanya! I pledges to take good, good care of it. Then I kin look just like y— I, I, I means then I kin gets outta these here rags… and I won't smells so bad."

"Oh, girl… I promise you I'll—"

"What the fuck?" breaks in Huong as he stalks back to the pair.

"By all means, Tanya, drag this walk out as long as

possible by stopping to gab. It's already taking forever and riskin' our ass, by having to nurse along this, this lame Spi— buddy of yours."

"Zip it, Houng, zip it now. But you're right, we gotta keep moving. And *you* can start by setting us a real good example: Get your ass back on point."

As the grumbling man moves off shaking his head, Shank quietly tells Tanya, "I'm sorry, I din't need takin' no restin' time. And I knows I'm slowin' you down and dangerin' you. I kin moves more faster... for you, not for none on his sayin'." And the crippled girl lurches off, rags flapping.

Tanya silently stays beside her, keeping the shoulder available. *This girl stopped in the middle of a shithole to tell me she wants a lab coat... the child wants a fucking lab coat... so she can be like me. Like me! Good Christ, what a bitch she's chose to imitate. Well... I'll damn sure get her one.* And Tanya smiles.

Huong suddenly crouches, raising a fist in the air. Motioning them to lay down, he squats lower, and begins a cautious duckwalk forward.

"Get down, girl," Tanya hisses as she kneels. Shank tries dropping to her good knee, and Tanya grabs her around the shoulders and crutch, laying her down. "Stay still and quiet," Tanya whispers, rising to a crouch.

Scuttling back to them in a fast low squat, a frustrated Huong speaks.

"I can't see shit through this fucking fog. There's an old caution light up ahead still flickering into the corridor, and it's showing something damned big has stretched itself across from room to room. I can't see well enough to know what it is, or if it's moving."

"I doubt if I'll see any better," sighs Tanya. "But I have to look. Shank, stay down, and better pull Lakker's old cannon out. If we come running back, be sure you don't shoot us."

"Ain't nothin' wrong with *my* shootin', in case you forgot," she answers, already digging for the pistol.

Creeping quietly forward, Uzis held ready, they strain to listen. But other than occasional clicks and whirs from the ancient machinery there's only silence. Squinting into the haze, getting closer, intensely peering, still closer, and... Tanya barks out a laugh, quickly stifling it with her hand.

"Well, Huong-y, in your defense, it is always better to fuck up on the side of caution. You blind idiot, it's that dead ass Coiler we had to walk around earlier. Of course that would be an easy thing to forget, considering its bigger than a tank, and it was probably all of an hour ago you saw it."

"Shit," says Huong.

"And fall back in it," returns Tanya.

Leaving Huong to admire his very dead Coiler, Tanya returns to the waiting, pistol clutching Shank.

"It was a mistake," she grins, telling the girl. "The thing is dead, and we'd already seen it on our way to you. Fuck-Nuts Huong is big time embarrassed."

"I'm powerful glad it's dead, 'cause what I just now seed back yonder sure ain't," Shank says, pointing with the gun barrel. "Way back down the hall, it come sorta pokeyin' out of one of them other ways we passed. And it was mighty big, it nigh on to filled the whole danged hall, and it had a big slather of what looked like red mouths all over it, and—"

"Where did it go?" interrupts Tanya.

"Rolled real slow up the wall, most like it was suckin' its way up'ards. Then the dang fog hid it."

"We've got to move fast, girl! It went up the wall, because I bet it can attack faster from up high. It's tracking us."

"Huong," she shouts, "I think we're gonna have visitors from above. Let's shift into high gear!"

"Of course we are," he answers, looking up. "What about your buddy Hop-A-Long? What *gear* you figure on shifting her into?"

"Mine! Now move your ass and keep looking up."

Helping Shank stand, Tanya tells her, "Don't you

argue; there's no time." Taking the crutch she drops to one knee, "Grab onto my back like before. Do it now, damn it!"

Carrying the girl, Tanya manages a staggering trot toward Huong, as the man keeps up a revolving forward jog. All while trying to guard the group's back, front and above them.

It's an impossible action to keep up. Constantly skipping over decades of debris, he finally trips, landing in a sprawling heap.

A fleshy tube the diameter of a pie plate immediately hits the floor beside him. With a sucking pop, it's yanked up, the fat red lips leaving a wet ring behind. Two more of the mottled pink and blue things smack down even closer.

Tanya screams, "Get into a room, get into a room," as three shots ring out, echoing down the corridors. Two bullets hit, and the tubes are jerked upward.

Huong scrambles through the nearest hatch, with Tanya stumbling in right behind, spilling the girl from her back.

"That there's how to shoot, Tanya, you hits what you aims at," cackles Shank, holding Lakker's pistol in one hand while rubbing her throbbing leg with the other.

Breathing hard, Tanya looks at the girl silently for a few seconds.

"Oh, child! You are really something."

Shank blushes, struggles with a thought, and finally says, "You packed me agin. I thankee."

"You are very welcome. And that was pretty good shooting... for you. Almost as good as mine," she says smirking, and turns away quickly before Shank can get wound up about marksmanship.

Huong considers the room's ceiling, then leans warily out into the corridor. Looking up into the opaque, hazy dimness, he asks, "Is it only the rooms that have ceilings?"

"Some of the bigger ones don't, all the small ones seem to," Tanya says, walking up. Behind her, the girl reloads, grinning delightedly about the shooting remark.

"What in hell do you think that was?" asks Huong. "Those weren't tentacles, not anything like that dead Coiler has."

"Don't know, but those sucking tube things definitely weren't from a Coiler. Good Christ, Huong, this is the Waydowns... you've been down here enough times to know there's life here that never existed topside, or has a name. This place shits monsters."

"Yeah, it was a stupid question. So, is that red lipped bastard waiting on us? That's the real thing to ask."

"Well, it didn't get its dinner, so yeah, I'd say the

fucker is still up there and waiting. We need a breather anyway, maybe it'll go off hunting, or the Coilers might run it off."

As Huong continues staring up into the murk, he speaks. "Okay then, since we got time to kill, why don't you tell me about this plan to take 19."

Tanya watches the deadly, unreadable man for several long seconds.

"Okay, but first... credit where it's due, Huong. You did good as point, good when good wasn't possible."

"Thanks, I guess," he says, looking over at her. "But it wouldn't have been needed if we weren't dragging along your pet," he adds, gesturing with his thumb toward Shank.

Tanya glances over at the crippled girl, who's sitting quietly, sorting through the years of crap laying on the floor.

"That girl saved your ass out there, and you need to remember it."

"Maybe. Maybe she did, but it's because of her that we're not safe, not back at your cabin."

"She stays with us, Huong. I... *we,* don't leave our wounded. Either buy into it, or get out and try making it on your own. So... do you wanna hear about this plan or not? I've changed it quite a bit, and you've become front and center."

"Lucky me."

"Yep, I do believe you'll think so," chuckles Tanya.

Yes, Tanya has changed her plan. And Huong will indeed *think* he's lucky. But there are many kinds of luck, and Lady Fortuna is a very fickle woman. He should ask Dr. Moto about luck. Or Seevee.

The attack on Deck 19 will go like the spinning of an oddly bent coin.

Not too far away, Seevee's body lays in a congealing pool of blood; the bright red, stark against the dingy white deck plates. His eyes are slits, filming over with death's final curtain.

The sounds of rage from behind the locked hatch have ceased. Whatever took Seevee's arm has given up, realizing that path is closed. And it does have the arm, so its attempt at angling wasn't a total failure. Human fishermen have similar thoughts when looking at the paltry perch they're taking home while thinking of the big fat bass that got away.

Bare footsteps come softly from the adjacent corridor, stopping at the edge of Seevee's drying life pool. Small tendrils, where toes should've grown, reach out touching the blood and withdraw. A Spill, a Spill whose creators on Deck 19 had judged too deficient to bother with trimming its feet. It hadn't even been a candidate for organ harvesting, it was just medical waste. So, after microchipping for possible future referencing, into the Waydowns she went. The gender was marginal and of no scientific interest.

Kneeling close to Seevee, she slowly extends a multi-jointed arm, nudges and gently shakes him. "Seeev? Seeev?" she rasps out and then rubs her throat, as saliva leaks from the corner of a vaguely feminine mouth. Looking at the gaping shoulder wound and then over at the gore smeared edges of the hatch, she nods to herself. Something had been clever and it sure as hell wasn't Seevee.

Seevee had befriended her when she'd first been thrust into this mangled, bewildering nightmare of the Waydowns. He'd helped her survive, but friendship and nebulous thoughts of obligation often did not count for much down here. Especially toward the dead… and she is hungry.

Her stomach growls. Hunger: the constant companion. She drools, and nudges the body again.

***

Tanya walks over and squats beside Shank, as Huong stays just inside the room's entry. Wondering about his changing fortune... and if that sucking-mouth thing is still up there.

And a wet looking, fat tube slams down right at the opening, its mouth gnawing greedily at the deck. It's immediately yanked up with a sucking sound that echoes into the room, and steam rises from the wet mark left by red lips.

Huong moved in a blur when the tube landed, and now stands beside Tanya and the girl. His usual frown momentarily replaced with terror.

"You're right, Tanya, that bastard *IS* waiting."

"I sorta noticed. We better hope it can't make an elbow and reach in here. Or we won't be trapped, we'll be fucked."

Shank manages a chuckle at this, despite the pain of her broken leg. Its swelling has visibly increased since they'd started their run, the flesh pushing out against stitches and splint.

Of the three, she's the least affected by this new monster threat. Tanya and Huong are relative new-bies down here, whereas she grew up below on Lak-ker's deck. She's trekked the path through those eerily still yet fast plants, hunted un-believables among them, and seen behemoths break the surface of the not-water lake. So... this tube-dangler ain't no real shit.

"I'm glad you can laugh, girl," says Tanya, reaching

over to brush the sweaty hair out of Shank's eyes. She notices the light sprinkling of freckles across the child's nose have gotten brighter.

"Well, Tanya, I ain't much a'skeered of it, it's just sorta, just out there like lottsa things is. Least it ain't the Yellow; I'm powerful a'skeered of them Melts."

"It must not have a sense of smell, or it would've run," says Huong, fanning his face, and pointedly not looking at Shank. "And don't talk about that Yellow-Melts shit. I've heard enough to be plenty *'a'skeered'* without seeing the fuckers. Come on, let's hear about your precious plan for taking 19."

Tanya gives him a quick warning glare about the smell comment. Shank only looks puzzled, as if thinking she might have missed something.

"Okay, on to the plan it is, Huong. From what you've told me, Moto has left control of the grunts and maintenance to you. Right?"

"I don't know what he actually said to Gaust, but that's what he told me. And for what it's worth, *I* have never seen this Gaust, but the last meeting that old Jap had with her, literally scared the shit out of him. There must've been a big fucking change."

"You not knowing what she looks like isn't going to matter. The old bitch almost never comes out of her office, anyway. So, our first step is getting you back up to 19, for recon, then you—"

"Me! Alone?" breaks in Huong, looking like he's just found something nasty in his mouth.

"Yes, Wonder Gook, you. Listen for a second and let your panties untwist. You're not going in there to kill, not yet. You're still in khakis, so you'll look like any grunt coming back from Waydowns scouting. If you see Moto, say you couldn't find me, or that entrance, were attacked, and need the infirmary. Then you do a little recon about Gaust, gather info and ammo, then report back to me. And *then* you'll hear the really good part of the plan."

"The good part, huh? Listen, not to shit on your parade, Tanya," says Huong, looking like he's now swallowing that something nasty in his mouth. "But just how am I supposed to get back *into* 19? The elevator controls on this Waydowns side, are melted all to hell."

Tanya smirks at him, her good eye widening as the blind one darts about.

"Yeah, so they are, and have been for decades. But, unknown to our dear Moto, I saw him use those melted buttons, and more to the point, I saw how he did it."

Several thoughts immediately race through the quick and deadly Huong. *Agree with this one-eyed blond bitch, get to 19, and simply head up to topside.*

If I run into Moto, I'll gut him and dump his body in that ridiculous carnival room; that'll give me plenty of time. Without realizing it, an uncharacteristic smile flickers on his lips.

"And before you cum in your khaki's, Huong-y, you can forget about just hauling ass up to topside. You'd never make it past the decks above 19, much less through the reception building. All the geeks and labbies that come and go daily are big time monitored. I worked up there, remember? You wouldn't pass even if dressed like one. And no grunt is ever allowed above 19 unless escorted by Moto."

Huong looks like that something nasty has gotten back in his mouth again. "And what are you two gonna be doing to *aid the cause*, while I'm risking my ass on 19?"

"Bathing. But first, we've got to make it back to my cabin. It'll go faster if you carry Shank."

The nasty in Huong's mouth just got nastier.

"Fuck that shit, Tanya. I'm not carry—"

"I ain't need no totein' by the likes of you," spits Shank. "I can goes more faster, Tanya, and my leg's mendin' lots more better." This last is an obvious lie; that leg is bad and getting worse.

"Shut it, both of you," orders Tanya. "I'm running this cluster-fuck, and you both will do as I say. Huong can go faster with you than I can, Shank. We've got no food or water, so we can't wait a couple days hoping those red mouthed fucks go away. And we've got to get you to my cabin, girl. That leg needs work."

"Shit," mutters Huong. "No doubt you have a *plan* for getting back. I'd love to hear it."

"Not a good one, I admit. We rest for a few hours, hope like hell it leaves, and then make a run for it. *With the girl on your back.*"

"Shit," Huong says again, still savoring that nasty. Abruptly turning, he stalks to a corner furthest away from them and stretches out. He's enough of a real soldier to know you rest when you can.

"I ain't gettin' on none of his back! I done tolded you—"

"Shut it, girl! You're riding him, and that's final. Now, let's see if I can get your leg propped up while you lay flat."

A bit later, they lay side by side, with Shank's fractured shin resting on the remains of an office chair. Tanya can hear an occasional grunt and snore from Huong. *Damn the lucky son of a bitch, how can he sleep? Maybe the girl can. I hope there's some meds in that place Seevee found, there's not much in my cabin. I've got to get something on that leg and something in her... I know it's got to be hurting like hell... but she never complains... she's tough, got sand as she'd say. And I'm going to change her name... Shank is no fit name for her.* Tanya's mind boils away with some very disturbing, uncharacteristic thoughts. And always, the plan for 19.

"Tanya? You awake?" whispers Shank.

"Yeah, can't sleep, but I was hoping you could, it'd do you good."

"Maybe I can, but I first I wants to, I wants to... I gots something to... oh, hump a gourd! Can I gives you a, uh, a gift?"

Tanya raises up on an elbow. *What on earth can this be about?*

"Well, of course you can, child."

"It ain't nothin' much, onliest I finded it when I was lookin' through the junk stuff on this here floor." Shank blushes deeply, not looking at Tanya, and hands over a small flat packet, still in an unopened plastic sleeve.

"I thought of how... how... how even more purty it would make you," she runs the last few words together. If the blush could be any deeper, her skin would blister.

It's an eye patch.

Tanya swallows against a lump suddenly appearing in her throat. Not speaking, she pulls it from the clear envelope. It's black, complete with elastic strap.

"You, you don't gots to wear it, I, I, I onliest meant—"

"Hush, child," interrupts Tanya, quickly reaching over and placing her fingers over the girl's mouth. Swallowing against that lump, she says, "I thank you, this is... wonderful." And she slips it on.

"Oh... oh, you so purty, I wisht I could onliest look like you," Shank says, patting and smoothing Tanya's blond thatch with one hand, her eyes shining.

Tanya's swallowing again. Gently pushing the hand down, she leans closer, kissing the dirty, sweat smeared cheek. "Let's be quiet and get some sleep, we've got a hard run ahead of us."

Shank dutifully nods, closes her eyes, saying, "Yes, Tanya."

Laying her arm across the girl's stomach just missing that third breast, Tanya eases back on her side. That crack in her armor against the world has just gotten a lot worse. With her good eye very wide open, and the blind one dancing behind the patch, she thinks. *Good fucking Christ... I've got a, a damn kid. I won't cry, I don't cry. I won't. But what now?*

'What now?' is a good question for Tanya. Tanya who has had two abortions. Tanya who had them because she couldn't be bothered with a kid. Had them because she was too busy, too busy with nothing; with being nothing. Too busy being a party girl, being a tough, cynical, assey young woman who cared for nothing. Her body, her life, her choice. A woman who was proud that she didn't give a shit about anything.

But Tanya had cared. Deep within, throwing those babies away had cost her. Cost her dearly. A cost she would forever bear. A cost... a debt that she had nearly paid for with her own life. Her wrists still show that. 'What now?' indeed, Tanya. Where is that protection, that hard armor?

About three hours later, Tanya hears Huong pacing up and down in front of the opening. It has been a rough, soul wrestling period for her, but acceptance and a decision had come. She rises quietly from beside the sleeping girl. Touching her eye patch, Tanya smiles, finger combing and raking at her hair.

"Anything stirring out there?" she asks, softly walking up to the scowling grunt.

"Just that damn haze, so I still can't see squat up there," Huong answers, gesturing with the Uzi muzzle. "That bastard must've got tired by now and went hunting, don't you think?"

"Who knows, but we've got to try anyway. Hunger and thirst will drive us out of here, Huong. This room is too small to have a protein distribution tray, so we can't even get any crap cakes."

"That ain't much of a fucking loss, but I'd eat one

about now. More than food, I want water." He's noticed the eye patch, but doesn't comment. Why bother.

Studying the man a few seconds, she makes a decision. He's clever, he might try to side with Moto, just stay on 19, and wait for another chance.

"Listen, Huong, you're a shifty, smart and venal piece of shit. So, to keep you from getting too brainy for your britches and screwing yourself, I'll tell you the rest of the plan.

"Okay," he says, turning his gaze from the corridor, looking at her, his eyes and face totally expressionless.

There's no comment from Huong about Tanya's accurate character assessment. Why bother. It's true, and he knows it much better than she. And he sleeps just fine.

Quite some distance away, the Spill leans in closer to Seevee's body. Strings of saliva dangle from her chin, down to the open wound where his arm used to be. A low gurgling in her throat matches those from her stomach. Her teeth are a forest of wet horrors. Both hands open and close, spasming on his blood drenched shirt. She tries one last time.

"Seeev?" she rasps, dripping. "Seeev?"

And Seevee moans. The Spill sits back on her

haunches, shoulders slumping and face twisting. It's the Spill equivalent of: Damn! No lunch today.

"Seeev!" she says again, with no small amount of exasperation in her voice.

His eyelids flutter and then stay open. She gives a quite human sigh of disappointment. As memory floods back, Seevee slaps a hand to his empty shoulder socket, his eyes looking fearfully toward the closed hatch. Turning his head toward the Spill, he nods weakly, recognizing her.

"Ton," he croaks, and manages to point at the hall. "Ton... much bring Ton."

"Tuhn," the Spill says slowly bobbing her head in understanding. "Tuh," she says again, rising. She knows of Tanya, whom Seevee had pointed out once from a distance. Stepping to the corridor opening, she indicates left, Seevee nods as his eyes close.

The Spill suspects she may get that lunch after all, but there is enough human left in her to understand she owes, and wants to help. She will try, and off she goes at a trot, having only a vague idea where she's going.

But she will remember how to get back... there is still the strong chance of lunch.

———··———

"Huong, there will be no attack on 19," Tanya says quietly, hoping Shank doesn't wake. That busted leg needs all the rest it can get.

"What the fuck, Tanya? We're just gonna waltz into 19, kiss and make up?"

"Don't be an ass. We don't have to charge out of the elevator spraying lead like in some movie. You're pretty much in charge of the grunts already, and I know the workings of the place. All we have to do is get rid of Moto, and that bitch Gaust... Deck 19 will be ours."

Huong stares intently at her, his mind working on several fronts.

"Well... doing it that way makes it easier to take 19, but how do you intend to keep the fucking place? Hell, I don't even want to. *I* am interested in *me*... and getting my ass topside permanently."

"Yeah, I'm very much aware of what you want. Listen to me, I can make you rich, and give you topside freedom. I was a ranking member of staff and know the system. With me in Gaust's office, I can issue orders, regulate employee salary, and any other fucking thing I want. You stick with me up there for a few months, and then you can take off... with all the money that ass of yours can hold."

Huong actually smiles. It's not a pleasant sight, it makes him look like an oriental weasel. A rabid and greedy one. Slightly nodding, he says, "Okay, but it'll hold a lot. So what about the staff? How are *you* gonna explain *you*? We can't kill them all, somebody would come looking."

"When that bitch threw me to the Almosts, I'm sure everyone was told I had to take emergency leave. It's the standard explanation for any staff disappearance. Well, I've come back just in time for Dr. Lillith Sally Gaust to have her very own emergency leave. They're way over-paid fucking sheep; paid to keep mouths shut and eyes blind. They want those jobs, they'll accept it."

Nodding again, Huong says, "I'm in. I'll be your Wonder Gook. For the money, and only for a few months, and—"

A cry from Shank interrupts him, coming as the girl struggles getting her crutch ready.

"Don't move, Shank, wait for my help," Tanya calls, hurrying toward her. "And Huong," she says over her shoulder, "you fuck me, you fuck yourself."

Huong still smiles, but he doesn't speak. Why bother. He still plans to kill the blond cunt. After she makes him very, very rich.

CHAPTER 16

PRAYER & LOVE... IN ODD PLACES

"RL!" yells Jayderay. "Get in here, it's Elvis, he, he, he doin'... doin' somethin'... it's awful!"

Coming back from being shocked by Moto *not* doing anything, RL and Frankie tumble into the room. And freeze, looking in horror at what's on the bed. Yes, Elvis is indeed doing, or more accurately, has done... *something*.

"Jesus," breaths RL.

"And his Dad," responds Frankie.

"Sakes, RL! Don't you two just stand there, help him, get Moto in here. Land of Goshen, move!" Jayderay fumes at the pair, "I seen statues more lively than you."

Those two statues are slow to break their trance. Elvis is, well, they're not quite sure if it still *is* Elvis. Or what. On the bed is what appears to be... a long sack of lavender jelly.

"This is not good," says RL, sounding remarkably stupid, but knowing he's got to speak. Better stupid than maimed, and the wrath of Jayderay is standing right there... within harmful striking distance.

"Nothing gets past you, Boss," mutters Frankie, speaking for the same reason.

An exasperated Jayderay stares incredulously at them for a few seconds. She chews at her bottom lip, as both hands grab and clench at each other.

"That's it, RL! I'm goin' for Moto," she says, starting for the door.

"NO!" shout both men, as RL leaps, grabbing her arm.

"No, baby, don't go near that room. Moto can't help. He can't even help himself, he's... I don't know what he is now."

"RL's right," adds Frankie. "Moto has gone somewhere, his body is still in that room, but the Doctor is... out of the office. And I bet it's a permanent trip, with no sukiyaki served. You don't want in that room. I mean, really you don't; Moto is scary."

"Well, what do we do? I ain— I'm not gonna let you stand around bein' idiots. You both too good at it."

Through all this, Shadow has quietly sat beside the bed, staring intently at what used to be Elvis. Who is now a bag of goop. A long bag made of some translucent membrane, presumably part of the same lavender colored mess that lightly undulates inside it. Elvis has indeed left the building. He oozed out.

"It happened within the time a candle flame can flicker away and be gone," Shadow's whiskey voice says to the room. Her gray hands laying beside the bag of Elvis, the black nailed fingers gently kneading the bedspread. "My husband, my Elv-is... seemed to, to melt, as if, as if... I do not know the correct words. Yet, he is in there, I feel his presence."

Jayderay kneels beside her, an arm going around the storm-colored woman's waist.

"What do you want us to do, Shadow? Whatever it is, I will see to it," she says, her eyes darting toward and piercing the two idiots.

RL and Frankie shuffle their feet, look helpless, glance imploringly at each other, and mumble asininities. Inane comments starting with words like: "I want to, I'll do, I wish I," and so on. Idiots, well-meaning idiots... but idiots. Men are often so afflicted. It starts at conception.

"At this time," answers Shadow, looking sadly at what remains of Elvis, "I feel any actions would be of no consequence. I will be here, for him, with him, let come what may. He is my reason for being. I wish... I wish for you to remain with me, Jayderay. Only you. Will you please do this?"

"Oh, Shadow... I won't be leavin' you. Not till you tell me to go."

The men go. Very quietly they go. They didn't need anyone to tell them to go. They figured it out all on their own. And the curtains swayed violently with the wind of their departure. Frankie snatches at the door and manages to close it behind them, silently.

In the hallway after closing that door, Frankie turns to RL, nailing him with a disgusted, derisive look.

"Jesus, RL... what's the matter with you. 'This is not a good thing' ... of all the doo-lolly, namby-pamby things to say. Couldn't you have come up with something just a weensy bit *sappier*?"

"I know, I know, Frankie, and I knew it as soon as it was out of my mouth. And I also know I'm gonna pay for it. But what about you, what brilliance did you come out with?"

"Ah, but Noble Sire of mine, I am but your lowly serf. Pearls of wisdom aren't expected of me. *AND*... I didn't just get engaged to Jayderay. She expects better. She *deserves* better. You, you... you're a CLOD."

"You're right," RL nods, sighing heavily, "I am a clod. But good Lord, Frankie, you saw him, or what he's turned into. Is Elvis even in that, that, that quivering baggie?"

"A better question might be, what's he gonna come out as. Shadow said she could sense that he was still there... well, just in case you've forgotten; she's a tad different from us. What did she sense? His brain? His, his soul?"

"Frankie," says RL with dawning horror. "What if he comes out, you know, a, a monster."

"Don't Boss, don't go there. He might come out... carnivorous with a taste for human flesh."

"Don't Frankie, you're scaring the shit out of me."

"Well, you started it!" Frankie gives a strangled giggle, adding, "Just think, we'd have ourselves a gen-u-wyne Purple... People Eater."

"Oh, shut up, Frankie. Please."

Dr. Moto had known of, or at least expected a coming change to Elvis. But Moto hadn't foreseen him becoming a goop tamale; that had certainly never happened before. No one knew the Proby/Elvis creature better, inside or out, but Moto has been wrong about the boy before. Badly wrong. And Moto had also been frantically scheming to be *gone*.

RL was correct. This is not a good thing.

In the bedroom, Shadow turns to Jayderay. With

coal black hair framing forlorn eyes in a scarred face, her ebony lips speak.

"You and I have spoken in the past of our losing God, Jayderay. When we turned from that which never answered. Is it possible now to reclaim that, that... hope? Or would prayer fall upon an ear even more deaf than that of before?"

"Oh, Shadow, I don't believe God is gone, he here all right," Jayderay answers, her own eyes becoming misty. "He just never seemed to listen to you and me. If God IS some kind of a *he*. Fact is, I 'magine he must be, 'cause it seem likely to me a woman would act more kindly."

Shadow nods slightly, a smile flickering. "Yes, that is much in the way of my thinking. And yet, that must be as is. Can we... will you pray with me? Pray with me for, for Elv-is?"

"Yes, on my knees I will, with all of me I will," answers Jayderay, wiping at tears, meaning every word.

Together they kneel. And with folded hands they silently pray. They pray for a creature, an odd, lavender skinned being that is not all human. A thing many would brand an abomination without soul. A thing who loves. They pray.

Only a Man of God could find fault with this.

———•••———

And in the Waydowns:

Hearing Shank struggle with the crutch, Tanya hurries over, and kneels beside the girl. "Don't try and get up just yet," she says, "let's you and I have a serious talk first."

"Did I, uh, did I do something wrong?" asks the girl, her eyes widening. "I'm sorry if you din't likes the patch, you ain't gots to wears it, I onliest wanted to giv—"

"Oh, you silly little girl," Tanya breaks in grinning, "I *love* this patch, absolutely love it! I've had lots of guys give me tons of nice stuff, but I treasure this," she says reaching up and touching the black eyepatch, "more than anything."

"You ain't funnin' me? Really?"

Without thought, Tanya hugs the girl, saying, "No, child, I absolutely *ain't funnin'* you, not even a little." Pulling back, she reaches up, strokes the girl's hair lightly, and runs her thumb across the freckles.

"You do realize we may not make it to my cabin? That tube thing may get us."

"Well, 'course I knows, Tanya. They is always some kinda monsters out there and everywheres," she answers with a puzzled look. "I ain't a'skeered, you had oughta knowed that."

Tanya nods, "I do know it." *Besides Lakker, mon-*

sters are all you've ever had. "I imagine you're the only one of us that isn't afraid," she says smiling. "I know I'm definitely *a'skeered*, very, very much so. Because of that, in case we don't make it, I want to give you something; it's not anything you can see or touch, but I very much want to give it. From my heart, I do. And I need to ask you... to ask you *for* something."

"You, you, you kin have anything I gots! And you sure ain't gots to gives me no gift, just on 'cause I gived—"

"I'm not," interrupts Tanya, gently. After her long inner struggles during the rest period, she speaks without hesitation.

"Okay, here goes. You're just way too good and cute a girl to have a name like Shank. That's a name for shit-balls like Bert and Giney. I want to give you another. I'd very much like to name you Shanna. It kinda goes with Tanya."

"Shanna? Is I sayin' it right? Shanna?"

"Yes, *Shanna*, you're saying it perfectly. Do you like it?"

"Shanna," the girl breathes the name. "Oh, I, I loves it! I loves it fierce!"

And two smiles become... enormous. (being bestowed by Tanya, the name could've been Orglestrokeit, and had the same result)

Tanya takes a very deep breath, looking at this girl, this Shanna.

"And... *Shanna*, this next thing is for me, it's, it's hard for me to ask. I... I'm empty inside, and it hurts, it's been bad for me, and I didn't know it. Until I met you. I need someone. I need badly to care for someone. And I've come to... care for you. Can I... I want to— will you... could you think of me as..." Tanya falters, wanting to say words like parent and mother, but feeling those names should come from the girl.

"Damn, I'm not saying this right, Shanna. I want you with me; I want us to stay together. Will you stay with me, for however long we have?"

Stunned silence from the girl as she looks back. The smile slips away. She blinks rapidly, then her face twists, crumples and she buries the dirty, freckled face into her hands.

"I, I, I cain't, Tanya. I cain't. I ain't never had nobody, 'cept the Sherrf. I ain't fitt'n... I don't knows how to..." and she begins to cry.

Tanya had never expected this, and has no idea how to deal with it. So, she handles it without thought. Naturally. Taking the softly sobbing girl into her arms, Tanya silently holds the girl, gently stroking the greasy foul-smelling hair. Rocking her back and forth... as a mother does a child.

"You don't have to do or know anything, baby," Tanya whispers. "I only want you to be you."

Slowly Shanna slides her own arms around the woman's waist, hugging timidly, as if fearful this cannot be real. All her short time as a child, she'd been unwanted, a burden to everyone. Shunted from one hatch to another, desperately trying to please without knowing how. She had so ached for a parent. For the tender caress of a loving hand. For someone to show, to explain, to guide. Who does not?

The girl, this Shanna, has never gotten anything in life without giving something in return. Ever. It has become an ingrained response. She must give for what she's being offered. She must earn it; but she has nothing.

Still crying against Tanya's neck, the girl offers the only thing she can.

"I ain't gonna never let no monsters gets you. I'll goes with you if they does. Don't you be a'skeered."

Tanya holds the girl, softly stroking her hair. *She's giving me her all.*

Tanya is no longer protected from life... she's as armor-less as a baby's bottom.

Life without love, without caring, is an emptiness, a terrible, lonely void... and Tanya is through with that.

"What the fuck are you two doing over there? Lezzin'

out? God damn it, we need to get out of here," Huong's voice grates across the room.

"He's right... Shanna, we need to get moving," Looking at the girl, she reaches out, wiping the tears away, she continues, "You belong to... we have each other now; we're gonna make it just fine."

"Yes, Tanya," the girl nods solemnly. "Don't you be a'skeered."

They hobble across the deck to Huong, with Shanna using the ever-ready shoulder of Tanya as much as the crutch.

"I haven't heard or seen a thing from that fucking Tuber," the man says, leaning out into the corridor, scanning the haze above. "This is a damn spaceship; where's all this fog shit come from?"

"Well," Huong, no one knows how many thousands of years old this wreck is. I'd guess the condensers are deteriorating, like all the rest of this hulk."

"Yeah, maybe that's why the protein crackers taste so bad, but I'd pay good for some about now. And a lot more for water, even the ship's recycled crap. Did anybody ever analyze that shit, ever find out what it actually is? And I've been told they don't even know where the ship makes the protein. You ever heard?"

"*Huong!* What the hell's wrong with you? You're

gabbin' like an old woman, about shit that doesn't matter. You scared?"

"Yes!" he snaps. Turning from the opening, he continues. "I've had too long thinking about that thing just squatting up there, just waiting."

"Only crazies are never afraid, you fucking grunt," chuckles Tanya. "You've got battle jitters, just like me. Maybe that Tuber, as you called it, has gone; got chased away by Coilers. Who knows, and it doesn't matter, we've got to run for it, no choice. But we're close to my cabin, just keep that in mind."

"Yeah, but close ain't there. Fuck it, let's go. And I will back-pack that... the girl."

"My name is *Shanna!* And I din't ax you for no packin'—"

"Calm down," interrupts Tanya.

"No, Huong, *I* will carry her. And her name *is* Shanna. I will not hear her called anything else."

Looking at the pair, the man gives a slow shake of his head, but doesn't speak. Why bother. They're dead anyway.

"I'm guessing you're as short of ammo as I am... right?" she asks.

"Probably. I've got one spare clip, maybe a half empty plugged."

"I've got one in, and fuck-all for another. So, I won't

bother telling you to hold back. Have you calmed down any?"

"Fuck no, but I'm wired to move. I just looked, the way seems clear down the hall, but there's no telling about up there," he motions with the Uzi. "Maybe you two should go first, with me on your tail. I can look up easier, and keep watch better. Maybe."

"I agree."

After letting the girl climb on, Tanya grips the Uzi, and faces Huong.

"Don't trip out there, twinkle toes."

"Same to you. And Tanya… you're packing a load and you fucking well better give it your all. I'll do my job, but I'm not dying for either of you."

"Think positive, Wonder Gook, and it'll be an easy run. But if things do go bad, remember, small rooms off the corridor probably have ceilings like this one." And with a deep breath, out the door she trots with Shanna on her back, Uzi clutched in one hand, the other supporting the girl's bad leg.

The girl constantly squints up into the haze, waving Lakker's old pistol in one hand, the other arm wrapped across Tanya's chest. Loosely tied to her back, the crutch tags along. Both know it may never again be needed.

Huong looks on with a grim, disgusted expression,

giving them a slow count of ten. *That stinking little cunt bouncing on Tanya's back will get us killed... it's because of her we're in this mess.* And then with a low sound in his throat, he follows, matching their pace. His dead eyes and Uzi sweeping the drifting, vaporous murk above.

Tanya does give it her all, running full throttle with everything she's got. A woman no longer driven and consumed by the cancerous need for revenge.

Perhaps for the first time ever, Tanya truly loves someone. She loves a child. There is no stronger motivation.

The Tuber is not gone.

Seevee's eyelids flutter. Raging thirst and throbbing pain have brought him back to consciousness. Looking over at the closed, gore smeared hatch, he thinks the Spill equivalent of: You sneaky fucking bastard.

Horrifically injured and dying, he pulls himself toward a milk-colored support stanchion. Leaking condensation often trickled down their slick sides, creating small puddles at the bottom. Dragging himself through the sticky lake of his own blood, he briefly thinks of lapping at it, but there's too much human in him to allow that. Yet.

Gasping, he reaches the support's base, and moans, seeing a tiny phosphorescent pool. Beyond caring what the slightly glowing liquid is, he sucks at the deck, then licks as far up as his neck and tongue will stretch. Every drop is precious, delicious, life sustaining.

Laying his head down, Seevee begins to slip back into oblivion. There's no hurt or thirst in that soothing realm. Sliding away into the darkness, his thoughts are of Tanya. *Ton... Ton with duck feathers Huong, quack man Huong... he much Moto man... he much sneak snake... much no trust... Ton must no trust... Seevee luff Ton... much luff...*

Thoughts of Tanya jerk Seevee back to his here and now. Raising his head, looking toward the corridor opening, he breaths in and out deeply. *Much go Ton.* With his remaining arm he pushes himself to his knees, falling back against the metal wall. The empty shoulder socket explodes with more pain. *Much luff... much go Ton.*

Fighting to get one foot flat on the floor, Seevee pushes, and manages to slide upwards. With both feet now beneath him, he looks toward the hall, and takes a step. Both knees buckle and he falls, landing hard.

He lays stunned, despair washing over him. His mind no longer sending coherent messages, Seevee tries again. Pushing with the toes of his military issue boots, his trimmed-to-fit feet, an agony. With his one arm reaching ahead, fingers futilely clawing against the deck plates, he moves a few inches. And then a few more. And so on. All for Tanya.

———

The attack on Tanya's group came without sound. It came with fury, as two of the deadly pink and blue veined tubes smack down at once; followed seconds later by a third. All landing close to Tanya. With the girl riding her back she's the bigger target, and more of a meal.

The red lips are snatched up immediately, as Huong sprays a quick burst from the Uzi. Shanna does not fire, trying desperately for aim; she has very few rounds. As Tanya slows, attempting to turn and shoot, the girl screams.

"NO! Don't stop, Tanya, don't stop, runs! I kin shoots."

Tanya does run, putting everything into pumping her legs, while cursing herself for not letting Shanna have the Uzi. She runs.

Huong speeds up, closing the distance between himself and the women. Nearing them, trying to look up and everywhere, he starts a crab like sideways jogging, keeping the gun in a constant sweeping motion.

The next tube smacks down directly between Huong and the women, its red lips open wide. Both he and Shanna get off shots, with at least one of the bullets hitting, making the glistening horror jiggle as it's yanked up.

Another hurtles down, nearly taking Shanna's hand off as she shoots. As it's pulled back, still another comes, and it gets a short blast from Huong. Going limp for a second, it then seems to roll up, rather than be pulled.

"Find a room, find a fucking room," he yells. "We can't make it, we can't do it!"

Two more tubes plummet down, their red maws yawning. Shanna hits one with two shots, and it begins limply rolling up.

The other tube hits Huong, its mouth raking flesh from his arm as it comes. He goes down, sending the gun spinning across the deck.

Shanna fires again, scoring another hit, and the pistol clicks on an empty chamber. "It got Huong, he's down, and I ain't got no more bullets!"

Huong screams while the meat tears from his arm as he yanks it from the retreating tube. Immediately he springs away, holding the bleeding arm to his chest, and running for the Uzi.

Tanya manages to stop and turn, bringing up her

gun, and firing at the next incoming tube. The bullets ram into it, and it never lands.

"There!" screams Huong, scooping up the Uzi and pointing at an opening off the corridor. With blood dripping from his elbow and cradling the gun, he yells, "Get in the fucking room, we're finished." He runs to the doorway, but whirls about, pointing the Uzi up, ready for the next incoming. "Move your ass, Tanya!"

Another set of crimson lips smack down right at the opening, and another beside it, blocking the way. Huong falls as he leaps backward, sprawling without firing, the gun spins from blood wet hands, flying between the tubes into the room.

And a third tube descends. Tanya tries to shoot, but her Uzi is finished, there's nothing in it.

Huong scrambles up, knowing it's over, they've lost, but damned if he's going to die on his ass. "Come on, you bastard, send another," he yells, glaring up into the roiling haze.

"Don't you be a'skeered, Tanya. I'm here," the girl says quietly.

"I'm not afraid Shanna; I have you. And WE don't give up."

"Then runs! Put's me down, I kin makes it my ownself!"

"No, baby, we stay together. Huong!" yells Tanya, "Move your fucking ass."

Death comes.

A smeared bloody trail leads to Seevee's body. His tortuous, dragging struggle to reach the corridor has kept the wound scraped open.

He lays with about half his body extending into the hall. Seevee had labored hard for these few feet, despite his mind being unclear as to why. Was it for life? Was it to get help? To find more water? Hunger? No, it must have been for Tanya; he would not have suffered and fought this hard for any reason but love.

For whatever purpose, Seevee's bleeding, valiant crawl of those agonizing few feet, has resulted in exactly... jack shit. There was no help, no water, no precious Ton. And he had fainted again.

In keeping with Seevee's current run of luck, something comes from further down the corridor. Its ances tors may have been a rodent of some sort. Some sort indeed, those ancestors must've suppurated ugly. In ancient times, some bearded, toga wearing ass, profoundly stated that everything is loved by its mother. That deep thinker had never seen this.

The thing is a scuttling, nearly comic nightmare; it

looks like a painfully big turd with eyes. No mother ever loved this creature; it's a true product of the Way-downs. And it's the size of a small rabbit... with five legs.

This walking turd stops, lifting its bent snout into the air, smelling Seevee's blood. Snapping an amazing assortment of teeth, the turd resumes its scuttling. Heading directly to Seevee's wound, it sniffs at the congealing mess, licks tentatively, and then opens the impressive mouth.

Seevee's hand slams down on the creature's neck and shoulders, and bones snap as fingers curl and crush. Giving the turd a lesson: Don't trust the dead; they cheat.

It gasps out a sharp, whistling squeak, legs spasming, and goes limp. Jerking the quivering carcass to his mouth, Seevee rips into the hide and meat.

Trying repeatedly to swallow, Seevee finally quits gagging, and spits the chunks out. *Much, bad! Much, much bad. Coiler much no eat!* This is a supreme insult to the turd's remains. A Coiler will eat anything.

Slinging the dead thing away, Seevee lays his forehead to the deck, breathing deeply. Several minutes pass, and then he turns his head. Looking down the endless, trash strewn corridor, he whimpers, he sighs, and then... he crawls on.

There's no keeping a good man down. Or an Almost.

"Huong, move your ass," yells Tanya as she charges down the corridor, with the girl bouncing on her back. "There's gotta be another room!"

"There ain't shit," he calls back. Cursing and shaking his head in disgust, he continues glaring up into the haze. Waiting for death.

But this is the Waydowns. Here, anything can be interrupted. Even death.

Out of an adjoining wing jogs a tall, gangly, human shape. It stops, looks intently at the two women, and then starts running toward them. Waving its multi-jointed arms and shouting in a raspy, seldom used voice.

"TUH! TUH! TUH!" yells the nude, vaguely female form. "TUH!" She continues to shout and run, the untrimmed feet slapping the deck. Having recognized the blond thatch of Tanya's hair, the Spill knows her quest is over. She's found Ton, found help for Seevee.

But this is the Waydowns.

The three tubes blocking Huong's way into the safe room are suddenly snatched up.

Seconds later two more drop. One lands a few feet in front of the running Spill. The other lands on her head, sucking the body in past her shoulders, the red lips stretching obscenely. As legs kick, and arms flail against the blue-pink hide, she's raised slowly up and into the obscuring depths of fog. No one can hear the screams.

Too late the Spill has learned: No good deed goes unpunished. It is an ancient and accurate lesson.

Huong wastes no time gawking as the thrashing Spill disappears. Lunging into the room, he scoops up his gun and whirls back to the entry.

"Are you two playing with yourselves? Get in here!"

As the pair do a fast lurch into the room, he backs up to a wall. Sliding down, he examines the ripped arm.

"I din't think you had none, but you does, you gots sand, Mister," Shanna says begrudgingly as she slides off Tanya's back.

"What I've got is a fucked-up arm. Listen, Tanya, we might still have a chance, if we hurry. Maybe that bastard will stop hunting while it eats."

"Yeah, it's a big maybe, but it's a chance," says Tanya. "We've learned one thing for sure, waiting for it to go away won't work. How bad's the arm?"

"Bad enough. But there's no time to screw with it," answers Huong, ripping the remains of his khaki sleeve off. As he starts to wrap it around the worst part of the still bleeding arm, Tanya drops to one knee, helping him bind and tie it.

Looking on and nodding to herself, Shanna mutters, "Yep, you gots sand. Danged if you ain't... speshly for an asshole you does."

"Okay," says Tanya, "we're down to one gun that can shoot, and no choice. We've got to run, and do it now."

"I got a few rounds, but not enough to count on," says Huong. "So, our only hope is that the fucker eats slow, and we're fast.

"Tanya! Lets me stays behind, so's you kin runs more faster. You kin comes back with more bullets to fetch me."

"No, Shanna, I will not leave you... I can't. I won't. But after what we just went through, I think maybe we can move faster side by side," Tanya says, adding with a mirthless grin, "You, me and the crutch."

Huong listens to this as he stands, flexing his bandaged arm and wincing. *Jesus Christ, these two twats are crazy. What next? A marriage to Seevee? The little stink pot and that worthless Spill would be a match, all right.* But he doesn't say a word. Why bother.

As they steel themselves to head out, Tanya says, "Since we're nearly out of ammo, Huong, there's no reason for you sticking with us. Just run for it."

"No, I'm in for the count," comes his surprising response. "Hell, I've got no place to run anyway. If the fucker shows, I'll give it the short burst this Uzi has left, and then we're fucked. It'll be lunchtime for Tuber... again."

"Thanks, Huong. And I mean it," says Tanya, looking at the dangerous, unpredictable man. "Who knows, one final blast might do the trick and you'll kill it."

None of the three believe this, but it sounds good. Sometimes even that can help.

Off they go, and they don't fool around about it. Imminent death by being swallowed whole is a terrific stimulant. It leaves a wimp like cocaine in the dust, way back at the starting line.

True to his statement, Huong stays. Pacing the women, and rotating from point position to rear guard, he continuously strains to see into the mists above, waving the near empty gun.

Without bullets, neither Tanya or the girl bother with looking anywhere except where they're putting their feet. Strewn with wrecked office/lab pieces, splintered bones, and the debris of chaos, the danger of tripping is constant.

No one speaks. The only sounds are those of their fast-shuffling progress through the eerie, dimly lit halls. An occasional cry or scream from an unknowable creature far away echoes through the haze. Some may have been made by a human. Or things that once were.

Shanna has one hand on Tanya's shoulder, the other

tightly gripping the crutch, and the two manage a quick, lurching advance.

Panting, sweating, her rags flapping, every step jarring the infected, throbbing leg, Shanna never cries out, never drops a tear. Through gritted teeth, she keeps on keeping on.

Tanya marvels at the girl. *She's so God damn tough... and I am so, so proud... so proud. I will not fail this child. I will not. I cannot.*

Either the Tuber was full and having a nap, or the bony Spill had disagreed with its delicate gullet, or maybe it had rolled away for a soul satisfying shit. But for whatever reason, there were no more plummeting, red lipped flesh tubes. This is the Waydowns, after all, maybe something ate the bastard.

So, the group catches a break, and without any further assaults from anything, not even a turd, they make it into Tanya's cabin. Miracles do happen, even in the Waydowns, but they're damn few, and slow in coming.

Immediately helping the girl onto the bed, Tanya begins stuffing pillows under her leg. "I'll bring you some water and something to eat, you stay put, girl."

"Huong, there's plenty of crap cakes and some old military issue packs, help yourself."

Huong is guzzling water and doesn't answer, sucking on the faucet. When he finally comes up for air, Tanya starts filling a glass for the girl, saying, "And don't take the chocolate bars. They're old, but I bet Shanna's never had any candy."

"Boo-fucking-hoo," responds the man, already rooting through the food. "Damn, this stuff really is old, it can't be from before the mutiny. Or can it?"

"No, can't possibly be," answers Tanya, "They're some packets Seevee rustled up. I figure they were left by grunts during one of Gaust's reclaim expeditions she sent down. You don't have to eat it, Wonder Gook. There's plenty of crap cake."

Huong doesn't speak, just nods, ripping into something. As Tanya passes by, she grabs the two chocolate bars. They look like military versions of a Hershey's with nuts.

Shanna is straining to look everywhere. This is where the worshipped Tanya lives. Tanya's home! It's much bigger than Lakker's, and to the girl's thinking, clean and fabulous. And it still has running water. Such opulence!

Handing the girl a glass of water and some tablets, Tanya says, "Get these down, baby, they're old, but should help some. And then you're in for a treat!" she continues, holding up the chocolate.

"Princess Shanna ain't the only one hurting," comments Huong.

"Don't twist your panties, Huong-y, I've got you some too. But ladies first. And there's some ointment that might help that arm.

"I'll take the pills, but pass on having this arm fucked with. It's worse than I thought, and it's feeling hot. That red color on the Tuber's lips might've been venom. Christ, this God damn Waydowns keeps on giving."

"Yeah, Huong, I've kinda noticed that. Look, since we're planning on you going back to 19 anyway, let's get you there sooner. The infirmary can inject antibiotics, and slap some plasti-skin on that arm. Hell, you'll be taking over 19 in no time."

"Good thinking. And I can get something to eat that's not a million years old. Hell, let's make sooner, *now*."

"Okay, you got it. I've got a couple Uzi clips here, so at least we can have fire power again. Let me see to Shanna's leg, and then we get your invalid ass to the elevator."

"Yeah, we will if the Tuber lets us," replies the ever-cheery Huong. "If that Seevee was here, we could use him as a decoy. Maybe he'd be good for that."

After issuing some stern and serious orders to the girl about not getting up, and keeping the leg elevated, Tanya gives her a grin... and unwraps the chocolate. Tanya has come late to parenting, but she's catching on quick to spoiling. And worry. Both are important.

Either the Tuber is still napping, or applying lip balm, or maybe the bastard died of indigestion, but the creature doesn't show.

What does show, is a Spill. Shambling out of some smaller hallway, with hands raised, calling "Ton, Ton."

"No, Huong!" Tanya shouts, pushing aside his gun as the man wheeled toward the creature. "It's one of mine, and it's got hands raised."

"Fucking Christ, Tanya. I need meds, not another of your... adoptees. Get rid of the filthy bastard."

Ignoring the exasperated Huong, Tanya steps toward the Spill, with one hand extended, palm outward. "GO," she says, and points back the way it had come. Gesturing with the Uzi toward the murk above the corridor, she adds, "Much new killer, much not Coiler."

Its feet have been trimmed, indicating it had initially been considered intelligent enough for training. The Spill slowly nods, looking warily up into the haze, while lowering its hands.

Pointing again back toward the smaller hall, Tanya repeats, "GO."

With a curt nod and another, "Ton," it shuffles away with some speed. Evidently this was its version of: "Yes, Ma'am! New killer... you won't have to tell me twice."

"Why do you bother, Tanya? You don't need those fuckers anymore."

"They trust me, and it's stupid to throw away friends or allies. That might be something you should think about, Wonder Gook. And why the fuck are you dithering around? Are you playing with yourself? Let's go!"

With wounded and pissed Huong, Tanya makes the elevator run with no more talking and no further interruptions. Not even an attacking turd.

Breathing hard, Tanya immediately grabs the edges of the melted control panel, twists, pushes, and off it comes. Inside, a keyed control has been added; open or close, idiot proof simplicity.

"Fuck," says the carefully watching Huong, shaking his head in disgust. "Real space-age security that is."

"Yeah, but it worked for decades; not many brains down here. Okay, Huong, you know what to do. Don't kill Moto, we're not ready for that. But if you have to, then hide his body. Find out if Gaust still stays holed up in her office, but don't try anything with her. The bitch is deadly. *WE* will deal with her together." She grins, "And then, I'm gonna make you one rich mother fucker."

"Yes, you are," quietly replies Huong, his dead eyes looking at her.

"This should go quick," he adds. "I'll get my arm fixed, the plasti-skin might take a couple hours, and I can pick up the latest deck talk from the medic. He's a mouthy shit who never shut's up. Moto is always around and usually alone. I've been wanting to kill that Jap prick, but I'll hold off, and talk only. And I got absolutely no intention of screwing with Gaust."

"All good. I'll be waiting for you back at my cabin... unless the Tuber gets me on the way back," she says, glancing up into the haze. She looks at him, her eye-patch giving her a rakish appearance.

"One last thing, Huong... I need a favor," she adds, reaching behind the melted controls and keying the door to open.

"A favor! I'm about to practically hand you Deck 19 on a platter, and you ask me for a favor?"

"It's a small one. There's a rack beside this elevator door, it's always got lab coats hanging on it. Grab one, toss it in, and send it down. That's it. I'm even saying please."

Huong frowns, turns, steps into the now open elevator, and pushes 19. He doesn't speak. Why bother.

Tanya waits doubtfully, while eyeing the ever-present fog above, keeping the Uzi ready. In about a minute, the door opens. Three coats are laying there.

Huong will not find Moto. He will find Dr. Gaust. The new version.

CHAPTER 17

AT THE ROATON HOUSE

In the bedroom, Shadow and Jayderay kneel in prayer. While RL and Frankie stand in the hall… doing a terrific job of scaring the shit out of each other speculating about Elvis. Or what he's turning into.

"Enough, Frankie, enough," RL tells him. "Let's just shut up about Elvis turning into the Borneo Booger."

"Huh! 'Borneo Booger'… that's not too bad. But, how about the Borneo Butt Beast instead? That sounds more—"

"Frankie!"

"Okay, okay, you're the Boss. Then let's talk about something really soothing… like what we're gonna do with Moto."

"Oh, thanks a lot. You really are toilet paper, Frankie. The entire roll."

"That's me, Boss; soft, but strong to the end. Well… what about him? I've got the Heebie-Jeebies more about Moto than I do about what Elvis is gonna be. And that room he's in is way, way too close to Jayderay."

RL takes a deep breath, and looks at his business partner, whom Jayderay often refers to as... my *other* crook. She loves them both... and knows them well.

Eyeing Frankie, RL speaks casually, easily, in an off-hand, friendly manner.

"Well Frankie, ummm, how about you take Moto to—"

"NO! No, you don't, Mon Capitaine! I am but a mere minion, and such an undertaking requires the firm hand of leadership. *Your* leadership. He's possessed, and he might start spewing green pea-soup at me, like in that awful movie. No, '*WE*' have to do something with Dr. Exorcist Moto. We, as in you and I."

"Yeah, you're right, it needs to be both of us. But what can we do with the— Hell, Frankie! Let's take him to the basement and toss that son of a bitch into the Waydowns. God knows we've got an entry into it."

"You do have your moments, Boss, yes you really do," Frankie replies with admiration, wishing he'd thought of it.

"But remember, RL, only Shadow can open that Waydowns door, and she is not going to leave Elvis, period. Not even for a few minutes."

"Well... then we can at least lock him in that closet

down there. That's a lot safer than leaving him where he's at."

And off they go to shovel the Moto Manure. RL might say something profound about this. Something wise, something sage, something like: This is not a good thing.

As Frankie unlocks the oak door, neither man exactly rushes in. There's no need for haste, no need to jostle one another. And they wouldn't want to startle the good Dr. Moto. They don't.

"Well... are you going in?" Frankie asks softly.

"Are you?" RL hisses back.

Both men become silent as they peer in. Their eyes are open wider than usual. The pair would say wider eyes makes it easier to see... and they would be brimming full of truth. Along with a lot of something else.

Inside, it is a room in stasis; where all is still. The portrait of the man with the elephant's ass chin still hangs on the wall. His chin still looks like it needs a bowel movement. The disintegrated curtains still lie on the floor. Dust motes still hang motionless in the window's light. And it is still cold. It is still very cold... and there is still Dr. Moto.

He appears much the same, standing exactly where they'd left him. The green syrup seeping from each ear is now crusted over, no longer dripping. Perhaps the eyes have never blinked, just continued staring straight ahead. Moto sees that which is unseeable. He sees this with great clarity. It is an agony to him. But it is a joy to others... to the girls who visit. A delight to the girls who slip from beneath the door. The girls who enter him... and play.

"I am here, Round-Eyes."

Frankie and RL flinch at the sudden sound from Moto. It is a voice without nuance or modulation. A voice of someone who is not dead, but wants to be.

"It is a long time here... where we are. A long, long time. When you are dust, I will be here. For all eternity I will be here. When all that you have known has faded and withered for a long, long—"

"How'd you like a pineapple stuffed up your ass?" interrupts Frankie. "I bet that would last a *long, long* time." Looking over at RL, he says, "Boss, I've had about enough of Mausoleum Moto. Let's herd this son of a bitch into the basement."

"Yeah, you're right. The more he talks, the less scared I am of this graveyard shit. I think that voice is all he has left."

"Take me where you will, Round-Eye. I am here. I am here forever," says Dr. Moto. He has never once looked over at the two men. His bright and clear eyes have continued looking intently at what only he can see.

Neither man wants to touch Moto. They haven't totally lost their fear of him, but they're really tired of dicking around with this ghastly husk of a man. So, with gentle pokes by Frankie, using his trusty razor, the doctor is guided to the basement.

Moto moves jerkily, as if by strings. He does not speak, he does not blink, he simply judders along. RL leads the procession, with Frankie in the rear judiciously applying the razor. He knows the razor is no longer a threat to this once a man, but... but Frankie really doesn't want any contact with the bastard. It might be catching.

Behind them, two ropes of dark gray fog follow. They constantly touch, entwine, and part from one another.

Arriving at the basement, Moto jerks his way into the indicated closet, looking straight ahead. Frankie closes the door on him, and turns to RL.

"Will this hold him, O Noble Leader? Is he just going to stand in there, giving the wall that thousand-yard stare?"

"Yeah, I think he will. I don't believe he *can* do much of anything, he's just kinda *not here,* in a terrible way. This should work just fine, till we can get Shadow to open the Waydowns door."

As they leave, Frankie giggles, "Damn! I wish I could've used a pineapple."

RL doesn't ask; he knows better.

But RL is wrong about Moto. The Doctor can still do many things... if properly motivated.

Behind the departing men, two loosely braided tendrils of dark mist float across the basement. Uncoiling at Moto's closet door, they glide beneath it. They've come to join their sister. They enter Moto.

And a good time will be had.

CHAPTER 18

MEANWHILE, BACK IN THE SHIP

Tanya arrives back at her cabin, huffing but smiling. The run had been quick, uneventful, and a success. Before opening the hatch, she examines the lab coats. One is totally pristine, and redolent with a pleasing but unidentifiable perfume. *She's gonna absolutely love this. I'll surprise her with it after I introduce her to the Groomer. I love her... but Lord, how my Shanna does stink!*

Carefully folding the coats, she places them just outside the hatch for some very quick, future grabbing. And the joy of giving. Parents get a lot of mileage out of giving.

She opens the hatch, expecting the gratification of hearing great relief expressed by her child. Of hearing the girl's boundless joy over this safe return, of feeling the love. She opens the hatch.

"Oh, Tanya! Oh... *Chuk-lit!* Ain't nothin' never been gooder, is they more?"

Parenting does not always go as expected.

Bursting with laughter, Tanya grabs her in a hug.

"You little greedy-gut, you. No, there's not any more *choc-o -late*, but there's gonna be. Where we're going, there's mountains of it."

With eyes staring in disbelief, Shanna says, "No! Don't be funnin' me, cain't be that much of nothin' so good. But I... Oh! Are you okay? Was they any more Tuber fightin'?" This is a child from a violent environment, danger and fighting is always expected, no big deal.

"Well! It's about time you asked, little Missy Chuk-lit. I'm fine, there were no attacks, and that butthole Huong-y is now up on Deck 19."

"I'm powerful glad you're okay. Fierce, powerful glad. But I ain't gonna miss that Huong none."

"Nor am I, baby. He's not a good man, not some-body to trust. But he can be bought, and that's valu-able in any person. Especially in a man, and it's some-thing we're gonna use. But never mind him right now, because you, young lady, are gettin' out of those awful, te-rrrrrr-ible smelly old rags, and into the Groomer."

The girl blushes, and looks away. "I knows I stinks, and I'm, I'm fierce shameful. I wants to, to smells like you."

"Shanna, you are mine, and I — I love you, child." Reaching over and turning the girls face back. "Don't ever be ashamed of something you can't help, not ever."

"Yes... Mama," nods the girl. "I, I, I loves you back, I loves you fierce hard."

A thrilled Tanya, grabs the girl in a hug. Fierce hard. *She called me Mama! She said... she said...*

Yes, Tanya's heart is now totally defenseless. As unprotected as a naked intestine. She once would've considered such a state beneath contempt. Things change; some people grow. And it always requires someone, it requires someone to love.

"Oh, child, oh, Shanna," is all that she can manage.

And to the Groomer they go. After some brief operational instructions, and quite a bit of in-depth hygiene suggestions, Tanya leaves the child. Leaves her to a wondrous world of hot running water, the delights of soap, shampoo, and many, many wash cloths. Lots and lots.

As he'd predicted, Huong gets plenty of information from the medic. The guy prattles away as he trowels plasti-skin thickly on the wounded arm. He also cautions Huong: "this may sting a bit."

It burns like the pits of hell. Huong wants to stuff

some of it up the chatty bastard's ass. A lot of it, going deep.

But Huong restrains himself, grinds his teeth... and learns spit. Gossip aplenty, like his rumored new command over Security, but very little about anything he needs to know. Of use: Moto hasn't been seen making his usual rounds today, and maybe not yesterday either. As to Gaust, the mouthy intern had suddenly become very reticent. He hadn't seen *Doctor* Gaust, not in a long time. And that ended that.

Fear will cure a loose mouth.

Flexing his arm, gently rubbing at the new skin, Huong heads to his dorm, a quick shower, and fresh khakis. Most of the grunts are out, probably on hated maintenance details. Those that are there, nod curtly, and a couple offer decidedly limp congratulations on his coming promotion. The limpness isn't jealousy; Huong isn't liked; he's feared.

And Huong, doesn't give a diseased rat's pellet. Being in charge does not require affection. Terrorized obedience will work just fine.

Walking purposefully as if following orders, Huong scouts the area of Moto's desk. As he widens his search, he hears a voice from somewhere within the Proby creature's area. It sounds female. Sort of.

Padding softly now, he follows the sound. And

wishes he hadn't. It's Gaust. That vastly altered Gaust, and exhibiting some new capabilities. Huong watches, hiding behind some ridiculous game machine. Sweat beads appear on his face, and without thought he pulls his knife. He has no intention of attacking her, the blade is instinct. *No wonder Moto pissed himself. What has she become? Who the fuck is she talking to?*

Laying on the floor a few feet from Gaust, is... her head. The old, putrefying head she'd ripped off and dropped. Resting on one cheek, the eyes blankly stare in Huong's direction. They blink slowly as the tongue slips from withered lips, and then pulls back in. Ignoring the ill-mannered head, Huong focuses on Gaust. This new Dr. Gaust.

Illuminated by the Bowl-A-Rama's strobing sign, she stands at the front of its cabinet, both hands grip the sides. Her knuckles shine like polished bone in the light of the flashing words.

STRIKE! PLAY!

Leaning forward, her upper torso has stretched far beyond possible. And the neck continues on, its circumference now that of her wrist. Before the yawning cave where the bowling pins set, it has made a single, rising coil. Her still human sized head poises there, framed in the opening. Above it, the sign silently screams:

STRIKE! PLAY!

The mesmerized Huong watches. Gaust is speaking into the opening. He cannot hear clearly, as the room swirls with game sounds. And the sign strobes:

STRIKE! PLAY!

Gaust's head slowly extends further into the shadowed opening. For long seconds it becomes rigid. The sign continues to pulse. The room still echoes with muted sounds from devices of fun. And Huong still watches, unable to move.

The Gaust head darts back... vibrating on its coiled neck, speaking louder.

"It is done. I am you now. The switch will soon be activated... soon we will cloak this world." Gaust slowly contracts until she stands erect. Turning, she walks toward her office.

Behind her, the sign flashes: STRIKE! PLAY! Gaust's eyes are brimming wet, glistening full... full of the Yellow... full to near drooling out. STRIKE! PLAY!

At this moment, far below within Lakker's area, the Yellow quit being busy. All the Melts stand motionless. Before being consumed by the mold, they had all once been totally human. But now someone new has been added to their colony. Someone who was not all human. The Yellow, these Melts, this sentient hive of Leprosy... now have a leader.

Even centuries after this asteroid-battered ship

rammed into earth, humans had not yet risen above the ridged brow, knuckle dragging stage. Many still haven't. The spaceship brought future extinction for these evolving excretions. That extinction begins now.

Huong, managing to break his fear paralysis, slides further back among the games. From the time he'd first heard the rumor about the switch, he had figured it did actually exist. It made sense.

Any species intelligent enough to build a starship, would never send it into deep space without a self-destruct. Without some device capable of not only destroying the craft that carried it, but also obliterating any attacking forces as well. The switch had to be a, *'Last one left; flip this; then shit.'* kind of device. One of horrific power.

Huong had no idea what the switch might do to a planet, but he certainly knew what it would do to a Huong. And Huong is a man who is *very* close to getting *extremely* rich. So, screw any dying crap.

Finding Moto no longer matters, Gaust has got to be stopped. She said switch activation will be soon... that could mean any fucking thing, and I don't think I can kill the bitch alone. Those fucking eyes... yellow eyes... is it the Gunch Yellow? Tanya said she's not sure that shit can be killed. I've got to get Tanya.

A highly motivated Huong heads to the elevator at

a pace that wouldn't draw attention. As the elevator opens into the Waydowns, a highly agitated Huong... runs as if someone had stuffed plasti-skin up him. Deep.

In her office, Dr. Gaust is finding her hive connection exhilarating. She is eager to use the switch. But not quite yet, she has one last pleasurable chore to perform.

That long ago group that found the switch had correctly guessed its purpose, and managed to estimate it's power. They had joked, calling it the 'We're Fucked Switch.' It would not destroy earth... no, just atomize the ship along with most of New Mexico and a big chunk of Texas. Some joke.

Gaust intends to do just that. And in the process, send countless billions of the Yellow spores into the jet stream. Her family. She will be with them as they cloak this world. She will be immortal... with an entire planet of humans to devour. An entire planet to be Yellow. To be Leprous.

But first: the killing of Moto. She has long wanted to slaughter that little oriental, perverted swine. Kill him in some innovative way that would take an exceedingly long while. But she now feels that would waste too much time.

So, eating Japanese will suffice.

———•••———

"Mama! You din't tells me it was gonna blows me dry," says a steamy, fragrant child, limping out from the Groomer area.

Her panties are on backward, and Shanna's holding a bra. "It nigh on to blowed me outta the danged thing. I loves it, mama! When can I does it again? And what's this?" she finishes by dangling the bra in front of Tanya.

Tanya laughs delightedly. The girl is a bit slump shouldered, a little flat faced, pug nosed, slew footed... and has a perky third breast about mid stomach. All this beauty, and an enchanting light spray of freckles across nose and shoulders. AND, the hair, freed from grease and dirt, is a bit blond. Tanya thinks she's the most beautiful wonderful child that ever was. Parents often see strangely.

"That thing is a bra which I put with your panties by mistake. Don't worry about it. For now... how about you try on this!" Tanya says, whipping out the perfumed lab coat from behind her.

"Mama!" she squeals, dropping the mysterious bra and reaching. No prom dress was ever more cherished. Not even close.

As Shanna hugs and buries her face into the aromatic coat, the hatch is thrown open.

And that highly agitated Huong tumbles in.

"Tanya! It's Gaust, she's Yellow, her eyes, she's going for the switch, we've—"

"WHAT! Gaust is Yellow?" she interrupts, her face turning white. The switch statement hasn't registered.

"I saw it, that yellow gunch shit is in her eyes, and I heard her talk about the switch. The switch, God damn it, Tanya! That switch exists!"

Tanya's mind spasms with too many thoughts. Immediately, her head snaps toward the girl. *No! Not now... this can't happen now... oh, Shanna... not now.*

The girl stands there, silently hugging her coat, eyes growing huge. She didn't understand what was happening, but she'd heard the word, Yellow. That word she certainly understood.

"I always knew that switch rumor had to be real," Tanya mutters. "Did you see it. Huong? The switch, did you see it?"

"No, Gaust headed to her office and I ran. Is that where it is?"

"Jesus, how the hell would I know! I've only heard—"

"Fuck! You're the one that's supposed to know all about this—"

"Shut up, Huong! There's no time for you to have your period."

Turning to the girl, grabbing her shoulders, she says,

"You've got to stay here, Shanna, there's no time to explain, I've—"

"I heard Yellow, Mama, I kin fights, and I knows—"

"NO, SHANNA! Your leg, child, you can't run. You wait for me, and you don't leave this cabin. I'll leave you the Uzi, you kill anything that tries to get in." Hugging the girl, she adds, "I love you. I *will* be back for you, I promise."

And then the two adults scramble through the hatch and are gone.

Shanna holds her coat, which has suddenly become much more precious. Looking at the closed hatch, she nods saying, "Yes, Mama. Don't you be a'skeered." Her trust is absolute.

But a parent should take care when making promises. Not all can be kept.

Huong and Tanya run, a full out, leg churning, panicked run. The switch must not be used. Neither of these two gives a fly fuck about saving the world, or humanity from anything. But!

For Huong, the gut-wrenching urgency is for Huong. That almost rich Huong. That spending lots of money Huong. That playboy Huong. That Huong who has become precious to Huong. For Tanya, it's for the girl, it's for her daughter. It's all about Shanna.

Reaching the elevator door, both gasping, Tanya

immediately yanks at the deceptively melted control panel.

"Wait, God damn it," pants Huong. "I screwed up on 19. I never picked up another Uzi, and lost my knife when I ran. Your weapon is with the girl. What are we gonna do, shit at Gaust? We need some kind of an attack plan."

"Well... Okay, I've got one, sort of." she answers. "Guns are no good, any hope we have of pulling this off, in stopping her, keeping and running 19, is in stealth. We go directly to Gaust's office. If we're seen on the way, hell, you're in khakis and I'm wearing a lab coat, we can pull that off."

"That's not the part that's worrying me, Tanya."

"Yeah, me neither. From what you've said, Gaust is not totally a Melt. Maybe it's necessary for her not to be, to get at, to operate the switch. So, if she's not all Yellow, then maybe she's killable, or at least stoppable. I always carry a scalpel, and you're not exactly helpless."

"That's our plan?" snorts Huong. "Christ, I was almost rich."

The trip to Gaust's office door is without incident; there is no one about. No member of staff ever wants close to *that* area.

Standing at the door, Tanya looks at Huong, then

over at the button. Slipping her hand into a pocket she grips the scalpel.

"Fuck it," she says, pushing the lighted disc.

As the door glides open, Dr. Gaust, deep in the euphoria of her new found oneness, has not even glanced at the monitor screen. There was no need; it had to be Moto. Turning, she slowly draws her head back, as if poising to strike.

"Well, well, well, isn't this a pleasant surprise. Ho Chi Huong, escorting... I believe the name is Tanya."

The pair step slowly into the room. Gaust is shocking... by appearing vaguely the same, yet somehow totally different. She's much taller and her body seems constantly in motion, even as she stands still. The eyes are almond shaped, and definitely Yellow. Molten, as if they will gush out at any moment. Her cocked head rocks slightly in an incessant tick-tock motion, and the voice has a lisping, sibilant similarity to the old.

Looking directly at Tanya, Gaust says, "Come in, come in, by all means come in. I must compliment you, Tanya, on your positively amazing survival abil—"

Her head darts forward in a blur, aimed at Huong. The neck stretching, upper torso elongating, as the jaws unhinge. Gaust has fangs now.

Huong manages to deflect her with an uppercut that lands just under the gaping mouth.

As the head strikes, Tanya slashes out with her scalpel. One of Gaust's arms surges, its hand closing around Tanya's wrist, twisting it back until the blade drops.

Huong, landing the uppercut and deflecting Gaust's lunging face, is caught by her vicious kick that knocks his feet from under him. Landing hard, he scrambles forward, desperately grabbing Gaust around her knees.

Tanya, forced to drop the scalpel, wrenches loose and dives for Gaust's neck, trying to keep that striking wedge shaped skull away.

With Huong around her knees, and Tanya's hands clutching her throat, Gaust topples backwards onto the floor. Kicking and bucking the man loose, she wraps both legs and arms around Tanya.

With her hands clutching the woman's throat, Tanya feels the immediate crush of the Gaust creature's limbs encircling her. They tighten, vice-like and increasing; Tanya feels the breath mashed from her lungs.

Stunned when kicked away from Gaust's legs, Huong pulls himself erect using her desk. Trying to clear his head, and looking frantically for any kind of weapon.

Feeling her grip on Gaust's throat weaken, Tanya fights to breathe as the woman's arms and legs continue crushing like winding bands of steel.

As Tanya's fingers loosen, Gaust's neck becomes free enough to stretch, pushing further up, lengthening to coil beneath the lethal head.

Huong, looking down on the desperate struggle, sees Tanya losing her grip on Gaust and her own consciousness. Her eyes are rolling, showing white. Spotting Gaust's prize glass display container, he lifts the heavy jar, smashing it down into Lillith's face.

This ends the fight. Maybe.

The jar containing Lieutenant Bastrop topples from the partially crushed head, rolling a few feet across the floor.

As Gaust goes limp, Tanya pushes away from the body, gasping for breath, she manages to stand.

"She's not dead," pants Tanya, massaging her chest while looking down at the body.

"Not dead! Her head's damn near a pancake, she's gotta be dead."

"She's fucking Yellow, Huong, and she's probably healing herself right now. Hell, I can see her breathing."

Picking up Tanya's scalpel, he says, "Let me fix that, I'll just cut off her—"

"No, not yet, Huong. And besides, cutting her—"

"Not yet? We can't wait for this bitch to wake... Oh, shit! Where *IS* that switch?"

"Exactly. We've got to question her."

"Fuck," replies Huong.

"Exactly."

CHAPTER 19

A MIRACLE... BUT FROM WHERE?

Shadow sits on the floor beside Elvis's bed, leaning against it with her head on folded arms. Waving ringlets of black spill across a tired, worry-sick face. From the adjacent chair, Jayderay occasionally reaches over and pats the woman's back. A gentle, stroking reminder that she is not alone.

Neither woman has spoken of the fervent prayers they had offered up. There is no need. Like all prayer, either it will be answered, or it won't. Usually the latter.

Or perhaps answered in some convoluted, unfathomable way. For Shadow, it had been an act of love and desperation. For Jayderay, it was more an act of commiseration. She had put all her heart into the prayer, all she had. But she also doubted.

Jayderay truly loves this strange woman and her not exactly human mate. They had saved her life. Literally rescued her from hell, a hell known as the Waydowns. But she felt her own praying was tainted, marred by thoughts of all the awful times when her supplications had been ignored. If not downright shit on.

But God, prayer, and weevils work in mysterious ways.

Thoughts always wander in a sick room. And especially in a sick room where the patient is a sack of grape Jello.

Shadow's thoughts are about her wonderful husband who had freed her from decades of aching want and loneliness. He's also currently the sack of Jello, but that's not his fault.

Jayderay's thoughts have also drifted. They concern another man. Actually, two other men, neither of whom could be termed wonderful. Not hardly. She loves them, but also knows them. Knowing these guys has a tendency to negate any wonderfulness.

There's often plenty of wonder, though.

Those two idiots... standin' there lookin' at what's happened to Elvis... and RL says "This is not a good thing." Not a good thing? He must not been able to think up anything stupider, which is kinda surprisin' for him. And Frankie wasn't no better. And just what are they doin' out there with that Moto? I bet they scared... both of them likely to be man sized goose-

bumps 'bout now. When I get a chance to talk to them two, when Shadow won't hear, I'm gonna tell both of...

Yes, Jayderay has all the makings of a very good wife. Men do need minders. Some more than others, and with some... the need is nearly terminal.

While both women are lost in those drifting thoughts, there has been movement within the bag, that sack of Jello. Lots of roiling, blending and bubbling. Lots of something.

From within the gelatinous membrane enclosing what had been Elvis, the lavender jelly pushes out. A bump begins to appear about half way down that translucent covering. Tenting out, the membrane silently tears as skeletal fingers force through. The entire hand and wrist follow, sliding out from the sack. Then the arm, reaches out. Skeletal... but not.

That arm and hand are not bare bone, there is a thin layer of flesh beneath a rather slimy, scaley lavender skin. It looks like it should be scrabbling out of a fairly old grave. Or into somebody's fresh one.

Shadow still has her head pillowed on folded arms, so she sees nothing as the spectral limb reaches nearer.

Jayderay does *not* have her head down. She *does* see. She catches this movement from the corner of her eye. Her expression does an Oscar winning job.

For an instant, she's a plantation mammy getting an unplanned enema.

As the awful thing lowers to Shadow's hand, Jayderay grabs the woman's shoulders, preparing to snatch her away.

But as those emaciated fingers touch Shadow, the woman speaks.

"My Elv-is! I knew that you would come back to me." Lifting her head, she smiles looking at that thing extruding from its membrane. "Yes, Elv-is, I knew you would return. I prayed for this."

At this moment, Jayderay is unsure *who* has answered the prayer. "Shadow, are you... okay?" she asks.

"Oh, yes. All is good, my true friend. God, our God, has answered. I wish for you to spread my joy, please go and tell the others." Her eyes are radiant, glowing violet, enraptured.

Jayderay is not sure about this joy, very unsure about it. But she does think leaving the room is sort of a good idea. Has God answered? Or maybe someone else has. Someone not usually associated with heaven.

Prayer? Could be. Why not?

In the hall, she finds Frankie and RL. Who, having just deposited Moto, are indeed, goose bumps. Jayderay makes three.

"It's Elvis... I think. He back, least ways... maybe," she tells the other two bumps.

"You don't know?" asks Frankie, thinking about purple, people-eaters.

"It's only his arm, it come pokin' out of that skin bag thing. It looks horrible."

"What does Shadow say?" Frankie's eyes are growing.

"Oh, she just sure it's really him. But... but, well... we prayed, and now she full of religion and believin.' But I ain— I am not. Suppose what's comin' out is not *really* Elvis anymore?"

"I think she'd know, Honey," speaks RL, with more hope than conviction.

"Well, if she wrong... we all in trouble. We all in big, serious trouble."

Frankie's eyes get bigger. He's thinking. He's thinking about *The Teeth From Titan*, and that *Saturn Shiteater*.

"Boss, I'm glad you and Shadow are comforted by this, but I agree with Jayderay. What if it's not him? Before we find out, and while Shadow is all religiously at ease... maybe she'll leave Elvis long enough to open the Waydowns door. Then we can dump Moto. At least we can get rid of Dr. Death before we get another bigger problem."

"You're right," RL says. "That would solve the—"

"While you solvin' you not thinkin' which is kinda usual for you two," interrupts Jayderay. "Shadow might leave that bedside, *if* I stay with Elvis. That's a mighty big if, 'cause I'm scared of, of whatever might come out of that bag."

"I'll stay with you," says RL. He's not being brave, he's in love. Some say it's the same thing.

"So! I guess *I'm* elected. Discarded and abandoned by friends, compelled to sally forth against the dastardly evil that lurks down in the basem—"

"Oh, don't get started, Frankie," says RL, tiredly. "You'll have Shadow with you."

"And this is your idea," adds Jayderay.

"True," replies the silly bastard. "But stir not the bitterness of my cup which—"

"FRANKIE!"

"Okay, Boss, okay. Don't get prissy."

Frankie is not really afraid of going to deal with Moto, not if he has Shadow with him. But on the other hand... he's a little frightened of Shadow as well. Maybe more.

"Take the gun, Frankie. When Shadow opens the Waydowns door..." RL doesn't finish.

"Right," says Frankie. "There might be a greeting

party waiting." He doesn't giggle. He's thinking of good Ol' Saturn and Titan.

Being ecstatic over *God* having, sort of, returned Elvis to her, Shadow agrees. If, RL and Jayderay will stay with the transitioning bag of Jello, she will accompany Frankie. And, away they go.

Opening the closet door, they find Dr. Moto, exactly as the Bobbsey Twins had left him. Starkly staring straight ahead. Staring at something that fascinates him. If his eyes are any indication, it's certainly not anything a human would want to see. Even a Moto.

"Ah! I'm ever so glad you've waited, my dear Doctor. May I say how delighted I am to find you in tranquil repose. I do hope—"

"Yes, Round-Eye," interrupts the sepulchral voice. "I am here in the long time. We will always be here in the long time. Forever, I will remain—"

"Oh, golly-gosh, there you go again," breaks in Frankie. "I'm so impressed. I wish I'd brought both of those pineapples... one would be for your mouth."

"Frankie, I desire to return to Elv-is quickly. Please do not make this last."

"Okay, Shadow, I understand. Remember, the second Moto clears that door, close it."

"Yes, I well recall our last encounter with this entryway. I've no wish to prolong another."

Looking at Moto, Frankie says with a giggle, "Okey-Dokey, Karaoke, your next adventure awaits you. I do hope and believe that you will find many, many in there who will remember you."

Moto is silent, as if he does not hear, or care. He will.

Frankie nods to the gray woman, who places her hand against the wall. A brief shimmering area appears, and then a door materializes.

As it slides open, Frankie prods Dr. Moto with the gun. And in a jerking, puppet like walk, he judders forward through the door. He steps on some fragments of its exterior controls, the remnants of Tanya's little visit. It doesn't bother him; few things could. He keeps going, and the door slides shut. Unseen others ride along with Moto. These daughters will not be pleased.

Frankie heartily wishes Moto had been carrying a Pineapple... without using his hands. And he's almost disappointed that Ol' Saturn and Titan were not on hand to greet the doctor. But that's okay. They have worse cousins in the Waydowns.

That door isn't magic, it's the product of an alien science. A science badly misunderstood by humans desperately trying to end a world war. Which resulted in a screw up that created the Waydowns and placed the door where it couldn't possibly be. A door that goes neither up or down; it opens directly into the bowels of a buried starship. It just can't be so. There ain't no such animal!

Returning to the bed room, and the intense relief of RL and Jayderay, Frankie makes his report. Due to Shadow's presence, he doesn't embellish it any. It hurts him, and it squelches his style, but he manages. Just the facts: Moto is gone.

So, three of these four, go back to worrying about Elvis. Frankie strongly suspects that what will blossom forth may indeed be Saturn or Titan. Maybe both! Maybe twins!

Being considerably less theatrical than the silly bastard, RL and Jayderay settle for just plain old worry. Plain old worry is quite sufficient to drive anyone to an early grave. Or somewhere not as inviting.

And Shadow... Shadow has rekindled her faith in God and prayer. This could lead her down the proverbial garden path. She's been there before. Maybe the path should worry.

The unlamented Moto had thought the Prohy/Elvis creature might've been shocked into an early skin-shedding. Which really wasn't anything serious, and was an almost yearly occurrence. One for which he and Gaust had simply tossed the congenital teenager into a hibernation tube for the duration. The pesky little shit.

But Moto had also thought the severe battering Elvis had taken, that put him into a coma, might very well result in physiological changes. Possibly catastrophic changes. Changes Dr. Moto definitely had not wanted to see, and certainly hadn't wanted to... *experience*. No one but Gaust knew exactly what *ingredients* had gone into the creation of the lavender mutant.

So, what will this Elvis be, and as Frankie had so eloquently asked: What will it eat?

So, the worriers are left with prayer. There is always prayer and that garden path. World without end... maybe.

CHAPTER 20

THAT ELUSIVE SWITCH

"Gaust has got to be interrogated, Huong. We *have* to find that fucking switch. Let's tie her up and—"

"Tie her up! This snake-cunt won't stay tied. The minute she comes to, she'll be out of anything we use."

"Yeah, you're right... okay, then let's get her into a Cryo-Tube.

"A what?

"A hibernation cylinder, one of those will damn sure hold the bitch while we ask questions. They've got built in restraints. If she won't tell us where the switch is, we freeze her, if she does... well, we freeze her anyway."

This is Tanya. Tanya to the core.

In the Waydowns, a child sits on Tanya's bed wearing her new lab coat. It's comforting; it came from her mother. Staring at the closed hatch, the Uzi lying beside her, she waits. If Tanya does not return, she will use the gun. Her leg has started throbbing again. Ignoring the pain, she speaks softly to the empty room.

"I love you, mama. Don't you be a'skeered."

She had understood very little of the frantic exchange between Huong and Tanya. She only knew that her wonderful mother had gone to that dangerous place they called Deck 19. Had gone with that mistrusted asshole Huong to fight a mysterious Gaust, and take something from it. Something they were afraid of. And she had heard, Yellow.

A noise at the hatch. Something scratching, something trying to get in. Some thing. Buttoning the coat, Shanna picks up the Uzi. This girl is crippled and in her early teens, but she'd been brought up quick and rough; about as jagged a rearing as can be. She definitely *ain't a'skeered.*

Clicking the guns safety off, she limps to the door. The scratching becomes clawing, getting louder. Gripping the Uzi with one hand, she braces herself with the good leg, reaches out and yanks open the door.

———•••———

"Damn, she's long and heavy, will she fit?" asks Huong, as he and Tanya carry Gaust from her office.

"Yeah, she'll fit. Those cylinders weren't made for humans. I've been in there a couple times, that's how

I knew about this private entry. Those alien bastards were tall drinks of something, this stringy bitch will fit just fine."

Avoiding any staff encounters by using Gaust's back way, they lug her into the never used Cryogenics Department. Well, hardly ever used; Proby had been banished into the tubes on a regular basis. Usually for long periods, when the good doctor was tired of fucking him. Or of him getting into things, or going where he shouldn't. Or when he shed. And while inside one of these cylinders, he'd be subjected to an endless barrage of old movies, TV shows, and advertisements. This had given the mutant many odd ideas about life and love.

Carrying the limp, disturbingly flexible body, they enter a dim, very, very quiet room. The low ceiling is imbedded with small, inverted bowl shapes. Starting in the center, they spiral out, ending where the walls meet. Intense, intelligent, scientific analysis had declared them to be part of the ship's hibernation time-treatment system.

And they might also be part of a space pig's ass. No one knew what they were.

Two rows of long, curve-topped cylinders are melded to the room's deck plates. Evidently the aliens stepped in to, rather than climbed up on, their deep sleep spaces. This will save Tanya and Huong a lot of difficult lifting. So far, so good.

Each space is lit from within by a soft, glowing blue, shining through their clear covers. Various buttons line the edge of one side. Making a lucky guess, Tanya pushes the first one, and the lid is sucked back, curving down into the deck. So far, so good.

Wrestling the body into the cavity is fairly easy, and as soon as Gaust was fully reclined, thick straps auto-extend from one side, crossing the body, and enter into the other side. So far, so good.

And then... not so good. They find out for sure that Dr. Gaust is definitely not dead. Not even a little. They also discover that her crushed skull has not diminished her vigor. Not even a little. *AND*, the strap that had so obligingly fastened itself across her forehead... is not worth shit. Not even a little.

Neither of the humans were prepared.

The slack, flaccid body erupts, bucking, twisting and lunging against the restraints. That strap over her brow doesn't break, but it hadn't been designed for any creature this rabidly supple.

Spitting a clear fluid and shrieking in a high-pitched, whistling whine, Gaust stretches her neck, forcing her head up and out of the belting. Immediately the neck telescopes into a half-coil beneath the fanged head, preparing it to strike.

Her shoulders begin elongating, their straps become loose, and the head darts out, jaws unhinging, gaping maw open.

Back in the Waydowns at Tanya's cabin:

With her finger on the Uzi's trigger, Shanna yanks the hatch open... and *almost* sprays lead into the ship's last *Almost*. Seevee lies collapsed at the threshold.

What saves Seevee from being riddled with bullets, is his missing arm, the smeared blood trail leading to the hatch, his huge terrified eyes, and a gasping, timorous, "Ton?"

Not lowering her weapon, Shanna limps a step closer, taking in the khakis, the military boots and the horrific, still bleeding wound.

"Ton? Does you means Tanya?"

Pathetically nodding from the deck, he whispers, "Ton... much Ton... much fren, me Seevee fren."

"Tanya is *my* Mama, *she* named me Shanna," the girl says, with pride glowing in each word. "But she ain't heres, and I don't knows as she would wants me to lets you in."

This is beyond shocking to Seevee. His stunned mind

swirls incredulously. *Mama? Mama?... Seevee much gone, much gone long!* His eyes flutter, closing as his head thuds back to the deck.

"Dang... don't die," mutters the girl, "if you really is a friend, my Mama might be fierce hurt about that." She studies the collapsed Almost a couple seconds, then looks up and down the corridor. With a deep breath, she decides. "My Mama says we don't never leave no wounded, so's in you come."

It's an agonizing struggle having to use her broken leg. Grinding her teeth, straining with her good leg, she drags the unconscious Seevee inside enough to close the hatch.

Examining the wound, she says, "I don't guess you can hear me none, but talkin' is comfortsome to me. I ain't gots hardly no doctorin', but I'm gonna try. Maybe it'll help do gooder till my Mama gets back. My Mama will knows; my Mama knows everything."

Smearing on the ointment Tanya had used for the leg, she continues.

"Hump a gourd! Whatever gots hold of you done a right powerful job. Hardly never seed no worser." As she presses a bandage over the goo, Seevee moans.

"Wa... wa," he croaks, opening his eyes.

"Water? Okay, my Mama gots bunches of water," and away she hobbles, returning with a glass full. Holding the back of his head with one hand, she tips the water as he drains it.

"Seevee much... much tha—" and his head lolls, eyes closing.

"Dang! There you goes ag'in. I cain't never gets no talk outta you. 'Course with that there blood trail you left, it's a mighty big wonder you ain't come a cropp—"

A crashing boom interrupts her. From out in the corridor comes huge thrashing echoes. They're repeated. And then again, getting nearer. A big something is coming, and the something is serious. Powerful serious.

Massive and repeated thuds of flesh against the deck and white walls of the hallway sound closer. And closer. Whatever it is, it's making for this cabin, and it isn't dawdling about.

Shanna forces herself upright, grabbing the gun. This is her Mama's home, and the girl will not let it be taken. She will not let this thing get inside. She's going out to fill it with lead.

Yes, this does indeed sound like the daughter of Tanya.

Seevee, wakened by the sounds, knows immediately what's making them. Seeing the girl start toward the hatch, he grabs her ankle.

"NO! Much no go. Much Coiler come... much no

fight Coiler." *Seevee must save Ton Girl... for Ton... bad leg girl much no fight Coiler...*

Seevee is right. A crippled girl, even with a Uzi, would be no match for the many writhing, quick snatching tentacles of a giant Coiler.

An explosion of battering muscle slams against the hatch. The Coiler is no longer coming, it's here.

Tanya and Huong had been lulled into stupidity. With her body as limp as an old man's dream, Gaust was no longer a danger. Hell, she's near death, got a crushed skull and is secured by those restraining straps. Dr. Gaust is finished.

Right.

That *finished* Gaust erupts into a venom spewing, squealing, writhing nightmare. With teeth. Big sharp ones.

The coiled neck launches her fanged head at Tanya, as the shrinking torso stretches out from beneath the straps.

Leaping back, Tanya narrowly escapes getting her face imbedded with fangs. But she's not quick enough to avoid the snapping jaws sinking those teeth into her coat's flapping lapel.

Grabbing both sides of Gaust's head, Tanya pushes

back, trying to free herself. The coat doesn't tear, and she's inches away from those hot Yellow eyes. Almond shaped and pulsing, throbbing with a liquid need. A need that nearly gushes out. Tanya can feel their heat.

From behind, Huong seizes the lithe, twisting neck. He might as well be jerking on a Boa constrictor. He *is* helping Tanya some, aiding her to keep that poisonous head back. But it's a losing effort against a tube of solid squirming muscle.

Gaust's elongating upper body is rapidly freeing her vice-like arms and hands from the restraints. That will totally end this fight. And little Huong-y and Tanya will find their asses stuffed into the vacated cylinder. What's left of them.

Those long teeth are snagged in Tanya's coat. Her constant pushing back, coupled with Huong's pulling are keeping Gaust from freeing the fangs and striking again. But they're losing, and the head inches closer to Tanya's face. The slanting eyes, those burning, sulphureous yellow eyes are huge now.

The only sounds are the constant keen from Gaust's whistling, muffled frustration, the tearing cloth, and grunts from the straining, losing humans.

There is nothing in this room Huong can use. Nothing. Tanya cannot let go of the advancing hot face of

Gaust. And the creature's arms are rapidly clearing the restraints.

Bravery is the result of thought. Heroism is born of despair. In an unthinking move, Huong let's go of Gaust's neck with one arm, and raising it, he drives his elbow into the jar-crushed area of her skull. Again and again, he hammers into the wound. Spit drips through his clenched teeth and sweat streams as he pounds into the weakened, softening bone. Again, and again, and again.

As the breaking bone is beaten further inward, the skin stretches with it, but does not split open. The bitch is practically indestructible... and the desperate Huong batters away.

Without warning... Gaust collapses, her body goes slack, and she hangs from Tanya's coat lapel, the limp neck trailing to the deck.

Shaking Gaust's head, ripping it free, Tanya lets go, and it flops beside the Cryo-Tube, the neck looping inside.

"Jesus," she pants. "Fuck the questions, let's freeze this bitch."

Huong simply nods, he doesn't speak. Why bother.

Kicking the head and neck completely inside the cylinder, Tanya pushes the same button that had opened this hibernation trough. It's curved lid instantly slides out of the floor, and closing with muted internal clicking. Freezing would logically be the next button in line. Even aliens should know that. They did, and it is; the tube quickly fills with a white mist. Within seconds the vapor is gone, leaving behind a lovely, frozen Dr. Lillith Sally Gaust. In all her splendor.

"Okay, then what about that fucking switch?" asks Huong.

"The switch? I'm going to be damn careful about taking over Gaust's office, that's what about the switch," answers Tanya. "It's got to be in there, and the fucking thing has been hidden for decades, so I'm just gonna let it stay that way."

Nodding, he says, "Yeah, that might be... best. Maybe. So, what now?"

"Well, first... thank you. I owe you big time."

"Yeah, you do," he answers, tearing his eyes away from the frosty fresh Lillith Sally. Looking directly at Tanya, he adds, "Super Gook saves the day and all that shit. Like I already asked, what now?"

"Now? Right now, you are going to start swaggering your oriental ass around this deck. Making it known that you officially are Moto's replacement, and that '*I, Tanya Denise Evans,*' now run Dr. Gaust's office. That doctor who has," she inclines her head down at the occupied Cyro-Tube, "taken emergency medical leave."

Huong actually smirks at this, and still breathing heavily, he speaks.

"I think I'm gonna be Colonel Huong, now... *Tanya Denise.* So, what about Moto? I think the Jap bastard deserted."

"If he did, then he's gone. If he shows we kill him. Easy-fucking-peasey. Don't get stupid on me... *Colonel.* And while you're off strutting about, *I'm* grabbing a gun, and going for my daughter. Shanna *IS* coming here with me." And off she strides.

Watching her go, Huong thinks. *Yes, go get your precious stink pot. She will be my insurance policy should you forget what you owe.* He doesn't speak. Why bother.

As Huong thinks his Huong thoughts, Tanya walks back through Dr. Gaust's office. Former office, as it's hers now. Absolutely hers, and Tanya will have no problem assuming authority. Not a bit, but other's may. They will be *attended* to.

Tanya briefly stops, surveying the spot where she and Huong had first battled with the now frozen doctor. *How did we make it? Fuck and wonder, how did we do it? That little bitch Huong-y... he does come through at times.*

A glint of light from the floor catches her attention. It's the jar that Huong had slammed into Gaust's face.

Through the glass, its murky interior seems to move a bit. Which is to be expected after its recent activity. Or perhaps it's only the light penetrating the curving glass. Probably just that.

Maybe the preserved Lt. Bastrop knows what causes those tricks of perception. Maybe his pickled brain has some ideas. He's certainly been in there long enough to know any peculiarities the container might have.

And maybe... just maybe... Bastrop is dead as a Do-Do's dick.

Shrugging off thoughts about that ugly jar, and anything else except getting her child, Tanya stops at the door. Buttoning coat, adjusting eye patch, and raking fingers through her hair; she must start showing an authoritative look around her old stomping grounds. Smoothing the fang ripped lapel, she pushes the door's button, and steps out. There's no one.

Being Tanya, she's a little disappointed. She's the boss now. The *real* fucking boss of 19, and she wanted to start that ball rolling by being seen. A brief glimpse of her and that sporty eyepatch, just a little something to get the rumor mill activated. But that can wait, getting her daughter can't.

As she importantly stalks to *her* private elevator, Tanya spots a grunt. It will not be a good day for him. This unlucky bastard has been sent on some hated maintenance detail. He's also got an Uzi hanging from one shoulder. Having the weapon is more bad luck for him, as it reminds Tanya she needs a gun.

"Private!" she barks. "Surrender your weapon at once." Tanya can give orders; it's so Tanya, it's so in her DNA.

The grunt, already in a foul humor about being assigned some pissy, make-work job, is not impressed. All he sees is some Labbie bitch with an eye patch. Huh!

"Well, *Pirate Polly*, you wanna cracker? Or a big prick up your ass? Just who in the fuck do you think you are? Labbies don't give Security Personnel any orders, so you gotta be a fresh-fish. Let me give you some advice on—"

He's interrupted. He's rudely interrupted. He's agonizingly interrupted.

As Tanya's knee smashes into his groin, she rips the gun from his shoulder, and steps back. Leveling the weapon at him, she speaks conversationally.

"You were saying, Private? I really do like being instructed."

The grunt responds by making soft and sincere goo-goo sounds. He hunkers, pigeon-toed, knock-kneed, and clutching his crotch. His scrotum has been filled with insanely mad hornets. Enormous hornets. Poisonous hornets. This is not being a good day. And it's not over.

"So, Private... I see you've met our new Commander," comments Huong, as he comes striding up. "Off to a good start are you?"

"Goo, goo... Huo... Huo... Huong," gasps the bent over, bedeviled grunt.

"That's *Colonel* Huong, to you. Let me properly introduce *Doctor* Tanya, who has replaced Gaust. And you will stand at attention in my... *our* presence. But there's no need to grovel and bow like you're doing. Stand up straight, man!"

"Goo, goo," responds the Private.

<hr>

On the way back to her cabin, carrying the appropriated Uzi, Tanya worries about the switch. Sooner or later, it must be found. Where is the bastard? What will she do with it? Where would it be safe? Could it ever be safe? And so on. But first, she will get the girl.

<hr>

Far, far below on Lakker's old deck, the Yellow stop all activity. In the instant that Dr. Gaust became frozen, the membranes growing over their mouths began silently pulsing. As if attempting to blow bubbles.

Then, all together, the Melts begin making their way down to the power place. There is nowhere else they can go, the Waydowns hatch is beyond their abilities to open, and there is no longer any need. They will wait for dispersal into the jet stream. The diaspora has been temporarily delayed. Their new leader has become a bit cool on the idea. For now.

The Yellow trek back through a village the child Shanna had once called home. The village where they had once lived. This place is nothing to them now. And the only sounds are the sucking slosh of their dissolving feet.

Single file, they trudge through the broken hatch of the power place. The hatch where the girl deputy had made her lethal mistake. Down the forest trail to the shores of the not-water lake they slump.

And then the Yellow; these Melts; these... Lepers, walk into the liquid stillness. They will wait. They are patient. Most toadstools tend to be that way. They have a leader now. A leader who is coldly asleep. Sleeping for now.

Far out in the lake's center, an enormous, scaled back breaks the surface.

⸻ ✦ ⸻

Back in Tanya's cabin, her daughter holds the Uzi, grimly staring at the now quiet hatch. There is only silence from the other side. A silence that is worse that the hammering, pounding sound had been. A brooding silence. A deadly silence.

Seevee, keeping hold of the girl's ankle, whispers, "Much no go, much no fight, is Coiler."

"Well, I cain't just stands here," she mutters back. "My Mama's gonna be comin', and I don't wants her to be a'skeered."

"No go," repeats Seevee. "Coiler follow blood... will much go."

Shanna nods, thinking of the smeared red trail that marks Seevee's tortuous journey down the hall. But the trail ends at the hatch. At this door. *That thing's powerful dumb if it follows that there trail back the ways it gots here. I ain't gonna lets my Mama get et. Dang it, I'm goin—* She feels Seevee let loose of her ankle.

"Yep, I figgerd you was due for another nap," she says quietly to the once again unconscious Seevee. "You seems purty reg'lar about them. Well, that's more gooder, 'cause I'm goin' out there. I cain't let nothin' gets in my Mama's—"

A staccato blast of flying lead from the corridor halts her one-sided talk. Another burst of death immediately follows, and is joined by piercing squeals from the no longer silent Coiler. The sounds of its thrashing retreat echo away down the hall.

Tanya has arrived.

The mother and daughter reunion is totally wonderful. As they should be, but often are not... both being women and all. It's full of chattering statements like:

"Mama! You ripped yore coat, you can wears mine." And, "This here Seevee, he conks out fierce reg'lar. How's we gonna git him up to that there 19?" And so on. Shanna is a teen, so Tanya doesn't get a chance to say much.

There was one particularly important question. A hugely, immensely, exceedingly, incredibly important question.

"Mama... did you, uh, did you finds any more Chuklit?"

But during all this joy, Tanya continues to be niggled by the switch problem. Obviously, the former Dr. Gaust cannot be questioned; she tends to be difficult. No, Gaust must remain frozen in her cozy hibernation cylinder.

Tanya begins to realize that she really can't ignore the whereabouts of the switch, of that... *control*. But she doesn't even know what it looks like, or its size. Even though this thing has remained hidden for decades, she must find it. *Carefully* she must find it.

Screw humanity, fuck the world and its population, Tanya has a much more important consideration: She doesn't want a certain mother and daughter to go wafting about in the stratosphere as particles.

To locate that elusive, ghastly important, damn all to eternity, device... Tanya will not have to look very far. She need only to check with Lt. Bastrop. He knows.

He's been sharing a very confined space with it for many years.

CHAPTER 21

THE CURTAIN

Back in town, a few miles from the Roaton house, other things are happening.

Theresa Ann Penny, called Tap by Frankie, is a nice person. She thinks this of herself. She says this of herself... to everyone. All the time.

But nice is only a wrapping. Nice is a covering for what lies beneath, be that what it may. Nice does not mean good. Nor does it mean moral. Nor does it mean ethical. Nor does it mean anything. In reality, nice means jack shit.

At this particular moment, *nice* Theresa Ann Penny is sitting with her feet soaking in a concoction to ease an itch that has taken over the tootsies. She's also harboring suspicions about that silly bastard Frankie.

This nice woman also has a deep, sanity-consuming itch somewhere else. So... she has an exceptionally large ice cube poked up her butt.

How nice.

Elsewhere in town, an elderly couple, who resemble a pair of Hummels, take turns with a tube of Preparation H. They argue about where this awful itch came from.

They've been married forever... so naturally each blames the other.

Also in this town, a single mother holds her sobbing baby boy. He is precious to her. He is her darling. He never does any, any, any wrong. And he is almost 18 years old.

Obviously, this bundle of joy has never had a father around to slap the living shit out of him. It shows. Painfully, it shows.

This much-pampered and revered orange haired reptile has a twisting, braided bit of a goatee. It sprouts from his manly chin. The mother tells him it makes him look so masculine. He readily believes this. He eagerly believes this. He has to believe this... there's never been any other evidence.

This prize specimen of America's future has freshly arrived home. More accurately, to his *mother's* home.

He has been to a free clinic. The taxpayers owe him, and have limitless money.

The medicos had been shocked, astounded, and enraptured by their examination of the... *boy*. Many tests have been ordered, and absolutely must be ran. None have ever before seen anything like this... *child's* affliction: the fusing of filthy underwear, pubic hair and... flesh. Oh, dear! The tests that must be ran. Oh, my!

To further the likelihood of those tests, the little darling had been told: Amputation of the affected appendage was imminent. And probably its dangling attachments as well.

This would not be a great loss to the world. But the tests will be run... repeatedly. The mother and child will insist on this. It is their right. The politicians have told them so... repeatedly. And the taxpayers will bend further over. It's a position they know well.

———◆◆———

And in this town, RL and Jayderay have arrived back at their old homes. Leaving the ominous recovery of Elvis in Shadow's gray, ebony nailed hands. Frankie volunteered to stay with her.

Which was a bit unusual, normally the silly bastard doesn't want to be anywhere but the shop. Where

Frankie can be Frankie with complete impunity. And make money in any way he chooses. Well... he can unless RL is around and in one of his particularly prissy moods.

Frankie staying with Shadow caused a brief flicker of *hope* with Jayderay. She adds it to one of her 'worry about' files. And one of those mental folders definitely needs some hope. Women seldom miss things, and they always keep archives. Having RL and Frankie to deal with, has made Jayderay's stack of files like that leaning tower over in Italy. But considerably more dangerous.

As George basks in the sun on RL's back porch, he's also looking across the drive at his human.

Just look at that lazy ass, sitting over there with Jayderay. As if he hadn't a care in the world. He's probably thinking about a nap! And I grievously know he's got important unfinished chores. After he rudely disturbed my sleep, for no more reason than a miserly bit of petting, he didn't even check my litter pan. Nor did he freshen up my water and feed bowls. And, I had to ASK to be let out! The unmitigated shame of it, this life I have to endure. George yawns, rolls slightly to get more sun, licks one paw, and his eyes close. *The abuse is too severe, I must rest.*

George loves his human, but being a cat, he knows

it's best not to show this too much. It might spoil RL, might make the man even more no-account.

Across the communal drive, Princess lays directly in front of her humans. Princess, being a dog, has no reserve about showing her adoration. She's quietly worshipping the pair. Intensely loving this man and woman who have been her salvation. Tail softly thumping the grass, her brown eyes follow their every move. This pair are truly her world. She wants eagerly to please them. With chin resting on her paws, she further shows her love... by drooling. Yes, Princess is a dog. A very, very good dog. Her humans know this. More importantly, they show it.

Sitting beneath the branches of towering Pecan trees, sipping iced tea, the newly engaged couple should be at ease. And one of them is. This will not last, there's a file about to come out.

"RL... do you think there's ever been any kinda... *history* 'tween Frankie and Shadow?"

"WHAT? Good Lord, no, no way! Not with any woman. Why on earth would you ask that?"

"Oh, I was just wonderin' is all."

Women never 'just wonder' about things. They think. Such a statement of 'just wondering' usually precedes a large amount of feces hitting someone's fan.

"Oh, RL... I am sorry. I'm tellin' a lie. The truth

bein'… the truth bein' I was kinda hopin' they was some history," she says, shaking her head. "I'm talkin'… I'm meaning bedroom history."

RL sets his glass down, leans forward in the metal lawn chair, looking directly at her. He is no longer at ease. For Jayderay to even begin a lie is pretty serious.

"Baby… what's this about?"

Looking over at him, biting her bottom lip, she takes a deep breath and says, "Well, if they *was* somethin' been goin' on 'tween those two, it *might kinda* make what's comin' easier. Maybe."

"Tell me, Jaderay. You tell me right now," he softly demands. RL is totally lost. Engaged or married men often are. But this must be really important to her, so it has become front and center for him.

"Shadow told me she pregnant, RL. If that baby belong to Elvis… and I guess it do, what in the world is it… is it gonna be? He not all human and we don't really know *what* Shadow is."

"And in our new home," moans RL. "Christ!"

"Yeah, well… all of us liable to be callin' on *HIM* before too long," she says, setting her tea down next to RL's.

Yes, Shadow being pregnant is big news to RL. It may well be horrendous news. But it's not nearly the bomb that's going to drop.

That little atom splitter will land when Jayderay tells him... that she is.

THE END

Want more of this couple? And want more Frankie, Tanya and the rest? Then be sure to read their first two adventures: THE COOL THING and LAB SPILL.

And join these misfits in their next whirlwind:

SÉANCE!

Go where you'll wish you hadn't.

———

Lush praise, constructive criticism... or constipated complaints, can be directed to:

Rife6000@aol.com

And thanks for reading. Robert Rife

———

This scribbling reptile lives on an island off the coast of Washington. Under a rock. Only Santa and large women of dubious morals are allowed to visit. Santa often skips.

www.ingramcontent.com/pod-product-compliance
Lightning Source LLC
Chambersburg PA
CBHW060517160726
47991CB00001B/69